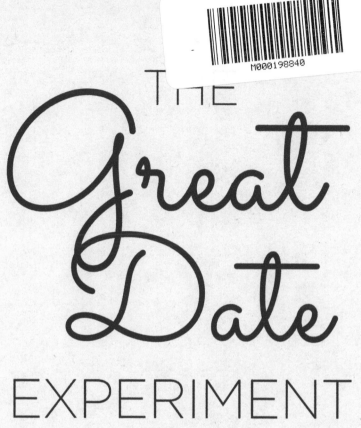

THE

Great

Date

EXPERIMENT

THE

Great Data

EXPERIMENT

21 Days. 21 Dates. 1,000 Views.
How Hard Can It Be?

THE

Great Date

EXPERIMENT

Ashley Mays

WhiteSpark

THE GREAT DATE EXPERIMENT

WhiteSpark Publishing, a division of
WhiteFire Publishing
13607 Bedford Rd NE
Cumberland, MD 21502

ISBN: 978-1-941720-93-6 (print)
       978-1-941720-94-3 (digital)

For my fourteen-year-old self.
We did it!
I'm so proud of you and your big dreams. I love you.

Chapter 1

THERE'S A HIPPO ON MY FRONT PORCH.

It's fuzzy, purple, and the size of a small cat. A polka-dotted envelope is tied to one of its legs. And in case there was any doubt as to who it's for, my name is scrawled across the envelope in letters so big the neighbors down the street can probably read it.

"Aww, Callie." My best friend Annabeth squeals behind me. She swats my shoulder. "Why didn't you tell me you've got an admirer?"

"I don't." I pick up the hippo and hold it by one ear at arm's length. "Where did it come from?"

"Who cares where it came from? It's cute. Read the note."

"I care." I stuff the hippo under my elbow as I work my fingers underneath the seal on the back of the envelope then read the inside of the matching card out loud. "I'm hippo-ing we can hang out sometime!" I wrinkle my nose. "Hippo-ing?"

"Hoping. I think." Annabeth peers over my shoulder. "Okay, it's a stretch. But still cute."

I stand there. Several seconds pass. "So. What do I do with it?"

"Take it inside?" Annabeth says it like a question because she probably thinks it's the obvious answer.

"And after that?"

"Gosh, Callie, I don't know. Put it in your room, maybe?"

"You're kidding, right?" She's my best friend, but she can be clueless sometimes. "I don't know who it came from, AB."

She snatches the hippo from my hands and squeezes it, nuzzling it against her face. "Fine. I'll take it home if you're worried."

"No way. The envelope says Callie Christianson, not Annabeth Mathis." I grab the hippo by the neck and step back inside. "Maybe we'll Nancy Drew it this afternoon and gather some more clues."

I can almost hear Annabeth roll her eyes as she shuts the door behind me. "Great idea. Maybe we could dust it for fingerprints too. Life isn't always a mystery, you know. Sometimes it's a romance. Can't you enjoy the romance for once?"

Not for once. For only. No guy has ever romanced me before in my life, so how am I supposed to know what to do?

I shake my head. "We don't know this is a romantic gesture. It could be some voyeur trying to put one of those nanny cams in my room."

"'I'm hippo-ing we can hang out sometime!'" Annabeth waves her hands in the air. "Yeah, that's exactly what someone says right before they end up the subject of some true crime documentary."

"That's what they'd want me to think. Lull me into a false sense of security." I toss the hippo onto the kitchen table but keep the envelope and the card, which I stuff into the back pocket of my jeans. Something about the blocky handwriting seems familiar, like I've seen it before, probably more than once or twice. But it's not Annabeth's. She still dots her Is with hearts even though we're seventeen.

"What does the timer say on the cookies?" I glance over at the oven, not quite able to see how much time is left. "They smell done."

Annabeth pulls herself up on the countertop and draws her knees to her chest without bothering to check. "They smell like cookies."

"Do they smell like award-winning cookies at least?" I ask as I grab a pair of oven mitts from a drawer and yank them on.

Annabeth shrugs. "I guess."

I squat in front of the oven door to peer inside. "I need more than an *I guess* if I'm going to have any shot at that mentorship thing."

"You mean the weekend with Raquel Martinez or whatever? The lady with that baking show?"

I frown at AB before turning my attention back to my triple-chocolate cookies. "Her name is Nichelle Melendez. And yes."

"Why would you want to do that, anyway? You'd hate being on TV."

"It's a sacrifice I'd be willing to make." A weekend with the woman who could help me figure out how to turn this baking hobby into a baking business would be worth it. One of the cookies burbles, a gooey chocolate chip oozing on the surface. I pop the oven door open and reach inside.

The doorbell chimes.

"I'll get it." Annabeth launches off the countertop and runs to the door.

I set the cookie sheet on the stove and slip off the oven mitts. "Who is it?" I call out to her. But Annabeth doesn't answer. She drives me crazy sometimes. If she's out there trying to convince a magazine salesman to come inside to try my cookies or something, we're going to have to have a serious conversation about stranger danger.

I head toward the front door and get there only to see

Annabeth peering around the large holly bush on the right side of the porch.

"What are you doing?" I lean against the doorframe.

"Looking for whoever rang the doorbell and left you those." She takes another step through the pine straw and points at a whole box of Moon Pies, the kind you have to buy to stock up a concession stand at a Little League game.

"Whoever it is, they wouldn't hide in a holly bush unless they were incredibly dumb. Those things hurt." I pick up the box. My mouth waters.

Junk food is my love language. Moon Pies have been my all-time favorite, even over any homemade treat, ever since third grade when I had my first one. The fact that someone knows this about me and left them on my porch is enough to make my knees as gooey as the chocolate chips in the cookies cooling in the kitchen. The fact that I don't know who that someone is makes me feel like I'm about to toss said cookies.

"Did you see anyone running away?" I ask.

AB shakes her head and pulls one of her copper curls free from her gold hoop earring. "Whoever it is, they move way too fast. Or they're wearing an invisibility cloak. If they ring the doorbell again, we're staking out your front porch."

I cradle the Moon Pies to my chest. "You think this person actually likes me?"

"I think they're in love with you." Annabeth goes back into the house, fluffing her hair as she walks. "But that's my opinion, so you know. Take it or leave it."

I rip open the box of Moon Pies. "I think I'll leave it."

Annabeth shrugs and reaches for a triple-chocolate cookie. She stuffs half of it in her mouth and talks through the bite. "I'm excited for you, Cal. Like, it's finally your moment to find love. Our entire summer break is in front of us, and now you've got this mystery person leaving you notes and fun presents." She sighs and swallows her cookie. "It's beautiful."

I tear a chunk off my Moon Pie and examine the edges before popping it into my mouth. "You think it could be a joke? Like someone's trying to make me look like an idiot?"

"Nobody's that mean. I'm sure it's some guy from your school. He was probably too afraid to say anything before summer started in case you'd shut him down and he'd still have to see you in the hallways every day."

The doorbell rings again before I can respond. Annabeth and I stare at each other for a whole second before she runs back to the foyer. I don't bother following her. Truthfully, I'm not sure I could. My feet may as well be glued to the floor in panic. Let's say it is some guy from school who likes me. What if he's out of my league? Or what if he's a total troll?

I hear Annabeth fling the door open. She groans.

"Still nobody?"

"Nope. Just a book this time."

"A book?" I put my Moon Pie down on a napkin on the kitchen table without taking another bite. "What kind of book?"

"An old one." Annabeth walks back into the kitchen, holding a paperback by the spine as though it's vermin. "Whoever it is definitely knows you, though. Julia Child? She's always been one of your inspirations, hasn't she?"

AB tosses the book at me, and I barely catch it. The pages slip and bend between my fingers. The front cover has a pencil-drawn illustration of Julia Child standing in front of the stove tasting something from a spoon. She looks confident. Strong. Familiar. A zing of realization shoots from my fingertips up my arms and settles into the hollow under my throat.

No. Oh, no, no.

"I left the door open, so we'll be able to see him if he comes back." Annabeth babbles on. "Try tiptoeing around here now, Mr. Shifty McSneakyPants."

I peel back the front cover. There's a neon green Post-it note on the front page. On it, in the same blocky handwriting from the envelope, are the words, *Find something you're passionate about and keep tremendously interested in it. –J. Child*

The Moon Pie churns in my stomach as I grasp the countertop suddenly breathless and dizzy. Why him? Why now? And why didn't I put the pieces together before?

"Um, hello?" a deep voice calls through the open front door. Annabeth bolts toward it.

I don't have to rush. I already know who's standing there on our front porch. He's been here a million times before, but it's been a while since the last time. A whole two years in fact.

I fold my arms over my stomach so tightly it feels as though I could possibly snap myself in half. Annabeth returns, grinning and dragging our visitor by the elbow. He's much taller now than I'd realized. He towers over both me and Annabeth, hovering somewhere over six feet. And his hair—it's turned dark brown. At some point throughout the years, he lost his signature stuck-a-fork-in-an-electrical-outlet poof, trading it in for a more sophisticated cut: longer on the top and shorter on the sides. I never imagined I'd see him in anything other than athletic shorts and a T-shirt, but here he is in khakis, a green and gray button-down, and a striped bow tie. He clutches a bouquet of white Gerber daisies in one hand, nearly strangling them.

We've passed each other in the hallway at school a few times, but my strategy during school hours has always been more along the lines of duck and run instead of stand and stare. But now staring seems to be the only thing I can do.

"Hi, Cal." Egan Pasko lifts the hand not holding the flowers in a sort of half wave.

Annabeth stands to the side, her eyes wide and glittery. She thinks he's my prince. But he and I both know the truth.

Egan's no prince. He's my ex-best friend.

Chapter 2

MY FACE BURNS. LITERALLY. IF I STAND HERE MUCH longer, I may spontaneously combust in a confluence of hives, confusion, and the memory of all the angry letters I've written over the last two years but never sent. And so I say, and do, nothing. For a full forty-five seconds, I stare. Annabeth's grin fades while Egan picks at imaginary lint on his sleeves. She looks from my face to Egan's then back to mine.

Finally, Egan pushes his glasses up the bridge of his nose and clears his throat. "I...wanted to return your book."

I stare at him without blinking, without smiling, without any indication that his sudden reappearance has surprised me. I barely even breathe.

He scratches the back of his head. "Sorry I kept it so long."

"Whatever." I lift an eyebrow in nonchalance. "No big." And then I cringe inwardly. Seriously? The first thing I choose to say to him in two years is, *Whatever. No big?*

"These are for you." He hands me the bouquet of daisies.

I just look at them.

Annabeth steps behind me, nudging me forward. "Take them and say thank you, Cal."

I know what she's thinking: I'm being ridiculously rude, even for me. But she doesn't understand what's going on here. She and I go to church together, where my grandparents and I landed after I'd begged them to try a new place, somewhere significantly less Egan-y than the church where he and I had grown up. And she goes to a private school twenty minutes away from my public school.

For all Annabeth knows, she was right and Egan is just another cute guy who roams the hallways with me at Creekside Ridge. Egan is a stranger to her. I never told her I had a best friend before her. Or that it broke my heart when he left me.

"Thanks." I yank the flowers from him and plunk them on the counter near the sink without bothering to look for a vase. I turn back to both Egan and Annabeth and cross my arms over my chest.

There's yellow pollen stuck to the front of Egan's slightly wrinkled khakis. He sucks in a deep breath through his teeth and looks around slowly like he's trying to figure out what's changed. "So. This is going well."

"Callie," Annabeth grinds out through clenched teeth. "What is wrong with you?"

"Didn't you have that thing? Tonight?" I grasp her wrist. "The thing you had to take care of immediately."

She wrinkles her nose. "Thing?"

Why she can pick up when I'm in the mood for stir-fry one minute and can't understand my not-so-subtle-wink-wink-nudge-nudge the next, I'll never understand. I pat her shoulder as though I think she must merely have a lapse in memory. "Isn't it your cat's birthday or something?"

After seconds of silent agony, Annabeth nods. Slowly. "Oh, right. I never miss the opportunity to throw a party for Mrs. Tinkles." She backs away but lobs a parting shot at me. "Don't forget, Cal. You said you'd be there later. In costume. Those kittens sure love Captain Catnip."

Egan chokes back a laugh, and as soon as she moves out of earshot, he raises an eyebrow. "Mrs. Tinkles?"

I trace a pattern in the granite countertop with my thumbnail. "Her brother named it."

"She doesn't have a cat, does she?"

"No. She doesn't." I drop the ruse and turn the brunt of my gaze on Egan. "Why are you here?"

Egan pretends like he doesn't hear me as he wanders around the kitchen island to the sink. He opens the bottom cabinet, pulls out an empty vase, fills it with water, then sets the daisies in it. "You should probably clip the bottoms so they don't wilt even more."

"Egan." I drop into a chair at the kitchen table and jam my hands under my thighs.

"I know. I went overboard on all this. But I needed to talk to you. I couldn't figure out another way to get your attention." He points to the chair next to mine at the table. "Can I sit?"

I review my options.

I could ask him to leave. But he'd likely ignore me and stay anyway.

I could throw sharp objects at him and hope the police wouldn't find out.

Or, the least appealing option, I could let him sit. Listen to what he has to say. And then send him on his way with no intention of speaking to him ever again.

I pinch the bridge of my nose. My hands are shaking. "Fine. Sit."

Egan pulls the chair out. The legs clunk and scrape across the floor, and I wince. He eases down and rests his elbows on his knees. "How're your grandparents?"

"Fine."

"They busy these days?"

"Busy enough. Grandma has a partial caseload now, but she's still working at Creekside Counseling on Thursdays and

Fridays. And Grandpa technically retired a couple years ago. But he's consulting for the police department now. Are you really here to ask about them though?"

Egan drags his hand across the back of his head and sighs. "No. But I'm not sure where else to start."

I look over his shoulder, refusing to meet his gaze. "Maybe with why you're here. Sitting in my kitchen. After two years of nothing."

He adjusts his glasses again, pinching the arm where it meets the rectangular frames. "You didn't want me around, Noog."

"I was hurt," I manage to whisper, caught off guard by the ancient nickname and the flood of memories that come with it.

"You took it too personally."

The searing ache that's fueled hundreds of one-sided morning mirror debates wells up in my chest. "How else was I supposed to take it, E?"

I still remember everything as clearly as if I were watching it play out in real time in front of me. Things had been weird between us for a few months. Sometime after Christmas I'd started comparing Egan's eyes to brown sugar and molasses instead of mud and old coffee grounds. It was dumb and cliché, falling for my best friend.

But it turns out it didn't matter because in February of freshman year Egan said he was too busy to go to a basketball game with me. Then I saw him sitting at the top of the bleachers with the track team while I played my clarinet in the band section. He promised to come to my birthday party but never showed up. He stopped saving a seat for me in the cafeteria at lunch.

I pretended none of it mattered, that we were growing up and he felt as awkward around me as I did around him and maybe that meant something. Or at least it's what I told myself until the last week of school.

Egan had sidled up next to me as I switched out my geometry book with my biology book. He'd peered into the mostly empty space of my locker and grinned. I remember the way my heart flip-flopped.

"Bet you can't fit in there." Egan had pointed to my locker, a spark in his smile.

I'd laughed and gazed at him wide-eyed. "Why would I want to try?"

"Because it would be hilarious, Noog. Come on. You're small enough to fit."

While junk food has always been my love language, stupid human tricks were always Egan's.

So, I set all my books on the floor, pulled myself into my top locker, folded my arms and knees inside, and leveled him with a smug smile. "Happy?" I'd asked, basking in the music of his laughter.

Seconds later a person outside of my field of vision slammed my locker door shut.

"Leave her in there," someone yelled as I blinked in the darkness.

"Yeah," a different person laughed, "Two-shoes deserves it."

Since I couldn't see him, I don't know if Egan hesitated, if he laughed, or if he turned immediately and walked away. But the point is, he walked away.

It took seventeen minutes for the school to locate the master key to get me out, and by the time I was free Egan was gone, and my crush and our friendship were both over for good.

Now I ask my question again, softer this time. "How else was I supposed to take it?"

Egan raises his shoulders. "It was a joke. A dumb joke, okay? I didn't think it was going to cost me…" He clears his throat and holds his hands in front of his body, palms up, fingers splayed out. "I didn't think it was going to cost me my best friend."

We stare at each other, and I count my breaths until I can speak again. "Why didn't you apologize?"

Egan looks away and leans back, sticking his legs out so his feet rest under my chair. He stuffs his hands into the pockets of his khakis. "Because I was fifteen. And monumentally stupid."

My lips twitch, but I don't smile.

He continues. "I didn't know what to do, I guess. You're a girl, and people were weird about us hanging out so much. I figured we'd had a good run and I'd leave it at that."

"It sucked."

"I know. It sucked for me too. Only it took me longer to realize it." Egan reaches over and grabs the stuffed hippo from the tabletop. He palms it like a football. "I'm really sorry, Callie. For everything."

Most of me wants to push him out of the house with a *don't let the door hit ya*. But then a tiny sliver of me has missed him, missed our friendship. Missed us. Nobody, not even Annabeth, knows me as well as Egan used to.

"I know what you're thinking." Egan interrupts my waffling.

"You do?"

"Yep. You're wondering how long you can drag this out so I'll bring you more Moon Pies."

I laugh. "So not what I was thinking."

"Oh. Well, I got nothin' then." Egan sets the hippo on the table then stands up and holds his arms out wide. He smiles. The single dimple on his cheek deepens.

I stand too but don't move toward him.

His smile disappears. He draws his arms back in and locks his fingers together in front of his chest. "I am for real sorry.

Forgive me?" His voice is low, deeper than I've ever heard before.

My heart pounds in my throat, and it feels like I've traded my T-shirt for a tight, woolen turtleneck. I hold my breath and count seconds. When I get to seventeen, Egan touches my shoulder with his fingertips. "Noog?"

I jerk away. "Don't call me that." I press my fingers to my temples and shake my head. "And I can't. Not right now."

"Oh." He whispers the single syllable. "Okay. Well."

"I'm really sorry," I say, then immediately want to cover my face with my hands. Why am I apologizing? He's the idiot here, not me.

Egan scratches the back of his head and looks away. "I get it. It was a long shot to begin with. I was just kind of desperate, and—no, never mind. It's not your problem." Without warning he steps close and crushes my cheek against his chest, curling one arm around me and holding me tight. The buttons on his shirt gouge my face. He smells like clean laundry.

"Anyway, it was good to see you again," he says.

"You…too." My voice is muffled. I stand there, arms dangling at my sides, because, of all the things I thought I'd be doing today, hugging Egan Pasko was not one of them.

Egan steps away. He backs down the hallway and holds one hand up in a stationary wave. "Have a good summer, Noog—I mean, Callie."

"Sure. I will. That is, I mean, you too." I start to wave back, but a loud clatter followed by a series of softer thuds in the front foyer interrupts.

Egan whips around and lunges toward the noise. I spring after him and nearly bump into his back when he stops suddenly in front of the open hall closet. My grandma's faux-fur winter coat, the hose from a long-departed vacuum cleaner, and Annabeth are in a pile on the floor.

"Annabeth." I frown at her as though she's a naughty toddler. "Seriously? What are you still doing here?"

"That's it?" Annabeth reaches for Egan's hand, gasping as though she's erupting from the sea. "Please tell me you didn't do all that—the hippo, Moon Pies, the book, the flowers—just for some lame apology."

"It wasn't…" I watch wide-eyed, my words dying in my throat as Annabeth tumbles out into the hallway while Egan tries to extricate himself from her clutches. The vacuum hose is tangled around her ankles.

Egan looks at me, his eyebrows raised over his glasses.

I square my shoulders and march over to grab Egan's wrist and pry Annabeth's fingers off him one by one. "This is not okay, Annabeth. Let go of him. You don't even know him."

She stares up at Egan and puts one hand on top of his shiny brown loafer as though it'll keep him from escaping, then pops upright and sticks her hand out. "I'm Annabeth Mathis. And you are?"

Egan gives her hand a quick, perfunctory shake. "Egan Pasko."

"So now that we know each other, there's more to it, isn't there?" A stray piece of her hair sticks to her nose, and she swipes it away with her free hand. She looks like a wild-eyed, auburn Medusa.

When Egan stays silent, I roll my eyes. "Okay, this is ridiculous. Bye, E—"

"She's right." Egan stuffs his hands in his pockets and looks away.

"Wait. What?" I squint at him.

Annabeth claps her hands together. "I knew it."

Egan nods. "Your friend is right. There is—was—more."

"And?" Annabeth asks when I say nothing. Her brown eyes are huge, nearly taking up her entire face. She leans toward Egan in eager expectation.

"And…" Egan turns his full attention back to me. He half-shrugs. "Well, it sounds weird now. But I wanted to take you on a date. Or, rather, I wanted to take you on twenty-one of them."

Chapter 3

ANNABETH SHRIEKS AND POPS UP FROM THE floor.

He's joking. He has to be. This is the guy who, up until we were fourteen, crossed his fingers to ward me off like an evil spirit whenever anyone mentioned the word "girlfriend" in front of us.

"You aren't serious. Are you?" My voice shakes and squeaks, and I hate myself for it.

Egan crosses his lanky arms over his chest and grimaces. "I kinda was."

"Why?" I shake my head. "We aren't a thing."

"But you could be." Annabeth jumps in again and grasps Egan's elbow. "Tell us more."

I press my fingers to my forehead and stare at the ground. This can't be happening.

"Well." He clears his throat. "You remember my brother, right?"

I draw a deep, less-than-cleansing breath in through my nose and nod. "Of course I remember Owen."

"We're kind of in a competition right now."

I raise an eyebrow. "You're always competing over something."

"But this time it's a real thing. With real-life implications."

I turn around and walk back to the kitchen. I don't want to hear the rest of this, whatever *this* is. I should have pushed him out the front door when I had the chance. Annabeth follows on my heels. Egan too, though he's slower. Probably afraid I'll bean him with a skillet.

I pretend like neither of them are there and pull a spatula from a drawer near the oven then scrape the nearly forgotten cookies off the sheet and dump them into a baggie.

"Owen and I both started posting videos online." Egan clears his throat and continues even though I've done nothing to encourage him to that end. "Whoever hits a thousand views first on a single video, wins."

I seal the baggie and set the cookies on the island then move to the sink to wash my hands.

"What would you win?" Annabeth leans against the counter.

Egan shrugs. "Bragging rights for the rest of our lives."

I look at them both over my shoulder then turn the water off and dry my hands on a navy kitchen towel. "That sounds dumb."

"And you," Egan points at me with both index fingers, "sound like an only child."

"I am an only child."

Egan smirks. "Well, my idea was to take you on twenty-one dates. We'd record them all and put it online. It would have landed us a *hundred* thousand views. People are obsessed with the idea of friends falling in love." Egan steps close but doesn't touch me. He dips to my eye-level and props one hand on my shoulder. He waves his other hand in front of us as though he's casting a vision. "I was going to call it, 'The Great Date Experiment.'" He straightens and steps away quickly when I reach for my spatula. "Anyway, it doesn't matter since you won't do it."

It also doesn't matter because we aren't friends.

I drop the spatula in the sink and press my palms to the cool stainless steel as I count the comforting *plunk-plunks* of the ice falling from the ice maker in the freezer.

"She'll do it." Annabeth grabs my elbow, yanking me back into the moment.

I weasel out of her clutches. "No. I won't."

"Cal, it's perfect. We were talking about how much you needed a summer romance, and now, poof! Here he is." She frames Egan's body with outstretched arms.

"We were not talking about how I needed a summer romance. That was all you." But even if I was into that idea, it wouldn't be with Egan. I glance at him, careful not to make eye contact. His mouth twitches, but he doesn't say anything.

Annabeth turns her back on me and tugs on Egan's sleeve. "When do we start?"

"We?" I ask.

"Yes, we. You're going to need a camera person, and I'm perfect for the job. I'll fade into the background, like curtains."

"Last I checked curtains don't butt into private conversations." I frown at her. "Why didn't you go home like I asked you to?"

Annabeth ignores me. "What kind of camera are you using? Just a phone? My dad has a nice professional camera, but I'm not sure he'll let me borrow it. Maybe if I tell him it's for a school project."

Egan covers his mouth with his hand like he's trying to hide a smile.

"Is anybody going to say anything?" Annabeth abandons Egan's side and grabs the bag of cookies. "Why aren't y'all listening to me?"

I barely stifle a growl. "Because nobody asked you to be here. You were supposed to be going home."

She harrumphs, takes a cookie, and drops the bag onto the counter. "Well, I'm here now, and it's a good thing. If I weren't, you'd have thrown this whole thing away for no good reason."

"I'm still going to throw the whole thing away, and I have plenty of good reasons." I reach for the unsealed bag of cookies.

"He's onto something." Annabeth leans close like she's telling me a secret, except we both know Egan can still hear. "Two words for you, Cal: Raquel Martinez."

My fingers still over the zip top of the baggie full of cookies. "Nichelle Melendez." I whisper the correction.

"You have to get a certain number of online supporters or something before you can do the show mentorship, don't you?"

Two hundred and fifty. I need two hundred and fifty fans of some sort across any social media platform just to qualify for the opportunity to submit my application. And for me, two hundred and fifty may as well be a couple million. But for Egan, I have a feeling it's a quarter of his phone's contact list.

"What's it worth to you?" Annabeth tilts her head to the side and taps her chin with her fingers. "Twenty-one dates, maybe?"

Egan's watching us, his eyebrows knit together in the middle. "What are you two—"

"I'll do it." The words tumble out of my mouth, feeling foreign.

"You're saying yes?" A slow smile creeps over Egan's lips. He touches my elbow, and I stare at his fingers. He pulls his hand back.

"I'm saying…" My voice comes out in a garbled whisper. I cough and start over. "Yes."

Annabeth claps and bounces on her toes like she's captain of my very own hype squad, heavy on the hype.

I point at Egan. "Twenty-one dates. That's it. And no re-dos either, even if you think a date was boring."

Egan's smile flattens, and he dips his chin and looks me full in the face. "Twenty-one dates. You have my word."

Chapter 4

I READ THROUGH THE LIST AGAIN.

- *Fresh berry puff pastry tarts*
- *Chocolate-chip banana cake with peanut butter icing*
- *Salted caramel pecan bars*
- *Pink lemonade pound cake*

My handwriting is perfect. The smooth pages of the yellow legal pad are perfect. Even my backyard surroundings, the humming June bugs and long shadows slicing through the golden sunlight, are perfect. It's a quintessential Carolina summer evening. But my stomach still churns.

All of this, everything I've put together here, it's too basic. Nichelle Melendez won't care about my recipes. Even a first grader could throw them together.

I yank the page from the notepad then crumple it in my hands before dropping it over the edge of the hammock. It falls into the mulch below. I squeeze my eyes shut and wrap my arms around my stomach. The hammock sways.

"Here we have the introvert in her natural habitat, in the backyard hammock. Let's try to get closer and see if she reacts."

My eyelids pop open, but the rest of me is frozen in place. Maybe if I stay still long enough he'll leave.

"Note the pile of waste. It looks like she's been here a while." Egan's voice is nearer now, and he sounds like an Outback Steakhouse commercial. "She's even kicked off her shoes. Note her hideous toe-talons. Have you ever seen such ridiculously small—"

"Your Australian is atrocious, E." I roll my eyes and curl my toes under to hide them, and my tiny toenails, from his scrutiny as my heart rate inches upward.

Suddenly, he's beside the hammock, his phone pointed at my face. He grins when I look at him. "Crikey! A screech. What a delight to hear her excitement at our presence."

"It's more like a warning sound. Like, hey, turn off the phone and get it out of my face." I swat it away and miss.

He touches his phone's screen then crams his hands and the phone into the pockets of his jeans. "So. Hi."

"Hi."

He rocks back on his heels. "How are you?"

I bite my lower lip and fight the urge to count the stripes on his gray and navy T-shirt. "Fine. You?"

"I'm okay." He nods a little bit and motions toward the hammock. "Can I?"

"With me?"

"I'm not kicking you out of your own hammock, so…" Egan half shrugs and tilts his head to one side. A tiny smile plays around the corners of his mouth, and he steps closer, wrapping his fingers around the edge of the hammock.

"Oh. Right. I mean, I'd rather you—" Before I can finish my sentence, Egan rolls his whole body into the swing next to me. "Not," I finish with a whisper and a frown.

Egan folds his hands behind his head, his elbows splayed out above us. But our sides still cocoon together, my arm pressed into his rib cage and our ankles touching. Close. Too close. "Ah," he sighs loudly. "Relaxing."

I move away but keep sliding to the middle, weighed down by his body. All I manage to do is poke my whole arm through the holes in the hammock. I give up and cross my arms over my stomach, staring into the purpling sky above.

"I made a promo video." Egan doesn't waste much time with quiet.

"Wow. That was fast."

"It's been twenty-four hours since you said yes. Don't really need more time than that. Want to see it?"

I lift my left shoulder, the one nearly crammed into his armpit. "I guess."

Egan bumps me with his elbow. "Don't get too excited."

My nose twitches. "I probably shouldn't have said yes."

He's silent for two whole seconds. A record. "But you did."

"I still have questions." Lots of them. Like, is there any chance the outcome of this thing isn't going to be an utter disaster? And why does my stomach still feel like a deflated, twisted up inner tube? And how do I stop my mind from replaying moments from the last hour of our friendship, moments I thought I'd long since buried?

Egan doesn't say anything, and I pick at the hem of my shirt. Finally, he turns and tucks his hand into his cheek, using his elbow to support his body. "Well?" he asks.

"Well, what?"

"What are the questions?"

"Oh. I mean, there are a lot of them."

"I'm not busy."

"I am."

"Then ask fast."

Ugh. "Right. Okay." I scramble to come up with a legit question. A logistical one. One that won't make it seem like my baker's block has everything to do with his sudden reappearance. "Well, first I guess I want to know who's going to pay for these dates. They're going to add up. I mean, even if we went to Dollar Cone every day, it'd still be at least forty-two dollars."

Egan smirks. "I'm not taking you to Dollar Cone twenty-one times. And I'm paying for everything. All of it. Of course."

"Seriously? With what cash?"

"I found a wad of hundreds taped to the inside of the trash can on Naylor Street. Think that'll work?"

My eyes grow wide.

He laughs. "I work, Callie. After school, on weekends. Even during the summer."

"You work."

He rolls his eyes. "We aren't fourteen anymore. I'm a responsible, contributing member of society now. You don't have a summer job or anything? I'd have thought your grandparents would be all over that."

I shrug. "I might help Annabeth babysit sometimes if she's desperate. But it's the summer before senior year. I think they're kind of hoping we get in some family time. Memory building and all that."

"That's cute." Egan pats the top of my head. "Pretty sure my parents are counting the minutes until I'm out of the house so they can save on groceries."

"That's fair. Where do you work?"

"Creekside Quick Wash. Is this an interrogation?"

I look away like I'm not at all interested in the conversation. "I said I had questions." When I turn back, I see he's still watching me, the barest quirk of a smile lifting the corner of his mouth.

"Okay, then, what else?" Egan presses his index finger into my shoulder.

I look down at my hands, curled into fists. I force them to lie flat against my stomach instead. "What about privacy?"

glance over in time to see Egan's eyelashes flutter against the lenses of his glasses.

"I think it's important? Are you talking in general, or what?"

"No." I shake my head. The hammock sways. "I'm talking online. There are a lot of weirdos out there, you know."

Egan nods. His glasses slip, and he pushes them back up the bridge of his nose. "I don't plan on posting our addresses or our phone numbers or the codes to your grandparents' security system or anything."

"You still remember the codes to the security system?"

Egan ignores that question. "We'll be smart. Just like we are with any other social media, you know? Of course I won't broadcast where we're going ahead of time. If you want, we won't even use our real names. I'll call you Noog the entire time."

I flinch. "No, thanks. Besides, I already told you not to call me that."

"What's wrong with Noog?"

"I remember what it originally was."

"Ah, yes." Egan nods thoughtfully. "Noogie Woogie Boogie Pants."

I roll my eyes. "Exactly."

"Owen and I were insanely creative back then. I still don't understand why it bothered you so much."

"Maybe it had something to do with the fact that you also paired it with noogies? Just a thought."

"That's right." Egan snaps his fingers as though he'd merely forgotten after all this time. He shifts like he's going to drag me into a noogie for old time's sake.

I not-so-accidentally jab him in the ribs. With force. For old time's sake.

He coughs, holding his hands up in surrender. "Okay, no more noogies. I get it. But the name is still fun."

"No way. I don't want it living online for all eternity. What if I'm looking for a job in ten years and some prospective employer comes across this? I don't want them thinking I actually go by 'Noog.' And nobody's called me that in years."

"We haven't spent time together in years."

"Just don't do it, okay?" I rake my fingers through my hair, and my knuckles tangle around a knot.

"Fair enough. Any other questions?"

My mind grasps for something else and comes up empty. I press my lips together into some semblance of a smile and shake my head. "That's it. For now."

Egan pulls his phone from his pocket. He holds it in front of my face. "Great. Let me show you this, then. It's going to go live at midnight tonight." He swipes at the screen a few times then mashes the *play* symbol with his thumb.

A poppy, bright tune full of acoustic guitar riffs and maybe even a little piccolo or something floats from his phone. The words "Great Date Experiment" fade onto the screen in front of a black background. He's shaped them into the form of a cute bow tie.

It's much more than I thought it would be.

The logo fades into black, then white text appears.

Featuring Egan and Callie.

The music continues in one fluid wave, carrying a slideshow of photos beginning with Egan's fourth birthday party. It morphs into a picture of me, a couple weeks later, dressed up in my lavender Easter dress, strawberry blond curls springing from my head, while Egan stands nearby in seersucker and saddle shoes, nearly strangling a baby chick. His eyes are the same color as the remnants of a chocolate Easter bunny smeared around his mouth.

I almost laugh at the photo of us after Egan broke his arm trying some crazy stunt on the diving board at the pool. His dark brown hair is streaked with lighter mahogany, a side effect of all the chlorine and sun from earlier in the summer. There's a loopy grin on his face, probably from whatever painkillers he'd been given, and I'm trying to write my name on his camouflage cast in a straight line.

We get older and older throughout the show while the music bounces on until finally the most recent picture appears and grows. I know it's the most recent because it's the last picture we ever took together.

Both of us are smiling, him with his trademark open-mouthed grin, and me flashing my braces with the silver and teal rubber bands to the entire world. A piece of my hair is strung across Egan's forehead like a tawny, sunset-gold ribbon. Both my arms are wrapped around his neck, and he's got one hand on my elbow.

Our neighborhood was having a picnic, and, since there weren't any track team members living nearby, I guess Egan figured we were safe to hang out.

It was two weeks before our friendship melted down.

The video pauses and buffers, leaving me time to inspect my old joy and Egan's neon green shirt. The longer I stare, the blurrier the picture becomes. I blink several times and look away.

"Good job," I say.

"It's not done yet." Egan frowns at his phone.

"It's fine. I get the idea. Midnight, huh?"

Egan clears the screen and crams his phone back into his pocket. "Yep. Going live after midnight. No take backsies after that, so speak now or whatever."

Now's my chance. I open my mouth to tell him I'd rather not, but then my gaze catches on the crumpled-up list of desserts discarded in the mulch beneath us, and instead of saying anything I inhale deeply. The breath escapes me in a sigh.

I won't be able to do it without him. I need him. And I hate it.

I look away into the distance of the woods behind the next-door neighbor's house. "You can post it. It's fine. No take backsies."

Chapter 5

MY ALARM GOES OFF AT 5:15, SAME AS IT DOES every other school day, and I swat at it to snooze. But it doesn't stop. And that's when I remember—this is summer vacation. And it's Saturday.

I squint at the screen and barely make out the goofy picture of Egan imported from his social media when I put his number into my contacts last night. I don't have the energy to groan, so I pick up the phone and will myself not to heave it across the room. It goes to voicemail before I answer, and seconds later Egan calls back.

This time I manage to answer the call but drop the phone onto my pillow before I can get it to my face. It seems like too much effort to find it, so I merely mumble a lackluster hello.

"Callie?" Egan's voice sounds like he bathed in coffee grounds this morning, all chipper and sunshine-y. "You awake?"

I grumble a few not-so-nice words then hoist myself up onto my elbow and paw around for my phone. Once I find it, I move the speaker to my mouth. "I am now." My voice sounds like I've been hibernating for the last six months. And I kind of feel that way too.

"Great." Egan either ignores my disgruntled tone or doesn't notice it. "Sorry for the late notice, but I've got a great date to kick off the Experiment. Can you be ready in twenty minutes?"

I hold the phone away from my face and glare at it, my upper lip twitching in disgust. "You've got to be kidding me right now. I thought we were going to start this thing on Monday."

"It went live at midnight, remember? Besides, this is sort of time sensitive. I'll bring you, um. Something. Do you drink coffee now?"

"No. Ew." I let my head fall back onto my pillow. A spray of my hair sticks to my lips, and I spit it away.

Egan says something that sounds suspiciously like, "Maybe you should," before covering it up quickly with a cough and a chuckle. "How about a doughnut? Will that help?"

"Two doughnuts."

"O—kay. Two doughnuts, then. But you'd better be ready to go when I get there. You've got twenty-five minutes since I have to go pick up doughnuts now."

"I want sprinkles."

"Can do."

"And chocolate icing, too."

I can almost hear Egan rolling his eyes over the phone. "Anything else, my liege?" he teases.

Nobody should tease when the sun is still asleep. "Your head on a platter."

"I'm going to pretend I didn't hear that." His voice muffles, like he's pressing the phone between his cheek and his shoulder so he can get a head start. "And you should dress like we're going to gym class, okay? Athletic shorts. T-shirt. Ponytail. All that stuff. See you soon."

"What?" Now I really am going to throw my phone across the room. "This doesn't sound like—"

But Egan's already hung up on me.

I stuff my face into my pillow and groan.

It's only my love of breakfast pastries and Nichelle Melendez that compels me to ooze from bed to plod across my room to my closet so I can find the outfit I wore for gym class last semester. It's shoved behind literally every other piece of clothing I own because I detest gym class and I figured I'd never have to wear it again, hallelujah.

Until Egan.

"Wear my gym clothes. Stupid." I mumble and shake my head as I pull the hot pink shorts out from behind the dirty laundry basket. I find the black shirt with my church's seventeenth annual barbecue logo screen printed on the front and pull on the whole ensemble before squinting in the mirror.

I look like a yeti. My hair is everywhere but layered around my shoulders like it's supposed to be. My eyes are normally the unmistakable blue of a cloudless summer sky, but right now they're more of a soupy, hazy gray. And the freckles on my nose look like someone sneezed on my face.

In spite of the futility of the actions, I go about getting ready, combing out my hair, wiping down my face with a makeup removing cloth, and brushing my teeth.

I stomp downstairs with an entire minute to spare, though it's a gamble as to whether or not Egan will actually stick to his timeline or if he got distracted along the way. Somewhere in the pantry Grandma keeps a coffee maker for guests since neither she nor Grandpa drink it. And I aim to find it. Maybe today's the day for me to start drinking it.

My phone rings, and I scramble to answer it so quickly I drop it on the floor instead. It lands with an enormous smack, startling my fluffy, white cat, Hedwig, out from under the kitchen table where she'd been batting at one of her pom-pom toys.

"Shh," I shush it. "You're going to wake up the whole—"

"Cal? You're up early." Grandpa's voice cuts through my early morning fog, and I startle so much my shoulders hunch up toward my ears.

Never mind on the coffee. Now I'm wired.

My phone trills again. I send Egan to voicemail.

"Thought I'd start this summer a little differently." Or a lot differently.

"With Annabeth?" Grandpa raises an eyebrow. He's already fully dressed for the day, in jeans and a powder blue button-down shirt rolled up to his elbows.

"Sure." It'll take far too long to explain the reality of the situation, so I toss out a fib. I reach for my gray hoodie draped over the back of one of the kitchen chairs. My phone starts ringing again, and I silence it. "I've got to get going. Dinner together tonight?"

I step up onto my tiptoes and kiss his cheek. He smells like shaving cream.

"Yep." Grandpa pulls me in for a hug. When I move away he squints at me as though he's trying to read the rest of my story. "Choose a restaurant yet?"

"Not yet. But I will. I promise. Bye, Grandpa." I grab a banana from the fruit bowl on the counter and power walk toward the front of the house.

As soon as I emerge from the garage, Egan's car is waiting, parked in the driveway. When I open the passenger's side door, he grins and leans over the center console to pick up a flat, rectangular box from my seat.

"Hey, you followed instructions. Great outfit." He slides the box of doughnuts onto the dashboard.

I roll my eyes. "I always follow instructions. Do you?" I lift the lid and sniff the air. Chocolate icing.

"Two chocolate-and-sprinkle-covered doughnuts, for you and you alone." Egan reaches behind my headrest and looks behind us as he backs down the driveway. "And ten other doughnuts of various edibility because they told me I had to get a whole dozen. I have no idea what I'm going to do with them all."

"Eat them?" I pluck a doughnut with a bunch of red, white, and blue sprinkles all over it from the box and sink my teeth into it.

Egan shudders. "Nah. I don't eat much sugar anymore."

I raise an eyebrow at him. "Seriously?"

"Seriously. This body isn't a work of Twinkies and Snickers bars, that's for sure. But I won't judge you, don't worry."

"What," my breath gets stuck in my throat around a wad of doughnut, "is it a work of? Not like I've noticed or anything."

His mouth twitches. "Mostly salads. A few steaks. Some fruit. A lot of water."

I lick a glob of icing off my finger. "Sounds depressing."

And, judging by the way his bicep stretches the arm of his T-shirt, it also seems like it's working. But he certainly won't hear that from me.

He shrugs. "It's kind of a necessity. I have type 1 diabetes. Got the diagnosis the summer after freshman year."

"For real?" I glance over at him in time to catch his wry smile.

"Yeah, for real." He tugs his shirtsleeve up to reveal a small white box taped to the back of his upper arm. "I have to wear an insulin pump to help regulate my blood sugar. This one's called a pod."

"Oh." I wince. "Sorry."

"It's not your fault. I also get some swanky jewelry out of the deal." He holds up his left wrist, which has a simple silver bracelet dangling around it. There's a charm on the bracelet, and it looks like it's been embossed with a red cross-like symbol. "Medical alert bracelet. Just in case I keel over or something and the paramedics need to know my info." He slows and hits the turn signal.

I merely nod, unsure of what to say next.

Egan doesn't say anything else either, but he does start tapping his hands on the steering wheel and bobbing his head to some sort of silent beat while he waits for an opportunity to take his left turn.

After he's filed in behind a steel-gray SUV, I speak up again. "What sort of torture have you dreamed up for me this morning? Please tell me we're not shoveling poop or something. That's not any fun, you realize."

Egan laughs. "No, nothing like that. It's a fun run."

I almost drop my doughnut in my lap. "A what-what?"

"Fun run," Egan repeats as though I merely couldn't hear him.

"No, I know what you said. But those two words don't go together. In any context."

"Well, this one is awesome. Trust me."

"That's kind of the problem." I stare at my doughnut. Suddenly the icing tastes like tree bark.

"It's called the Oink and Moo 5k. Our entry fees went to local farmers, so they'll be able to stay in business over the summer. Sounds cool, right?"

"Oink?" I ask, unsure if I heard him correctly and unsure if I want to know the rest of it. "Like a pig?"

"Yeah. Oink and Moo. And it gets even better—we're going to dress like a pig and a cow. I've got your ears, nose, and tail in the back seat."

I look over my shoulder. Sure enough, there's a plastic pig's snout, pointy porcine felt ears attached to a headband, and a corkscrew pipe cleaner tail in the seat behind mine.

"You've got to be kidding me. You want me to dress like

a pig?" I stare at him, and for the first time realize his white T-shirt isn't only a little dirty. He's drawn black blotches all over it with marker. "And you're going to be a cow?"

He glances over at me, and his kid-on-Christmas-Eve expression falters. "You want to be the cow instead? I guess we could switch shirts or something if you want." He looks me up and down as I count passing streetlamps and wish I was somewhere else. Anywhere else. "I think my shirt might be too big for you though. Your barbecue shirt is awesome, by the way. Did you guess what we were going to do?"

I scrub my face with my palms. "No. And I don't want to be a cow. I don't want to be a pig either."

Egan slows for a stop sign. "They don't have any other choices."

"I'm saying I don't want to do this race thing, E."

"What? Why not?" Egan frowns then turns back to the road and hits the gas.

The box of doughnuts slides off the dash into my lap. I seize the opportunity and grab the other sprinkle-covered breakfast treat. I push it under Egan's nose. "Because I'm not a runner. I'm a junk food eater. A couch potato. A Netflix binger. Not a runner."

He sniffs and wrinkles his nose like the smell of the doughnut churns his stomach. "Aww, Noog. Give it one chance, okay? I'll stick with you the whole time."

"Don't call me that."

"Sorry." His eyebrows raise the slightest bit, and he stares straight ahead. "Callie."

The tires make a *thump-thump* sound as we ease over a speed bump. I sigh. "Do I have to finish the race?"

"I guess not. But it's only a 5k. You know, three-point-one miles? It's not that far, pretty easy."

Because I'm exceedingly gracious, I don't reach over the center console to rip his head from his shoulders. "Maybe three-point-one miles is easy for you, but I still don't run. Do we need to rehash the Netflix binging aspect of my lifestyle?"

Egan's fingers tighten around the steering wheel, and his knuckles go white. "So, it's outside of your little Callie box. It's okay to try something new every once in a while, you know."

I shove the doughnut box back on the dashboard. The corner crumples. "I try new things all the time."

"Like what? In the last month, what are all the new things you've decided to do?" The fuzzy dull orange of the rising sun in the distance makes his face look like he's been using too much cheap sunless tanner.

I cross my arms over my chest. "This."

"Besides this."

"I…" I flip back through my memories from the last month: studying for the entirety of exam week, signing the same yearbooks I've signed since kindergarten (excepting Egan's), eating Rocky Road ice cream out of the carton with Grandma and Grandpa in the living room after the last day of school.

Egan smirks at my hesitation. "Having trouble coming up with something?"

"No." I shake my head so hard a piece of hair slips from my ponytail. "I just—oh. I went to the new library that opened on Robeson Parkway last week."

"Wow. That's incredible." Egan lifts both his hands from the steering wheel and waves them in the air in mock celebration. "Way to prove me completely right."

I glare at him. "Just because I'm not like you doesn't mean there's something wrong with me."

"Didn't say that." Egan hits his turn signal and steers the car into a large gravel lot on the outskirts of Idaville Park. He pulls into a space, puts the car into park, then reaches into the back seat for the pig nose. "Look, I get it. This was maybe not the best idea for our first date."

"You think?" My stomach clenches when a group of girls our age walks past the car wearing hot pink tutus and snouts. When I glance back at Egan, his lips are curved into a half-smile.

"Time was of the essence, though. This race only happens once a year." He props his phone up on the center console then flips down the visor and peers into the mirror as he outlines an enormous black blob underneath his right eye.

"Are you using eyeliner?"

"Is that what this is? Mom gave it to me this morning." He fills in the spot. "Seemed like a better choice than Sharpie, which was my first idea."

I stare straight out the windshield.

"Look." Egan sighs and caps the eyeliner. "I'll stick close. We'll be a team the whole time. Exactly like old times, right?" He holds his hand out to me and wiggles his fingers.

I swat him away. "What if I can only make it a mile?"

"Then you can only make it a mile. No big deal. We'll set small goals and get through it."

"Those girls in the tutus will think I'm lame because I didn't train ahead of time."

Egan laughs and jerks his chin toward the gaggle of girls dressed like swine. "Those girls are too busy taking selfies next to that race sign to notice you exist."

I follow his gaze. He's totally right. They're all adjusting their curls and pursing their lips and probably applying filters. One of them turns around and tries to take a picture of the pigtail taped to her rear end.

"Come on, Babe. Give it a try." Egan tilts his head toward me, holding his phone at my eye level.

"Babe?"

"You know, like the pig? Because you said I couldn't call you Noo—never mind."

My face feels pinchy. I shake my head.

"Right. Sorry. It seemed like a good idea at the time. Callie." He glances away and coughs as though he needs to clear his throat.

"How about I stand at the finish line and clap for you as you cross it?" I look into the eye of the camera on his phone instead of at his face. "Is that good enough?"

He shrugs. "If that's all you're willing to do, fine. No skin off my snout." He dangles the pig nose from his pinky. "But you have to wear the costume anyway."

"I'll wear the nose. But not the tail."

"Fine, no tail. You have to do the ears, though."

"What is wrong with—"

"Come on, Callie." Egan lets the snout sway in front of my face. "Nobody likes a party pooper. Besides, I'm already recording, so…"

"Then stop recording."

"I would, but then we won't have anything to show for our first date. Without anything to show, we won't have any fans." He tips his chin upward and squints as though he's concentrating. "Who was it Annabeth said you wanted to meet? Maleficent Lopez or something?"

I have the worst case of heartburn I've ever experienced in my life. "I hate you so much right now." I yank the snout from his hand. "Give me the stupid ears too."

"That's the spirit."

Chapter 6

IT'S ALREADY HUMID FOR EIGHT A.M., BUT I STILL keep my arms wrapped around my stomach in an effort to hug away my nerves. Egan, meanwhile, looks like a grinning pinball, shooting from one person to the next handing out high fives as though they're energy bars. The race bib safety-pinned to the front of my shirt scratches the inside of my arms.

"All right, pigs to the left. Cows to the right." A man sporting an olive-green knit cap and a lumberjack's beard speaks into a megaphone from the direction of the starting line. He gestures with his free hand as he repeats himself.

Egan claps, cheers, and starts walking to our right, alongside the rest of the herd shuffling to that corner of the field.

I grasp his elbow, not caring that I'm gouging him with my fingernails. "Where are you going? I thought we were in this together."

He freezes, and his grin falters. "Oh. Right. I guess I didn't realize they were splitting up the cows and the pigs. You'll be okay though, right?"

"Um, no." I start looking for the exit. I'm definitely not doing this thing alone. "Where's the finish line? Or the spectator route?"

"Really? You don't want to give it a try?"

"I really, really don't want to give it a try."

"Oh. Okay. Well." Egan's eyebrows furrow. "I'm not sure.

Maybe there's a map or something? You could ask one of the race attendants. They'll probably be able to help."

A man wearing a hideous pair of hairy, plastic pig ears pushes between us on his way to the starting line. I take a step back to steady myself.

"Pigs to the left. Let's go." The man with the megaphone gets louder. "Countdown begins in sixty seconds."

"Look. That girl over there looks nice. Ask her." Egan points over the crowd. All I see is lots of pink and pointy ears.

"Who? I don't see anyone."

The crowd cheers. Two more cows and four pigs push between me and Egan.

"Her." Egan points again, jabbing his finger to my left. He raises his voice over the noise. "With the curly brown hair."

I stretch my neck, but still can't see the girl he's talking about. When I turn back again, Egan's gone. "E?" I squeak.

"Ten, nine, eight…" Both herds begin to chant.

I put my head down and push toward what I hope is the edge of the horde. But the countdown ends much too quickly, and suddenly the noise swells and all the pigs around me cheer and begin trotting in the direction of the trail through the woods. A middle-aged man in camouflage shorts and a bacon-printed T-shirt barrels into me, and I stumble forward into the mouth of the trail beyond the starting line.

"Wait." I try to stop, but the others around me have already sped up, hurtling closer to what appears to be a large sinkhole in the trail ahead and dragging me with them. I try to time my footfalls to sync with the guy in front of me so I won't get run over, but he's too fast.

My throat burns.

"Stop," I yell, but my voice gets swallowed up by the cheers ahead. "I'm not a runner. I don't want to be here."

A blond wearing hot pink shorts laughs as she jogs beside me. "None of us really do, but it's an addiction."

"Addiction?" My voice bounces with each step. "To what?"

She stares straight ahead. "The challenge. The adrenaline. The bragging rights."

"That explains a lot about this date."

"What?"

"Nothing." I'm gasping now. "Where's the exit route?"

She frowns. "No way. You can't give up now. We haven't even hit the best part yet."

My calves are on fire. "It gets better?"

"Oh, yeah. Way better."

Without warning, she stops.

I do too, doubled over with my elbows on my knees.

"You're running alone?"

I reach for a scrawny birch tree on the edge of the trail and nod as I gulp for oxygen and get humidity instead. Running is a generous way to describe what I'm doing, but she doesn't need to know all the details as to how I got here. So, I only nod. "Yep."

People stream around us.

"Not anymore." She grabs my hand and pulls. Hard.

I trip behind her, barely regaining my footing before plunging forward into a pool of slimy, chilled mud the color of manure. Sludge shoots into my shorts, into my armpits, into my nostrils. I open my mouth to scream and burble into the mud instead.

But my new partner hasn't stopped. She drags me along by my wrist. My knees scrape the bottom of the mud pit as I scramble to push myself upright. It tastes like I've swallowed ground up charcoal. After three exhausting minutes of slogging, I flop over the edge of the pit. A quick glance to the right reveals a huge grin on my unlikely partner's face. Her teeth stand out, practically Day-Glo white against the mud caked around her mouth.

Her smile falters, and she drops my wrist. "What's wrong?"

"I'm not supposed to be here," I growl.

"Oh. You look like a pig, though? Are you supposed to be doing the fun run instead of the mud run?"

Other runners stream around us again. A college-aged guy plows into my shoulder, knocking me forward. He shoots me a dirty look as though I threw him an elbow. I cross my arms over my mud-coated torso.

"No, I mean, I was only supposed to be a spectator. I got stuck in the crowd."

"Get outta the way," another runner yells, glaring at me as he effortlessly springs out of the pit.

I can't help rolling my eyes as I flop away from the maniacs and mud. "Gladly," I mumble. "How do I get out of this thing?"

"Get out?" My piggy cohort blinks at me as though she's suddenly lost the ability to comprehend language.

"Yes. Get out. Leave. Stop the ride. How do I do that?"

"I don't really know. I guess you could walk the rest of the way and skip all the obstacles. But that's kind of lame, right?"

I only stare at her. Maybe she doesn't know the actual definition of the word "lame."

"Come on. There are only five obstacles. I need a buddy." She grabs my wrist again and turns away without bothering to wait for a response. If she'd have bothered, she might have heard an expletive or two in conjunction with Egan's name. Several times.

But her grip feels like handcuffs, and she doesn't let go.

A fifteen-foot wall, three enormous culvert pipes half-filled with mud, and a squatty ceiling made of barbed wire later, I drag myself over the finish line two steps behind my mud run partner.

Onlookers cheer and congratulate me. I throw up on their feet.

It's going to take so much more than doughnuts to make up for this.

I down a bottle and a half of purple Gatorade and fold myself into one of those shiny tinfoil blankets before I even think about trudging back through the open field parking lot toward Egan's car.

I can see him from a distance, chin to his chest, staring at his phone. If I had any strength left whatsoever, I'd pick up a clod of dirt and hurl it toward his face. He's lucky my arms feel like shoestrings. It's not until I'm about four zombie-shuffle steps away that he lifts his face and notices me.

"Heyyy-ayyy." His greeting goes from hyped to horrified in half a second. "Whoa, what happened? You look awful. Did you fall into a pit or something?" Egan reaches for me but stops a couple inches short of my elbow.

I readjust my tinfoil blanket. A large hunk of dried mud falls off my arm and hits the ground with a dull thud. "Oh, yes. At least three of them."

"Three mud pits? Weren't you watching where you were going?"

"I didn't make it to the spectator's area. The pigs started stampeding, I got stuck in it all, and it wasn't a *fun run*, Egan."

He wrinkles his nose and tilts his head to the side. "Really?

I had fun. And I ran. Made good time, too. I think if I'd have timed myself, it might have been a personal record."

"I'm so happy for you," I say in the flattest tone of voice I can muster. "But the *pigs* ran a mud run. A five-kilometer mud run. With pits. And pipes. And electrified barbed-wire suspended over even more mud."

Egan scrubs his sweat-shined jaw with one hand as he steps closer. "That's, uh, terrible." He raises an eyebrow at me, as though he's trying to gauge how painful I'm going to make his penance, even as he scoots his phone out from the crook of his arm and does a poor job of covert filming.

"Terrible doesn't cover it." I scratch my forehead, driving more dirt underneath my fingernails. I glare into the camera. "Humiliating. Disgusting. Traumatic. Those are great words."

Egan winces and drops the ruse, moving the phone closer to my face. "So not a fun run, then?"

"Nope." I clench my jaw, and it feels like my skin is starting to crack underneath all the mud.

"Sorry. Maybe I'll do better tomorrow."

"Yeah. Tomorrow. About that." I lean out of the way as he reaches to open his car door then shuffle around the car to the passenger's side. "How about I plan tomorrow's thing?" There's no way I can call it a date at this rate.

Egan's eyebrows lift as though I've just relieved him of some huge burden. "That would be great, actually. I was having a hard time coming up with something."

"You hadn't planned anything already?" When I slide into the car, it leaves a huge streak of powdery dirt on the seat underneath my thighs. I almost sweep it away out of habit, then change my mind and wiggle my butt and rub my shoulders against the upholstery. He's the one who got me into this literal mess. He more than deserves an afternoon of vacuuming in his future. Besides, he works at a car wash. He'll be fine.

He drops his phone into my hand. It's still recording. "I had some ideas for tomorrow, but nothing was set in stone, you know?" Egan jams his key into the ignition and twists.

I stare out the window. "Because having a plan would take all the fun out of this."

"Huh?"

"Nothing. Are you putting this online when you get home?" I shake the phone, and the video bounces.

"We're going to have to work on your videographer skills." Egan takes the phone from me, hits stop, and drops it into an empty cup holder. "I'll edit the video before I put it online. Stitch the pieces together. I took video from my half of the race, and I'll include that."

"So, it'll be online tonight?"

Egan shrugs and pokes the power button on the radio. Music blares, and he turns the volume knob until the numbers reach twenty-seven. "Probably," he shouts over the bass as he bobs his head to the beat. "I love this song."

I toss him a tight-lipped, flattened smile as I dig through my bag on the floorboard for my phone so I can start doing my own research while he drives. With any luck, all I'll need is the one video. He'll post it, we'll go viral, and then I'm buying a plane ticket for Birmingham, where Nichelle Melendez does her filming.

It will happen. It has to happen. Because I can't do another fun run or whatever else he'll come up with in a pinch.

Egan glances over at me after he stops at a red light and grins like this is the best day of his life. The music playing on the radio vibrates through my chest, making it painful to breathe. He sings along, loudly and off-key.

I look back at my phone and Google opera houses or charity balls or modern art museums near Creekside. Because the longer this goes on, the clearer it's becoming that Egan needs a lot more culture in his life.

Chapter 7

ANNABETH SHOWS UP WITHOUT AN INVITATION thirteen minutes past eight p.m., immediately after her babysitting gig with the Townsends wrapped up.

"So," she sing-songs the second I open the front door. "How was your date?"

I shrug and start walking toward the kitchen without answering. "You want an ice cream sandwich?"

"No. I want details. What did you wear? What did he wear? Where did you go?" Annabeth follows me. Her bright purple flip-flops smack the floor with her steps. "Was it so romantic?"

I open the freezer. "My outfit included a pig snout and a curly tail. He wore cow ears and gym shorts. Does that sound romantic to you?"

Her smile falters the slightest bit, but she recovers quickly and takes the ice cream sandwich I offer even though she turned it down seconds ago. "It sounds like it has potential."

"I ran a muddy obstacle course by myself while he pranced around a paved pathway with a bunch of girls wearing udders. So pretty much we're getting married next weekend."

"Seriously?" Annabeth's eyes grow wide.

I put a hand on my hip. "About which part?"

"The obstacle course, obviously. You'd never get married with only five days' notice. Or at seventeen." She starts unwrapping the ice cream sandwich.

"True." I take a bite of ice cream and talk around it. "And

yes, I'm serious. This date was so bad. When I blew my nose afterward, the tissue looked like a rock quarry."

Annabeth grimaces. "Did he buy you flowers? An ice cream cone? A nice bracelet?"

"He bought me doughnuts." I lift one shoulder in a half-shrug. "But only because I refused to meet him at five-thirty this morning unless he brought pastries."

She gasps. "Five-thirty? In the morning? I thought you said this guy used to be your best friend. He should know better."

I open the back door to the porch and glance at her over my shoulder. "I know, right? It's not like that's changed at all over our lifetimes."

"Exactly. Nobody could ever accuse you of being a morning person." Annabeth follows me outside and leans on the back porch railing. She sighs. "So no sparks? Or butterflies? Or anything?"

"You can't light a match in a mud puddle, Annabeth." I hold my hand out for her ice cream sandwich wrapper.

"Hmph." She drops the wrapper into my waiting palm. "That's too bad. The whole experiment seemed like such a cool idea the way he described it the other day."

"Maybe."

"You're still going to finish the whole thing, though, right? Twenty more dates?"

I crush the wrappers in my palm then set them on the outdoor table. "I don't know. If tonight's video gets enough views and I can capitalize on those fans, maybe I won't have to."

"Callie." Annabeth's eyebrows knit together.

I stop brushing ice cream sandwich crumbs from my palms and return her frown. "What?"

"You promised."

I roll my eyes and wipe my hands on my shorts. "That was

before I knew our first date was going to be more boot camp than *The Bachelor*."

Annabeth harrumphs. "I thought you were a woman of your word."

"I am."

"Then why are you giving up so quickly?"

"I'm not giving up."

"You've been on one date. Give the guy a chance."

"This isn't about Egan, AB. This is about me and Nichelle Melendez."

Annabeth lays her fingertips on my forearm. "Have you never watched a good chick flick?"

"Of course I have. You make me watch them with you all the time."

"Then you should know all the greatest ones start out exactly like this. You're living a classic chick flick. Please promise me you'll let him stick around for at least a week. Who knows what could happen?"

"Permanent humiliation. Hiring a hitman. Life without the possibility of parole." I tick off the possibilities on my fingers. "I've already said my life isn't a romance."

Annabeth crosses her arms. "You keep telling yourself that. Has he posted the video yet?"

"Dunno." I shrug and reach for a lightning bug hovering inches away. It settles on my palm then relaunches.

"Well, what's the site?"

I shrug again. "You can probably search for 'the Great Date Experiment' or something. I'm not sure what the actual site address is."

Annabeth pulls her phone from her back pocket, shaking her head at me the whole time. "Your enthusiasm is lacking."

"Yours would be too if you swallowed a half-gallon of mud this morning."

She doesn't answer, ignoring me as she focuses on her new mission. Seconds later, she grins. "Found it. He's quick—it's already posted. Let's watch." She leans into my shoulder as I groan.

"I'm not watching those."

"Whatever. You've got to be at least a little bit curious." She hits *play* before I can answer.

The same poppy piccolo music from the intro video plays, but it's shorter this time and fades into shaky video.

"Come on, Babe. Give it a try," Egan says from behind the camera.

"Babe?" The video jiggles then focuses on my less-than-enthused expression.

Egan zooms in on the intense frown line deepening between my eyebrows.

"Oh, my." Annabeth sucks a breath in through her teeth.

I bite my lower lip. "The costume was—"

"Shh," Annabeth hushes me, waving her fingers in the air.

The video, and my excruciating embarrassment, continues.

Egan captured the guy yelling at me through the bullhorn, as well as my frenzied retreat. I thought he'd turned off the camera by then. He must have picked it back up when I turned around, after I lost track of him. The footage from his run is pastoral and exactly what you'd expect from a bunch of people dressed as cows. A lot of slow shuffling, and Egan's breath remains steady throughout as he provides a running commentary while he jogs.

I come back into the picture trudging up to his car after the race looking like I just escaped Alcatraz with a vendetta. It's not like I need to watch to remember any of it and seeing it all over again is making me queasy, so I turn away, cover my ears, and start counting my less-than steady heartbeat.

When the video ends, I glance up in time to see the logo appear on Annabeth's phone. She looks at me and blinks several times.

"What?" I ask. "Why are you looking at me like I need to go sit on the naughty step and think about what I've done?"

She sets her phone down on the railing. "That was a literal tragedy. It has nothing to do with him, though."

"It totally does. This whole thing was his idea, and he planned that date."

"Callie. You could have used your tone of voice to strip the paint off the side of your house. You never even smiled. It's less than inspiring to watch."

"I smiled."

"You grimaced."

"I was upset."

"Clearly." She sighs. "Cal, nobody's going to believe you enjoy hanging out with him if you don't throw the guy a smile every once in a while. You're supposed to be dating—maybe you could, I don't know, hold hands or something."

"We're going on dates, not dating."

"And you look angry. Nobody's going to watch that. He's going to lose to his brother if you keep this up. And you're never going to meet Raquel."

"It's *Nichelle*. Why is that so hard for people to remember?" I wince when Annabeth bites her lower lip and looks away. "Sorry. I'm not mad at you or anything. It's just, we aren't those kinds of friends, me and Egan. I don't even know if we're any kind of friends right now. I won't be all lovey-dovey on camera when we aren't like that in real life."

"What about that picture he put at the end? The one of y'all from a few years ago. You used to hug. It looks like you used to be really close."

"We were." I tuck my chin to my chest.

Annabeth pats me on the back. "Remember that, then. And quit being afraid to make some new memories."

"I'm not afraid."

"Oh, yeah? What would you call it, then?"

I lean on the porch railing and let out my breath slowly, counting to four as I do. "Cautious."

Annabeth raises a single ginger eyebrow. "I guess that's one way to put it." She falls into an uncharacteristic few seconds of silence, then slides closer and rests her head on my shoulder. "What did he even do to tick you off so much? Hold Hedwig for ransom? Fill your shampoo bottle with Nair? Cut your brake lines?"

"We weren't old enough to drive."

"What then?"

I give her a bulleted version of the story I've worked to forget for so long.

Annabeth stares. "And that's what he was apologizing for?"

I nod, once. "Yep."

"Did he seem sincere?"

I shrug. "I guess. He didn't get on his knees and beg or anything, but he wasn't laughing."

"But you still told him you couldn't forgive him."

"I need more time."

"For what? I thought you said this happened two years ago. Were you serious about the begging?" Annabeth shakes her head.

"Maybe I need proof."

"Of what? Income? Identity?"

I roll my eyes. "Quit being dumb. You know what I mean. I

need to know he's grown up. That he actually cares about doing the right thing. That he's actually a decent human being."

Annabeth smirks. "Well, he seems like a decent enough guy to me. At the very least, you should probably quit acting like he stole your cat. Nobody's going to want to watch twenty-one dates of dagger-eyed you insisting he pay for something stupid he did once upon a time."

"I don't have dagger—" Annabeth holds up her phone, frozen on my does-anyone-else-smell-that expression, and I stop short. "Okay, I get it. I'll try to tone down the weird faces."

"Good." She drops her phone into her pocket. "Now tell me where you're going on your date tomorrow."

I can feel her gaze on my face even though I'm staring out into the backyard. "I don't know yet. He told me I could choose."

"Any ideas?"

"Not yet. You have any thoughts, Fairy Godmother?"

Annabeth grins. "You could take a horse-drawn carriage ride through downtown at sunset."

"No."

"The rose gardens?"

"With all the couples getting engaged?" I shudder. "No."

"Dinner and a movie?"

"No. We'd end up with an hour of chewing videos since we can't film in a theater."

"Hmm." Annabeth goes quiet, and we're surrounded with a chorus of night noises. A few seconds pass and then she gasps. "Wait. I saw something online this morning about a cake decorating class. That seems like something you'd love."

I start to object on account of Egan's sugar intolerance. But then I stop. It's not like we'll be eating cake. Just covering it. With more sugar. And it's not like anyone will be forcing a pastry bag full of buttercream down his throat. "I like that idea. Send me the details?"

"Sure." She pushes away from the porch railing. "I told Mom I'd be back by nine, so I've got to get going, but I'll send it to you as soon as I'm home."

"Thanks. You're the best."

"Cal." Annabeth stills. She turns back to me, and I'm surprised to see the sudden shimmer of tears in her brown eyes. "I've never seen you smile like you were smiling in some of those pictures, when you and Egan were still friends before. I think that's worth running after again even if you have to work at it. Don't you?"

My breath catches in my throat. I stare at the ground. "I've had enough running for today, thanks."

Annabeth sniffs. "Yeah, okay. Make it a joke. I'll let you get away with it now, but later tonight I think you should watch this date all over again. By yourself. See if you like that Callie. If you do, great. Keep it up. But I don't think that's the real you."

"You don't—"

"I'm nannying until three tomorrow. But we'll rendezvous for dinner, okay?" She rakes the back of her hand across her eyes, then flutters her fingers in an airy wave as though she hasn't spent the last few minutes scolding me. "Love you," she calls over her shoulder as she walks away. When I don't respond, she stops. "I mean it."

"You know not everybody gets a happily ever after, right?" I cram my hands into the back pockets of my shorts.

The corner of Annabeth's mouth lifts in a lopsided, wry smile. "Nobody automatically gets a fairy-tale ending, Cal. But a lot of us have the opportunity to fight for them. I'm just trying to make sure you don't chase yours off with a pitchfork in one hand and a torch in the other."

I wrinkle my nose but still return her goodbye wave. And when I play the video in my bedroom a couple hours later, my stomach clenches and I can't help but wince every time I make an appearance. My voice sounds weird, a couple octaves too high, but what's more disturbing is the fact that I look like I'm going on a hunt for an ogre. Even Hedwig paces and meows around my ankles, almost like she can't believe that's actually her human on the screen.

I stop the video and turn off the tablet, letting my fingers linger on the power button. Annabeth was right. We have a huge problem.

And that huge problem, it turns out, is probably me.

Chapter 8

"I COULD HAVE PICKED YOU UP, YOU KNOW." EGAN sits in the passenger's side with his hands resting on his knees.

I pull up beside a street-side parking space and shift my car into reverse then hesitate. I don't usually have anyone in the car with me besides Annabeth. It feels different stretching my arm behind the headrest when Egan's sitting there instead.

His eyebrow twitches, and I stifle a grumble and plant my hand on the back of his headrest with enough force to give him a mild case of whiplash. Then I gun it and slip into the space before throwing the car into park.

"Could you have done that?" I ask, yanking my arm back into my personal space bubble as quickly as possible.

Egan's eyes widen the slightest bit before he scrubs his chin with his palm and looks away. "Ah, no. Don't think I could have. Your grandpa teach you that?"

"Of course."

"I'll have to ask him for lessons sometime."

I nod as I pick up my phone from the cupholder and drop it into my bag. "Yeah, maybe." I don't bother letting him know neither of my grandparents have any idea we're hanging out again.

"So, this date you've got picked out must be pretty swanky if we're downtown." Egan unbuckles his seat belt and unfolds himself from the car.

"It's definitely a step up from yesterday's." As soon as the words leave my lips, I mentally groan. Annabeth is going to require an on-camera retraction of that. "I mean, it's less gritty than yesterday's date. But it's not particularly fancy or anything."

"How much do I owe you?" Egan falls easily in step beside me as I stride down the sidewalk toward Henny Cakes at the corner of Henny and Finch Streets.

"Nothing." I reach for the silver door handle underneath the Henny Cakes logo painted in bright pink and glitter.

Egan pushes my hand out of the way and tugs the glass door open. He waves me inside with the sweep of his other hand. "Nothing?"

"Annabeth heard about this thing they're doing tonight, and it's free." As soon as I step through the doorway, the scent of the air transitions from summertime honeysuckle to sweet, buttery cake batter. I close my eyes and breathe deeply. My whole body feels warm and gooey and safe.

Egan bumps into my back, knocking me forward a couple of inches. "Exactly what are we going to be doing?"

I look up and my gaze connects with the slope of his neck underneath his chin. Suddenly I realize the extra warmth isn't from cake euphoria, it's from Egan's body towering over mine, his forearms resting on my shoulders. He's using me as a tripod while he holds his phone steady to record.

I duck away, and his shot dips. "We're decorating a cake. You'll be okay with it though, right? Even though you can't really eat it?"

"I think I can handle the temptation." He winks at me, stops recording, and drops the phone into the back pocket of his khaki cutoffs.

The front door jingles and three young women file into the store, smiling and laughing, as they carry tote bags looped over their arms. One of them is wearing a T-shirt from Creekside Community College, and the other two look like they're probably just a few years ahead of me and Egan as well.

"Oh, welcome." A woman my grandmother's age with gray spun-sugar hair and hot-pink glasses bustles out of a back room. "My apologies. I didn't hear anyone arrive." She glances at the girls with the tote bags. "I see you've brought some supplies. Very good."

I can feel my cheeks heating up already. Annabeth didn't say anything about bringing supplies.

"Do you need me to run to Paterson's? I'm sure he's got some cake decorating stuff on a top shelf somewhere." Egan's breath tickles the top of my ear.

I nudge him away and shake my head, wondering at the same time how he still seems to be able to read my mind all these years later.

"No worries, love." The woman smiles at Egan, having heard his offer. "I've got plenty to go around. The ladies here are regulars, so they've brought some new supplies they've wanted to try out."

My breath leaves me in a whoosh, and Egan musses my hair as he leaps into the conversation.

"Hey, that's excellent. I'm Egan, by the way." He sticks his hand out for the woman to shake.

"Sandy. It's so nice to see a young man here. And what a unique name you have."

Egan smiles as though he hears it all the time. Probably because he does. "It's my dad's best friend's last name. I like it all right. So, do you own Henny Cakes?"

"I do." Sandy beams and tucks her thumbs underneath her apron strings. "Going on two years now. It's a dream come true for an old lady like me."

"You can't be that old. Maybe in your forties? You're practically right out of high school."

I stop short of covering my face with my hands, but Sandy's face turns a lovely shade of bubblegum as she waves away his compliment.

"How do you all feel about a fresh, light strawberries-and-cream layer cake?" she asks.

"Yum!" The quick exclamation escapes before I can stop it.

Egan, Sandy, and two of the other women chuckle at me, and I can feel my nose start to tingle and itch. "I mean, it's been my favorite since I was a kid. My grandma used to make something like it for most of my birthday parties growing up."

Egan squeezes my shoulder. "I remember that. They were pretty good." There's a tinge of wistfulness in his tone, and I wonder if he's not as uninterested in the cake as he led me to believe at first.

"What a fun memory." Sandy smiles at me. Her glasses slip down her nose and she pushes them back up with the tip of her index finger. "Do you still like to bake?"

I nod, then stop short. "Yes, but I'm not a professional pastry chef or anything. I mean, I'd like to be one day, but I don't even have a chef coat or anything right now. So, I'm not all that legit, I don't think." But if Nichelle Melendez will choose me for her special, maybe I will be sooner rather than later.

"I'll bet you're closer to being a professional than you think." Sandy smooths the front of her apron with her hands. "I'm excited to see how you decide to make this cake your own tonight. Would you like to grab a couple of pints of strawberries from the refrigerator in the back? I've had them all chilling for the past couple of hours."

"I'll grab them." Egan steps around me and moves toward a

doorway near the back of the room. "Back here, Mrs. Henny Cakes?"

"Sandy," I mumble, embarrassed that Egan seems to have forgotten her name already, but he winks at me over the top of an industrial mixer.

Sandy only chuckles. "Yes, sweetheart. You'll see the refrigerator as soon as you go through the doorway."

"Is there anything I can do?" I ask because it seems like the right thing to do. It's foreign for me to be in a kitchen, standing in front of so many ovens, without doing anything.

"Why don't you go ahead and get situated at one of the stations?" Sandy nods toward some open counter space. "We'll be getting started here in a couple of minutes, and you seem like a gal who likes to prepare before she bakes."

I nod. She's right. "Okay. Thank you."

As I slip around the counter, Egan reappears from the back room, balancing four pints of strawberries in his arms. He slides them on the counter with finesse. "How's this? Think we'll need any more?"

Sandy tilts her head to the side and seems to weigh the number of attendees with the pints. In the end, she smiles. "Yes, I think this will work just fine." She pauses then lets out an amused chuckle. "I see you found my apron collection?"

Egan grins. I lean around the end of the counter and immediately want to melt down one of the drains in the floor. "Egan, stop it. Put that back."

"Come on, Callie. You don't think this goes with my outfit?" He holds both hands in the air and does a little step-twirl to show off the half-apron, four layers of pink eyelet fabric and lace wrapped twice around his hips.

I move close to him, so close I can smell the wintergreen gum on his breath, and stuff my fingers into the waistband of the apron and tug. He moves with the tug, smashing my nose into his chest.

I push him away, but my hand is still stuck in the apron, so I only gain inches. "We aren't eight years old anymore. Put. That. Back," I grumble, hopefully softly enough that Sandy won't hear.

"How adorable is that?" The girl in the college T-shirt laughs.

Egan and I whirl to see her pointing at him. He turns back to me for half a second, raises his eyebrows, and whispers, "At least *she* thinks I'm adorable."

I wrench my hand free from the apron and clench my teeth. I know Annabeth had high hopes for this date, but I'm pretty sure we're going to be lucky if I get out of it without a court date and a third-degree murder charge. Thirty minutes later, the feeling is confirmed when Egan swipes another fingerful of whipped icing.

I push his hand away from the mixing bowl, pausing my meticulous strawberry slicing to keep him from eating the whole bowl. "Stop it. I'm never letting you back in a kitchen again."

"What?" Egan blinks at me, his eyes wide and golden brown in the evening light streaming in through the storefront windows.

"I thought you said you were used to the temptation."

He half shrugs. "I am used to the temptation. And sometimes I give into it."

"But that's not sugar-free. You know that, right?"

His wide eyes grow wider. "Wait. What?"

I turn back to the strawberries without sympathy. "You dumped the cup and a half of powdered sugar into the icing yourself. What's wrong with you?"

"Yes, I know it's not sugar-free. It's not like we're baking with Splenda here."

"Then why are you eating so much?" I slice through a strawberry so hard the blade of my knife clacks on the plastic cutting board surface.

"Don't worry about it, Noo—Callie. Seriously. I know my body by now. It's fine."

"Just don't come whining to me when—" The tip of my knife blade runs across the pad of my left index finger. I yank my hand back and grab a paper towel to wrap around my finger. "Ouch!"

"What happened?" Egan's already close, as though he's been sling-shotted in my direction. He leans over my shoulder.

I peel the paper towel away and blood gurgles from my finger. I wince and hold it a couple inches higher so Egan can take a good look.

Egan stills, and his eyes go glassy and blank. He slumps forward onto the countertop like someone hit his hidden power button. He slides down, his bare forearms squeaking as he drops, until his whole body comes to rest in a heap on the floor.

"Egan?" I stare down at the top of his head, waiting for him to look up at me and laugh at his latest prank. But he doesn't say anything. All I hear in response are the whirs of mixers blending icing and the gentle chitchat of our classmates.

"Egan." I nudge him with the toe of my gold sandal. He doesn't stir. "Stop messing around."

Nothing.

The others are beginning to notice. The brunette who brought her own cake pans leans around the corner of her workstation and look at the floor. I raise my maimed hand at her in a half wave and plant my other hand on my hip. "He's fine. Just joking. He's like that. A jokester, I mean."

She grimaces. "Didn't I just hear you guys talking about how he shouldn't eat sugar?"

I start chewing on my lower lip and squeeze the paper towel even tighter around my finger which has started to throb in time with my increasing heartbeat. "He's diabetic."

She doesn't say anything else, and her grimace doesn't fade.

"Oh. Oh!" I crouch at Egan's side. "What do I do? He ate sugar. And he's diabetic. He's got this bracelet. See?" I wave his wrist in the air.

The rest of the kitchen turns into a rush of activity. "Someone call 911!" The brunette looks around at her friends.

I pat my pockets for my phone and only succeed in bleeding all over my shorts.

Sandy cuts across the kitchen and kneels by my side. "I've already called them, sweetheart. Someone should be here shortly. The volunteer fire station is just up the road."

"Thank you." My voice sounds weak and mousy. I reach for Egan's motionless hand, grasping his last three fingers with my right hand and holding on tight.

His eyelids flutter, and my heartbeat stalls. "E?"

"Noog? What happened?" His voice is cottony, and his lips move slowly like he's having a hard time putting the words together. He pulls his hand from my death-grab and loops his fingers around mine instead.

I can't scold him for the nickname, not when he's mostly out of his mind. "You passed out. Probably from too much sugar. I told you—"

Egan's shaking his head. "Not from too much sugar."

"You ate like half a cake's worth of buttercream. What do we need to do to counteract it?" I'm so scared and relieved at the same time that my voice shakes.

"Nothing." Egan tries to sit up, but I shove him back to the floor with a palm to his shoulder. "Seriously, it's not the sugar." The longer he speaks, the clearer his words get.

"Then what is it?"

"Blood. I really don't like to see blood." His fingers twitch around mine, and he nods in the direction of my flesh wound.

I frown and yank my hand away. "What? Are you serious? But you have to test your blood sugar all the time."

He sniffs and sits up, successfully this time, keeping his gaze turned away from my spurting finger. The paper towel has turned bright red, rivaling the ripe strawberries I'd been chopping moments earlier.

"I didn't say it made sense," he says. "Besides, it's different when it's somebody else."

Now that Egan seems to be on the up and up, Sandy turns her attention to me. "Let's take a look at that finger, sweetheart. Is it going to need stitches?"

I peel the paper towel away and shield my wound with my body when I notice Egan's face has turned the color of the powdered sugar we just used in the icing. It's a clean slice across my fingertip, and it definitely stings. But the bleeding looks like it's slowed to an ooze. "I've had worse, I think."

"Worse?" Egan's voice rivals my natural pitch.

I glance over my shoulder at him and shrug. "Last year. It was a bread knife. I sliced a bagel. Poorly."

He grimaces.

Sandy pats my shoulder. "It's still bleeding, but you're right. It doesn't look too terrible. Why don't you go rinse off in the sink over there? I'll get you a Band-Aid and some antiseptic." She nods at the sink in the back of the kitchen.

I stand and come face to face with Egan's phone in the hands of one of the other cake class students.

"What are you doing?"

She smiles. "He said you guys were recording dates or something earlier. I figured you'd want this documented too?"

It takes me a full three seconds to nod even though my inclination is to hide in a cupboard instead. "Right. Thanks. That's probably good." I hold my hand out to her, and she drops the phone into my waiting palm. I stop the recording before I set it on the countertop next to my forgotten cutting board.

How much did she get on camera? And how quickly can I get rid of it before Egan uploads the video of me, the girl who's supposed to be a professional, slicing her fingers up like she's never picked up a kitchen knife before?

Nichelle Melendez would take one look at that and kick me out of the running for sure.

"Evening, Sandy. What's the emergency?" A deep voice with a thick Southern accent comes from the doorway as soon as I begin washing my hands. The bleeding has stopped, and I grab a Band-Aid.

"No emergency," I say as I turn around, tugging the bandage from the wrapper. "I'm fine."

Sandy points to Egan. "He probably needs some tending to, though." She smiles, and I feel my cheeks warm.

"Oh. Yeah. Right." I'd forgotten it wasn't all a joke, that Egan wasn't really messing around because that's who he is.

"Did he hit his head?" One of the paramedics looks up at Sandy who looks at me, eyebrows raised.

"I'm not sure." I toss the Band-Aid trash into a nearby waste bin. "I was kind of too busy freaking out over the passing out thing. He's diabetic."

The paramedic leaning over Egan and taking his vital signs nods. "I see. Why don't we test your blood sugar while we're here?"

Egan shrugs. "Sure."

A minute later, after seeing Egan's blood sugar numbers, the paramedic starts stripping off his latex gloves. "Well, blood sugar looks fine right now. But you should probably think about going to urgent care or something like that if you start to feel badly, especially since nobody's really sure if you hit your head or not. Just have your girlfriend drive. Don't get behind the wheel, okay?"

If my cheeks were warm before, they're right on par with an oven on broil now. "I'm not—"

"She'll do it." Egan interrupts me and holds out his hand to shake with the paramedic. "Thanks for coming out for this."

"No worries, man. We were right across the street getting ready to grab dinner."

They file out the door, and as soon as it shuts behind them, I start gathering my keys.

"What are you doing?" Egan frowns at me and reaches for a stool nearby.

"Taking you to urgent care."

"They said I was fine."

"They said I should drive you."

Egan grabs a new cutting board from Sandy's stash in the cabinets behind us and switches it out with the one covered in strawberry guts and O+. He drops the latter in the sink and pats the clean surface. "Sit, Callie. We can enjoy the rest of our date, and if I start heaving my hot dogs from lunch all over the floor, then you're more than welcome to drag me to your car and take off."

"No, we need to…" My voice trails off as I realize the rest of the room has gone quiet. All I hear is the tick of an oven heating behind me, and when I glance around, Sandy and our classmates are watching as though Egan and I are suddenly on reality TV. They turn away as soon as we make eye contact.

I draw in a deep breath and look back to Egan, whose face has already started to regain some of its early summer tan. "If your parents ask, tell them I made you sign an ACA waiver," I mumble.

"ACA?" His eyebrows furrow then relax quickly. "Oh. Against Callie's Advice instead of Against Medical Advice."

I reach for the mixing bowl to give the icing a little swirl with a spatula. "Exactly."

Chapter 9

"YOU HELD HANDS." ANNABETH SIGHS SO LOUDLY into her phone that it sounds like I need to find a storm cellar.

"You can just text me, you know." I put the phone on speaker and drop it into the folds of my comforter next to my thigh.

"It's almost midnight. You would have ignored me."

I half shrug. She's got a point. "We didn't hold hands."

"On your date? Of course you did. I watched it like two minutes ago. Go to 2:10."

I sigh and grab my tablet from the nightstand. "I was there, AB. There was no hand holding or eye gazing or wistful sighing going on, as much as you wish that had happened. Egan is still Egan."

"2:10," Annabeth merely repeats.

"Fine." I pull up Egan's Great Date Experiment site and slide the time to 2:10. The video remains still since I haven't pressed *play*. Sure enough, it's a still of my hand wrapped around three of Egan's fingers, a shot from above.

I cover my face and drop the tablet next to my phone. "Ugh. I forgot."

"Forgot what? That you took my advice and held hands with the guy?"

"No," I grumble. "I forgot to delete the video that girl took at the bakery. It's not what you think it is. He passed out, and I was scared. It wasn't like I was trying to woo him or something. It was just—"

"Natural?"

"A lapse of judgment."

Hedwig leaps up onto my bed and pushes the top of her head into my palm. I scratch between her ears, and she purrs.

"Well, it's a good thing you didn't delete it."

"Says you." I flop over and bury my face in my pillow. Hedwig meows.

"If you had, you wouldn't be getting the comments you're getting."

"Wait. What? We have comments? How many?" Because if it's anywhere close to two-fifty, my dream is about to come true. I scroll down to the bottom of the page, but it stops scrolling way too soon. "You said comments."

"Okay, so a comment is more accurate. But it's better than nothing. And I didn't even write it." Annabeth starts to read it out loud, and I follow along on my screen. "'You two are the best together. I hope you get married at the end of the experiment. I'm a stationery designer, so give me a call when you decide to tie the knot. Here's my email address.'" Annabeth's voice trails off. "Oh. Never mind."

I roll my eyes. "So our only comment is from some girl trying to promote her wedding stationery business?" I shake my head. "Typical."

"Give it more time. I watched it and loved it, so I'm sure more people will too. Look, I'm sharing it right now."

"Thanks for the free publicity."

"No problem." Her voice is muffled, a sure sign that she's moved on to other distractions. "Talk to you in the morning? Maybe we can go to the pool. I've got a few free hours in the afternoon. When's your next date?"

"No idea."

"Sounds good. Update me when you find out. Sweet dreams. Preferably about Egan."

"Whatever. I think I'd rather dream about velociraptors."

Annabeth laughs. "Your choice. Goodnight."

As soon as we hang up, I push the slider back to the beginning of the video and press *play*. Hopefully this time I'll seem a little less angry and a little more approachable. It took a lot of effort not to cuss when I cut my finger, so I'd better get five new followers out of the disaster at the very least.

I watch the whole thing, on mute the first time because I can't handle the sound of my voice when I'm panicky. Sure enough, there's a ten-second shot of me grasping Egan's hand while he's slumped over on the floor. It's not exactly the stuff romance novels are made of, but I guess most people who are willing to waste their time watching this aren't all that discerning.

The second time I watch, I turn the volume up a couple of notches because I can't figure out what Egan's saying even though I was there. When the video fades to black, I sigh. He was generous with the cutting tool in his video editor, so it doesn't seem as horrific as the first one, but I still need to figure out how to get my face under control when I'm on camera.

My finger hovers over the X in the corner, but just before I close the window two shiny new comments pop up below the video. I scroll down to read.

> Can you believe this girl? She has her own car and a cute boyfriend and this perfect little life but she still stomps around and whines like everything is so hard. Give me a break.

What's that supposed to mean? I read it again, this time fixating on the phrase "perfect little life." Stupid. I've experienced a lot of hard things in my life but excuse me if I'm not all about airing my dirty laundry all over the internet. Egan and I are going on dates, not standing trial. And this isn't supposed to be about me, anyway.

I read it again and again, trying to find some clues as to who the commenter could be. Maybe someone from school? Someone from summer camp? Someone who doesn't even know me? But I come up with nothing, so I force myself to move on to the next comment.

> It's sweet to see how far you two have come in just two dates. I bet you're both going to be hopelessly in love after twenty-one of them. I'm calling it right now. Please invite me to your wedding one day. PS: Callie, I love your freckles!

Without thinking, I touch my nose where most of my freckles congregated the minute I stepped out into the sunshine for the summer. I'll take more of those kind of comments, please. Even if she is horribly misguided about where this relationship is going.

I scroll up to the top of the page to check out the number of times the video of our date-turned-disaster has been viewed. I freeze.

Two hundred and nine views? That's, like, twenty percent of the way to a thousand, Egan's goal. And if each of those viewers would just follow me somewhere, anywhere, this whole thing would be a done deal.

I'm not ready to admit Annabeth might have been right, that the façade of a closer relationship may be exactly what caused the bump in views tonight. But I don't know if I can say she was wrong either.

Tomorrow's date might be a good time to bring up adding a few "follow Callie here" links to the end of our videos.

Chapter 10

I'M NOT SAYING I'VE OUTGROWN GOING TUBING down Golden Turtle Creek on a random Thursday but it's significantly less appealing now at seventeen than it was when I was ten. Hopefully the commenter who thought I was spoiled and whiny is tuning in today, because nothing says down-to-earth like my backside wedged into the middle of an inner tube.

It took us a few days to get here, though, since we had to take it easy at my request after Egan's passing out incident. There was a date to the bookstore, where we almost got kicked out because Egan started a puppet show with some of the stuffed animals on display in the kids' section. And then we stopped by the mountain overlook at March's Roost to take in a sunset alongside at least seventy-two other couples. Yesterday, Egan almost forgot about the Experiment entirely, and we had to video chat our date at 11:47 p.m. I was half-asleep, so I'm not even sure how that one went.

"Ahh," Egan sighs as he folds his hands behind his head and squints toward the sun. "Nothing like some fun in the sun, huh, Noo—I mean, Callie? Just like the old days. Except for those things on your feet. What's up with that?" He gestures toward my boring, black water shoes with his chin.

I shrug and skim the top of the water with my fingertips. He obviously doesn't remember his "hideous toe-talons" comment from last week, even if I haven't been able to forget it. "There

79

are lots of creatures swimming around in here. I don't want them nibbling on my toes."

Also, I can only imagine what hundreds of commenters could say about my tiny toes and oddly-shaped toenails if I give them the chance. Yesterday someone called out the thickness of my eyebrows, or lack thereof, so I'm sure toenails aren't immune either.

"But we used to do this all the time back in the day. Don't tell me growing up means you got scared." Egan glances over at me with a crooked smile on his face. The camera strapped to his forehead makes him look like a cyborg cyclops.

"I'm not scared. But the wildlife is…" A bee or a gnat the size of a grape buzzes by my head, and I can't help my sudden spastic swatting. "Prolific," I finish as Egan floats beside me and tries, rather unsuccessfully, to quell his amusement.

"We can climb out at that crook in the creek over there if you want." Egan clenches his fingers around the black skin of my inner tube to keep me from drifting faster than him. "But then we'd have to hike back to the car with these things and drive to the rental place to return them."

I shake my head. We don't have any compelling footage yet. "This is fine. But we should try to move a little faster. My SPF 60 is no match for this kind of sunshine and my fair skin." I gesture toward my bare shoulders, growing pinker and pinker by the second.

"I think my problem is less skin tone and more that I forgot to put on sunscreen this morning." Egan pokes at his bare stomach, which resembles the warm caramel of a rotisserie chicken at the moment. His insulin pod thing is stuck to the back of his arm again today.

I pretend to stare beyond him at the creek's edge, though I can still see him perfectly fine in front of me. He's not ripped like some of the guys who stay late after PE to fit in a few more reps in the weight room, but he's annoyingly fit. And also not ten years old anymore.

I clear my throat. "I'd offer you my sunscreen, but it's in the car."

"I'm fine as long as you are."

I shrug.

Egan wrinkles his nose. "You *are* having some fun, right?"

"Of course. Why would you think I'm not?"

"Because you just shrugged." His eyebrows knit together, two well-defined lines which I can easily see now since he's not wearing his glasses in the water.

"I can do a cheer if you want."

Egan pushes his fingers against his mouth and nods. "Yes, please."

I shove his tube away from mine and laugh at his expression. "Yeah, no. But this really is fun, E. Almost like what we used to do before…" My voice trails off as I try to figure out a nice way to say it. "Before things got weird."

"You mean before I turned into an idiot."

"You said it. Not me." I run my fingernail down the seam in my inner tube.

"Fair enough." He falls silent, and when I finally build up the courage to look over at him he's staring off into the distance. "I did apologize. And the apology still stands." He raises his right eyebrow as he turns back to me. "I'm really sorry, Callie. Really."

"I know." I chew on my bottom lip and glance away. I believe him now.

He sighs. "I hate that I was such an idiot."

We both go quiet. The water burbles and bubbles over rocks and the creek bank, carrying us farther downstream.

"I don't think you are anymore," I finally say. "An idiot, I mean. For the record."

Egan chuckles. "Thanks. I think."

"How'd that happen, anyway?"

He shoots me a sideways glance. "Don't know. I guess I just grew up a little."

It's been bugging me the last couple of days, trying to figure out who he is and how he got there without the benefit of the last two years of memories. I study at him as though it will help me understand faster.

"That's not it." I watch his face, pausing on his damp eyelashes, looking for the spark that drives his easy smile and fast jokes. "It's like you're even more you now than you were before. You're a real-er Egan."

Egan ducks his head, and in spite of his tan, I think I see a little bit of color on his cheeks. "That's sweet of you to say."

"I don't mean it to be sweet. I want to know what happened to you." As soon as the words leave my mouth, I regret them.

But Egan doesn't seem to mind. "You really want to know?"

"I asked."

He sniffs and rubs the back of his hand underneath his nose. "Chess."

"Chess?" I repeat.

"Yes."

"Like, the game?"

"What other kind of chess is there?"

"There's a chess pie, too."

"Right. Of course there is." He shakes his head and smiles then gazes downstream again. "I'm still talking about the game. I didn't know it two years ago, but I'm pretty good at it."

"Yeah?" I can tell by the way he doesn't really elaborate that he legitimately has bragging rights.

"Mom and Dad were thinking about shipping me off to military school or boarding school or something. But Grandad talked to them and asked if he could have a shot at me instead."

"Military school?" I squeak. "Just because you shut me in a locker?" When he glances sharply at me, I backpedal. "I mean, not just. It was a big deal. To me, anyway. But not military school big."

For a brief second, so brief I wonder if I imagined it, it seems like a shadow passes over his soul. His lips tense and his gaze shifts to the shore. Then he reaches for my hand and drapes his fingers over mine. "Do you mind?"

I stare at our hands. Our fingers. Touching, and not because he's injured and I'm panicked.

"Callie?"

"What? Oh. No. Of course not. It's fine." I shoot a smile at the camera.

"Only when we're filming for the Experiment, of course."

"For sure." I look toward the shoreline and try to ignore the way my whole arm is starting to tingle. "Anyway, your grandad? Do you still get to see him?"

"Ah, no." When I glance over, I catch the tail end of a wince. "He passed away like a year ago. Almost exactly, actually."

My eyes widen. "Oh. My gosh. I'm so sorry. We should have sent a peace lily or something. I didn't know."

"How could you know? We weren't hanging out then, remember?" Egan's smile is not all there. "But it's okay. I got to spend a lot of time with him before he passed. And I learned a lot during those chess games."

"Like what?" I start to float a little faster, and Egan tugs my hand to pull my inner tube back in sync with his.

"Like how to tie a bow tie."

"The one you wore when you brought me the daisies?"

"Yep. He also taught me how to budget my money and how to get rid of groundhogs. Stuff like that." He rubs the side of his face with his free hand. "We talked about what he was like when he was our age. Grandad saw a lot of himself in me, I guess—" Egan stops abruptly.

"And?" I whisper, more than a little unsettled by our sudden role reversal. He's the incessantly chatty one who asks too many questions. It's me who keeps details buried deep underneath silence.

Egan clears his throat and shakes his head, still staring downstream. His fingers tighten slightly around mine. "And he flat-out told me I was stealing from my future by acting the way I was. That if I didn't deal with the junk I'd been ignoring it would start to take over my life and I'd forget who I was at my core." His eyes are swimmy when he finally turns back to me.

I have to look away. "That was bold."

"I guess I needed bold. I was headed down a nasty path."

"E, you shut me in a locker. You apologized, and it's been over for a long time." I inhale quickly. It's the first time I've ever said those words and meant it. I think.

"No." Egan lets go of my hand and lays his fingers across my forearm. "I get that there were a lot of little things that happened before it, but that was a big deal. If it weren't, we never would have lost our friendship. But it's also not the only thing I did."

"Oh." I watch a trail of goose bumps skitter across my arm.

"I hurt a lot of people and did a bunch of stupid stuff. But I got caught defacing a cop car at Christmas a year and a half ago. That's what pushed my parents to their end."

"You what?" I paw at the edge of my inner tube, trying to sit up, but I only manage to slip farther into the middle. My skin squeaks against the tubing. I end up leaning awkwardly over the edge, my elbow jammed into my ribs, as I openly stare at Egan. "Did Grandpa know about it?"

"Probably. You said he retired, but he's still consulting with the police force?"

I nod. "He officially retired a couple years ago, but he's still over there a couple times a week consulting. He never said anything to me about you, though."

"That was nice of him."

"Why'd you do it?" I ask.

"A couple of guys on the track team dared me. To be honest, that was probably the least stupid thing I did, but it's the first time I got caught. I'm glad I did, though, because at least I got the chance to learn who my grandad really was before he was gone. At the beginning of the summer last year, he fell when he was getting up to grab the TV remote, and he broke his hip. He never really recovered and caught pneumonia last June."

"I'm so sorry. That must have been terrible."

"It's fine. Really. It was sad. Still is. But Grandad loved God. He loved me. And I'm grateful he saw through my crap and cared enough to get in my business." He reaches up and brushes the side of my cheek. I barely notice that his finger feels like an icicle against my roasting face.

Egan smiles. "He liked you, you know."

I lean away. "He yelled at me for making mud pies in his garden when we were seven."

"He also really liked his garden."

We both run out of words at the same time. Egan drapes his arm over the edge of his tube and dangles his fingertips in the water, resuming proper tubing position. "Hey, Noog?"

"Callie," I correct him automatically.

"Sorry, Callie." Egan dips his chin downward in apology. "Thanks. Again. For doing this, I mean."

"You're welcome." It sounds like I'm mumbling so I clear my throat and force myself to speak over the babble of the creek. "I hope we both end up getting out of this whatever it is we're hoping for." Like a chance to launch myself into my dream. Or bragging rights for life. Or maybe even the slow resurrection of a friendship?

It's not his trademark open-mouthed grin, but Egan does glance over at me and smile, crooked and bright like a wedge of lemon.

He pats the side of my inner tube and pulls, drawing me close until we bump into each other. "Me, too, Callie. I hope we do, too."

Chapter 11

I WRITE MY INITIALS IN THE CONDENSATION ON THE side of my glass of iced lemonade, then wipe it all away. Annabeth sits across from me at the picnic table in my backyard with a legal pad, occasionally mumbling things under her breath.

"How much would you pay for a handmade poodle skirt for your hamster?" She taps the end of her neon green pen against the tip of her nose.

I raise an eyebrow. "I don't have a hamster."

She sighs. "Pretend, Callie. I'm running a business scenario."

"Ten bucks."

"That's it?" She chews on the end of her pen.

"Thirteen-fifty?" I follow up.

"Never mind." She scribbles on the notepad. "It was a dumb idea anyway. What are you working on over there?"

I glance at my tablet, which has gone dark because I just stared at it for so long without doing anything, and grimace. "My application."

"For Raquel?"

"Nichelle. Yeah."

"Ooo, let me see." Before I can object, Annabeth reaches across the table and grabs the edges of the tablet. She touches the power button.

"Stop, put it down. It's not done yet."

Annabeth scrolls with her index finger. "What do you mean it's not done? You've answered all these questions. And it says your three recipe samples uploaded successfully. What's left?"

I want to lie and tell her it's my social media numbers, but after Egan posted yesterday's creek-tubing date I gained enough followers to double the minimum platform requirements outlined in the contest rules. And I'm pretty sure Annabeth watches my numbers more closely than I do, so she'll know if I try.

"Cal? What's left?" Annabeth persists when I count the grooves in the picnic table instead of answering her.

"The deadline isn't for a couple more weeks. I think I'll just let it sit and marinate for a while."

"It's an application to make your dreams come true, not a chicken breast. Send it in."

I dig my thumbnail into a knot on the tabletop. "It's not ready."

"Don't you mean *you're* not ready?" One corner of Annabeth's lips lift upward. Her skin is dewy in the lingering humidity, and her eyes glitter in the early evening golden light.

My nose starts to itch with some sort of weird BFF intuition. "I'll get to it soon." I casually reach across the table and wiggle my fingertips as though I just want to glance at the tablet again, but Annabeth's on to me. She yanks the tablet away with a grin.

"How soon?"

"Tonight."

"Tonight? Like a few hours from now?" She sets the tablet down but doesn't relinquish her grip.

"Definitely before I go to bed."

"And you'll text me right afterward?"

"Promise." That I'll text, anyway. Something might come up, like I might find a disastrous typo or remember a better recipe between now and then. But she doesn't need to know that. Just saying.

Annabeth starts nodding. "Okay. Sure. Good." She looks at me and smiles. "This is a huge step outside of your comfort zone, isn't it?"

The rolling squeeze of my stomach confirms her words, but I'm grateful she seems to understand. "It's actually more like a flying leap out of my comfort zone."

"Definitely." She's still nodding. "And I'm really proud of you, you know?"

"Thanks, AB. That's sweet."

"But I don't believe you. Not even a little bit." Before I can reach out to rescue my application, Annabeth leaps away from the picnic table and takes off across the yard.

I try to extricate myself from my seat too, but I only end up falling face-first into the lawn. I push myself upright. "Bring that back."

"Or what?"

"Or I'll…I don't know, but it won't be good."

Annabeth is skipping through the yard now. Her auburn curls bounce against her shoulders, and she's grinning. My legs finally start working again, and I rush toward her.

Suddenly, Annabeth freezes. Her mouth opens in a tiny O, and her finger hovers centimeters from the tablet screen. I stop too. "Annabeth?"

She's breathing fast, like she's just run a marathon. "Don't hate me, Cal. You promised to send it anyway."

Now my heart's pounding. "You didn't."

"I didn't mean to." She holds the tablet toward me, and I reach for it.

"Annabeth."

"I'm sorry," Annabeth wails, nearly flinging the tablet into my waiting hands.

The screen no longer sits on my application. Instead, it's a confirmation screen. And in the middle of the plain white page are huge, black letters proclaiming, "Congratulations, Callie Christianso!"

My mouth suddenly tastes like I've eaten an entire sleeve of Saltines. "You've got to be kidding me," I manage to mumble.

"It's a good thing, Cal. Right? You needed that push. I think." Annabeth's voice gets higher and squeakier with every syllable.

"Callie Christianso?" I shake the tablet close to her face. "I am not Callie Christian*so*. I am Callie Christian*son*. Why did you press submit?"

Annabeth's face drains of its vibrancy. "I thought you needed the push," she whispers, clutching her hands underneath her chin. "I'm so sorry, Cal."

I close my eyes so I can concentrate on my breathing. "They're going to think I'm such an idiot. I can't even spell my name right." I sink to the ground and sit in the grass. It's cool against the back of my thighs. Cool, but itchy. I set the tablet down beside me and hang my head between my knees.

Annabeth drops down beside me. "They won't think that." She bumps my shoulder. "I'll write them a letter of recommendation. I'll tell them it was my fault. Everyone makes mistakes. They'll totally understand. Even Nichelle Melendez is human."

I glance up at her, swallowing back my sudden panic. "You got her name right."

"I do listen to you, Cal." Annabeth wraps her arm around me and squeezes. "Sometimes."

Chapter 12

TODAY'S BEEN A DRASTIC IMPROVEMENT OVER yesterday, and it's not even noon.

Last night, Egan and I went to the playground at our old elementary school for our date, but it was decidedly un-fun. I spent the entire time trying not to vomit every time I thought of Nichelle Melendez, then I had to blame it on the Merry-Go-Round when Egan noticed.

But this right now? This is paradise.

I reverently reach for Egan with one hand and press the other to my heart. "How did you know?"

"How did I know what? That you'd fall madly in love with me if I took you to a food truck fair?" He smirks. "Please. You're pretty much an open book when it comes to anything fried or sugar-coated. Anyone who spends more than two minutes with you can figure that out."

"Oh, come on." I shake my head and step away from him. "The only thing I'm falling in love with today is a gourmet grilled cheese. Or maybe a deep-fried s'more. I'm not picky."

He pulls his phone from his pocket and starts recording, holding it slightly above and ahead of us. He narrates as we meander through the empty fairground, but I'm barely paying attention.

Food trucks of every kind are parked around a portion of the grounds. There are trucks with cupcakes and doughnuts, gourmet hot dogs, tacos, and even a milkshake truck. This is as close to heaven as I think I'll ever be this side of eternity. And it smells like funnel cake and cheeseburgers on the grill. It's the best sort of distraction. Something to keep my brain occupied in the wake of my submitted application. As fun as it is to ride the wave of an adrenaline rush every time my phone gets a new notification, I'm looking forward to a chance to concentrate on something else. Maybe something else drenched in cheese.

"Which truck do you want to go to first?" Egan asks. He reaches for my hand and loops his fingers between mine. I glance up at him, curling my lip at the surprise hand holding, but he's got the camera turned toward me so I course-correct and grin, hoping it doesn't look too much like a grimace.

"How am I supposed to choose?" I wiggle my fingers, but Egan doesn't let go. "I don't know what all the options are."

"I got you a map."

"There's a *food truck* map? Best. Date. Ever." Hand holding ambush forgiven.

"You realize you sound like a super nerd, right?" He drops my hand to slip a glossy brochure from the back pocket of his jeans.

I rip the map from his hands. "Maps make everything better. And look at the cute way the artist drew all the trucks." I point to one drawing in particular, a pickle business housed in an old Airstream trailer called "Pickled Pink." "It's a giant hot pink pickle."

"That's just adorable." Egan nudges me over to a nearby picnic table and motions for me to sit down. "We're going to be here a while, aren't we?"

I don't even look at him when I answer. "You brought me to a food truck fair and gave me a map. What do you think?"

"I think you're going to need some time to strategize."

I merely nod. Egan holds his phone out in front of his

body and talks directly to our audience. "When we were in pre-school she bit me because I ate a Froot Loop off her cereal necklace. I learned an important lesson that day: don't get between this girl and her food."

He looks over the phone and half-smiles at me, like he's remembering that day. And the tooth marks I left on his shoulder. He graciously pokes around on his phone for a full five minutes while I build a game plan. I can tell I'm pushing it, though, when he stands, stretches his arms over his head, and feigns a huge yawn. "Are you having a hard time deciding? We can start at the doughnut truck. It's close."

"Actually, how does Curly Cue's sound to you? Spiral fries would be an excellent appetizer. I thought we could save the doughnuts for dessert. Well, my dessert, anyway."

Egan nods. "I see. You're playing the long game today."

"Of course. You're surprised?"

"Not even a little bit." Egan stands and squints into the noonday sun. "You think they have a salad truck around here somewhere?"

"I did see one on the map. We can find it after I have my fries." I shake my head as we walk past a bounce house full of screaming children.

It takes us a couple of minutes to weave through the rest of the gathering fair crowd before we get to Curly Cue's. It's a large box truck with a window cut out of the side, and it's been fitted with kitchen equipment. The truck itself is turquoise and the bumper is polished silver. Its name is painted across the side in glittery pink and silver paint. If I weren't here for the fries, I'd be here for the glitter.

There's already a huge line at least twenty people deep, but it'll be worth it to eat an entire plate of curly fries by myself. But before we get to the Curly Cue's line, Egan gasps. He squeezes my hand and presses it to his chest. "Callie."

"What?" I can feel the thud of his heartbeat through his T-shirt.

"That sign." He points over the crowd, obviously able to see something from his vantage point that I won't be able to see without a ladder. When I don't answer, he points again more forcefully.

"I can't see over everyone else," I finally say. "Just tell me what's so amazing. Deep-fried Oreos? Deep-fried Pop-Tarts? Please tell me it's not a kale truck—"

"It's not deep-fried Pop-Tarts or a kale truck." He wraps his arm around my shoulder and drags me through a huge crowd of people away from the Curly Cue's line.

"No," I groan. "This is off mission. You gave me the map so I could plan."

But then the people part in front of us. Egan drops my hand and holds his arms out like he's presenting me with some sort of gift. I squint and wipe a bead of sweat from my forehead as I read the sign in front of us. "Competitive cheeseburger eating contest signups until noon. Start time at 12:30."

"The fine print says the winner gets twenty pounds of bacon. Callie, seriously. Let's do it." He clasps his hands in front of his body and looks down at me with shiny molasses eyes.

What he means, of course, is not for us to do anything at all. He's got the appetite and the body of a boa constrictor—one big meal a week and he's good. He'd eat one and a half burgers and tap out, so what he's really asking is for me to do this thing. For us. For him.

"You were going to eat more than one cheeseburger anyway. Admit it." Egan squeezes me into a side hug and gives me an enthusiastic shake. "Think about the prestige. The bacon. The free publicity."

"Just because it's free doesn't mean it's good." My stomach curdles as I imagine myself as the main feature in a horrifying vomiting video gone viral.

Egan doesn't notice my hesitation. He points to the sign. "Black forest, thick-cut, sugar-cured bacon. That's good, right? And, again, it's free."

Egan once bought his mom a hundred-dollar basket of warm vanilla sugar hand soap because the purchase came with a free shower cap. The siren's song of free has nothing on my voice of reason. But I try anyway.

"How about I buy you twenty pounds of bacon? I've got some cash saved up from my last bake sale and then we can still enjoy—"

"But this is your destiny. You know none of these people will expect it when twiggy little you climbs up there on that platform and eats twenty-five burgers like they're handfuls of popcorn. It would make this the most epic date of all time." He crouches and leans in so our cheeks touch. "Just say the words, Callie. Say, 'I volunteer as tribute.'"

I shove him away and rub my face.

"I don't know, E. It seems like a bad idea." But my voice is too measured, too rehearsed.

Like a shark who just caught the scent of a drop of blood in the water, Egan steps closer. He drapes his arm around my shoulders. "The sign also says the winner takes home $500 cash."

Every shred of cool I had melts around my feet. I grab the sleeve of his T-shirt. "I could do so much with $500."

"Exactly. You could get a million new baking books. A cotton candy machine for your room. A mixing bowl at that fancy kitchen store where you like to torture yourself by going in but never buying anything." He encroaches on my space again, leaning so close his hair tickles my temple. He whispers, "I believe in you."

And because he's the Pied Piper of Dumb Ideas and because I really would love something from Williams-Sonoma, I suddenly agree, telling myself all the while that I'm only agreeing because of the cash and nothing to do with the weird way his whisper sent a shiver down the back of my neck.

"Where do I sign up?" I ask as I pull a purple hair elastic off my wrist and begin gathering my hair into a ponytail to keep it out of my face for the competition.

Egan punches the air. "That's my girl. I'll get you a pen."

Chapter 13

HALF AN HOUR AND SEVERAL FORMS LATER, I'M sitting behind a long table and sandwiched between a man with a beer gut the size of a large, lumpy loaf of brioche and a college guy who keeps kissing his biceps every time a girl in the crowd bats an eyelash in his direction. The table is on a stage, and spectators watch from a grassy area below. I glance down from the platform at Egan who's holding his phone heads above the rest of the people gathered nearby.

He grins and shoots me a thumbs-up. "You got this, Callie," he yells over the crowd.

I press my hands under my thighs and try to time my heart rate though it's faster than usual. You'd think by now I'd know not to let Egan lure me into doing these things. The college guy turns toward me. I see my reflection in his sunglasses, all pale and hunched over as though I'd rather melt through the floor than take part in this contest. I'm the only girl up here. Easily the youngest participant too since the college guy has to be four or five years older.

He shakes his head and chuckles. "It's so cute that you think you can do this." He winks and holds his hand out for me to shake. "I'm Shawn. Maybe after I win, you'd like to finish out the meal with some drinks?" He adjusts his visor, flipped backward and upside down, and smashes his bangs up.

I scowl. "I'm seventeen."

His eyebrows move upward. "Whoa. My bad."

I roll my eyes and turn back to the long table in front of us just in time to see Egan hopping up and down like he's trying to start a mosh pit.

A girl with two dark brown braids slides a tray of cheeseburgers in front of me. And they're gorgeous, gooey from the melty cheese. There have to be at least twenty of them on the tray in front of me. My stomach rumbles.

A man wearing a red and white striped paper hat and a name tag that says "Rich" picks up a cordless mic and taps the end. It echoes out over the crowd gathered in front of the cheeseburger truck. He leans in and begins to speak. "In front of each of these contestants, we're placing a platter of twenty-five cheeseburgers. Each cheeseburger is a quarter pound of grass-fed, organic beef."

I meet Egan's gaze, and he sticks out his tongue and crosses his eyes. I look away before I start laughing.

Rich keeps talking, half a step below a full-out yell. "Each cheeseburger has a piece of perfectly melted Colby Jack cheese, three pickle slices, and a splash of ketchup and mustard. All ingredients have been weighed out to ensure complete fairness. Our contestants will begin after we ring the bell, and whoever eats the most cheeseburgers by the final buzzer will win the bacon and that $500 in cash. Can we get some enthusiasm going here?" He waves his hands up and down.

The crowd cheers and hollers but none of them as loudly as Egan. He cups one hand around the corner of his mouth and yells. "Yeah, Callie! Take those guys to school."

I frown slightly at his smack talk, but Egan doesn't seem interested in backing down. He keeps yelling.

"Your boyfriend's got a big mouth." Shawn leans over and grumbles inside my personal space bubble.

I scoot as far away from his breath as possible. "He's not—"

A bell chimes and all the participants except for me start shoving piles of cheeseburgers into their faces. It's mesmerizing, really. And disgusting, all the cramming and chewing and spittle.

"Callie! The burgers," Egan screams.

"Oh!" I blink then grab two burgers in one hand and start eating. It helps that they're cooked to perfection, not super-well-done but not so rare they're falling apart. Also, with each bite I can tell they used some sort of spice rub with paprika and salt and a touch of something else tasty. Even this cheese is amazing. I lose count of my cheeseburgers after four, but my stomach doesn't seem to be too concerned. The only thing I'm concerned about right now is wondering why I'm not able to unhinge my jaw like a python.

A quick glance reveals that both men on either side of me have slowed down considerably. Shawn's chest heaves, and he dunks half a cheeseburger in his glass of ice water before cramming the rest of it into his mouth.

Long before I'm willing to concede defeat the crowd starts their final countdown. It only spurs me on to eat faster, and I down another cheeseburger and a half before the final buzzer sounds.

Shawn groans and drops to the table, doing a face-plant into the stack of his remaining burgers.

The crowd is utterly silent. A baby cries somewhere in the distance. A napkin blows off the table and swirls to the ground below. The only one smiling, and it's a killer, is Egan. His grin splits his entire face, almost as though it would be too much work for him to keep it contained. Egan is fully alive.

And, under the weight of all this scrutiny from the crowd, I just wish I were dead.

Rich hovers over my shoulder. "I believe we have a pretty

clear winner here, but, to keep things fair, can I ask my associates to please gather what's left over so we can do an official burger count?"

The girl who placed the platter of burgers in front of me takes the tray away while the others' burgers are gathered as well. I reach for my cup of ice water and take a sip.

Before I set the cup back down, Rich has returned with the microphone. "Ladies and gentlemen, I'd like to pronounce this summer's Cowaburger Truck Challenge champion." He stands behind Shawn, not me. I sigh, a violent rush from my lungs, instantly flooded with equal parts disappointment and relief.

"With fourteen-and-a-half burgers, our winner is Callie Christianson." Rich grabs my wrist and hefts it over my head in victory. My whole body follows, albeit unwillingly. Shawn pounds the table with his closed fist.

"Congratulations, Callie." Rich pulls me around the table to center stage and plunks at least five pounds of ice-cold, plastic-wrapped bacon into my arms. "So, how does it feel to be a winner today?" He plunges the microphone into my face.

The crowd in front of me morphs into a blurry mess. I drop the bacon onto the table and cross my arms. My fingers find my elbow, and I start tapping.

"Callie?" Rich waves the mic in front of my face.

I swallow my panic and try not to start counting the number of hats I can see from the stage. "It feels great," I whisper. My voice sounds choked and raspy.

When Rich only stares and presses the microphone closer to my mouth, I lean forward and add, "Thank you. A lot. Thanks." Feedback squeals from one of the speakers, and I cringe.

Rich clears his throat then takes a step back as he seems to try to rally the conversation. "I don't think anyone expected you to do so well, much less win. Do you do a lot of competitive eating?"

"Um, no. Not really."

"You didn't train for this at all?"

I shake my head. "I didn't even know this was going on today. We were here on a date thing." I look out into the crowd for Egan, but he seems to have disappeared. "We saw the sign and I—I eat a lot of junk food. So."

"Wow. That's remarkable." Rich nods. "And what do you plan on doing with the prize money?"

I try to peer around him to find Egan, but Rich keeps blocking my field of vision. My insides are starting to gelatinize. Remembering my earlier conversation with Egan, I say the first thing that comes to mind. "I'm going to buy a mixing bowl."

"A mixing bowl." Rich blinks at me.

I nod and try not to panic about the fact that I've suddenly been abandoned by the only person here who believed in me. "Yeah." I keep nodding, feeling more and more out of control. "I like to bake. Cookies. And breads. And stuff. So it would be a nice thing to have." I feel like the whole crowd is just staring at me as a disappointed herd. "I guess I could buy a new hand mixer too. And a lottery ticket. Or something."

"You said you're seventeen. They won't sell you a lottery ticket," Shawn says behind me.

"Oh. Right." Never mind that I'm not even sure how you go about buying a lottery ticket in the first place. I'm about two seconds away from shoving Rich out of the way and leaping off the stage so I can run away from the stares and the awkward silences. With or without the bacon and the cash.

"Hey," a woman yells as she's bumped from behind. Her sunglasses fall off her face and hit the ground.

"Wait, kid, you can't—"

"You won!" It's Egan. He's running toward me, across the platform, arms outstretched.

I nearly melt with relief and reach for his hand so he can drag me offstage. But he doesn't take it. Instead, he makes a grab for Rich's microphone.

Rich doesn't let go. He grunts, and his face turns red as he struggles against Egan's wiry strength. "Stop it. You're not allowed to be up here," Rich says away from the microphone, trying to keep his voice from being broadcast over the speakers. He's unsuccessful.

Egan tugs on the mic again, and this time it pops from Rich's fingers. The heavy end with the batteries hits me full on in the eye. I double over, pressing my hands to my suddenly throbbing face.

The girl who took my burger platter rushes to my side and touches my shoulder. "Are you okay?"

"I'm fine." I wave her away, but she still hovers nearby.

"Everybody, let's cheer for Callie one more time." Egan doesn't seem to notice my distress as he takes a couple of steps toward center stage. Rich scowls and swipes for the mic again, but Egan ducks away.

"What are you doing?" I whip around to grab his elbow, but the motion sends my stomach into a state of mutiny, and my fingers only barely graze the inside of his arm. Out of the corner of my eye I sense more movement at the bottom of the stairs to the stage.

"If you want to see more of me and Callie, look up the Great Date Experiment online. We're going on twenty-one dates and—" Egan squawks and drops the mic. It falls to the ground with a dull thud, and he starts running away from two men wearing windbreakers marked "Security."

Rich cuts in front of me to give chase as well. His shoulder connects with my chin when he twists to avoid Shawn's feet poking out from beneath the table behind us. More white-hot pain explodes across my face, this time emanating from my lower lip.

Now the girl who had, seconds earlier, laid gentle fingers on my shoulder grabs my wrist and drags me off the stage, trying to get me the heck away from the maniac tearing across it. The maniac I'm sort of dating.

My confusion turns to mortification as Egan jumps off the platform and zigs and zags through the crowd, evading a security guard with a sizable paunch.

My handler, or whoever she is, yanks my arm when I try to stay put. "Come on. You can meet up with him after the paramedics take a look at your…" She gestures around her face.

I touch my rapidly swelling lip, and my fingers come away bloody. The burger rush combines with the adrenaline of Egan's escape and the realization of my injuries, and my senses converge in an overwhelmed, swirling amalgamation. My knees give out, and it's all I can do to close my eyes and hope for the best.

Chapter 14

ANNABETH BALANCES HER PAINTBRUSH BETWEEN her fingers and considers the paint on the paper plate in front of her before she slathers it on her snail figurine. "He's probably embarrassed."

"I'm sorry. Have you met Egan?" I glance up from my ceramic hedgehog, which sits blank and white in front of me. My paintbrushes rest beside it, unused. Painting is Annabeth's therapy, not mine. I need a brownie.

"Maybe he's waiting for you to call him and give him the all clear."

I pick up a paintbrush and tap it on the table. "I did call him. Three times. He never answered." Now every time my phone gets a notification, I spend agonizing seconds wondering if it's something from Nichelle Melendez, an email about BOGO candles, or proof of life from Egan. Super fun.

"Did you leave him a voicemail?"

"His box is full."

"Did you text him?"

"Yes. And I spammed all his social media."

"How many times?"

I let my hand fall to the tabletop. The paintbrush water ripples. "I don't know. Like ten times, then I felt desperate, so I quit. The Experiment's over, okay? I'm not going to throw myself at him anymore. If he doesn't want to hang out, he doesn't want to hang out." I try to sound casual about it, but as soon as the last words leave my lips, I have to look away to hide the sudden tears springing to my eyes.

I don't know why I'm emotional. I knew it would end. Worse, I knew it would end like this.

Annabeth covers my hand with hers. "Maybe he's been working a lot and can't answer."

"For two days straight?"

She wrinkles her nose. "That is pretty implausible."

"Excuse me?" A clear, pure voice interrupts my unwelcome emotional deluge.

A girl about our age, wearing a red Paint Perfect employee apron and a high ponytail, stands in front of our table. She blinks at me from behind the large black frames of her glasses.

"You aren't really supposed to take the paint back to your table," she says, gesturing toward the bottle of lavender paint Annabeth set down in between us. Her name tag says ELIZA in big block letters.

"Sorry." I grab the bottle and hand it to her. "She won't do it again."

"No problem." Eliza shrugs. "It's kind of a dumb rule anyway." She starts to turn around then stops and looks over her shoulder. "Sorry, this is awkward. But did I hear you guys talking about an experiment?"

I sit on my hand so I can't reach up and touch my fading black eye. "It's just a dumb thing we were doing for the summer, but it's—"

"She's supposed to be going on twenty-one dates with her best friend and recording the whole thing. They post it online. They're totally falling for each other." Annabeth doesn't even look up from her snail.

I glare in her direction then turn back to Eliza. "I think it's over, actually. I haven't heard from him in two days. And we aren't falling for each other."

"Has he said it's over?" Annabeth crosses her arms over her chest.

"No, but—"

"Then you don't get to say it's over."

Eliza doesn't seem to hear us, or if she does, she doesn't care. "Wow, this is so awesome." She drags a folding chair away from one of the other tables and drops into it. "I thought it was you, but I didn't want to be all awkward and in your business and whatever, but it really is you. Wow."

Annabeth and I both freeze. "You actually watch the Great Date Experiment?" I ask.

"All the time. At first I wasn't sure about you two because you're such a strange couple and you don't seem like girlfriend material, but the more you post, the more I get sucked in. I'm pretty much addicted now. You have to finish all twenty-one dates. There haven't been new videos lately, and I was getting nervous."

Annabeth elbows me in the side and grins. But I'm stuck on the "strange couple, not girlfriend material" comment. There's another sound bite that's going to get stuck in my mind for days.

Eliza rests her elbows on the tabletop and plunks her chin in her hands. "I didn't think you two were good together at first, especially since you guys didn't hold hands or smile at each other or anything."

Annabeth clears her throat. I ignore her.

Eliza continues. "But it's funny to watch now since you're so different from each other and stuff. He's all crazy and you're all…not."

I'm not sure why it feels like an insult to be called the

not-crazy one. "Well, hey, thanks for watching so far. I don't know if we'll finish, but if I hear from him, I'll tell him what you said." I force myself to smile and turn back to my blank hedgehog, hoping Eliza will take the hint and return to her job of policing the painting supplies.

But she leans in closer instead. "Do you think you two are going to last beyond the Experiment? Because that would be the best love story ever."

I bite my lower lip and inhale. How many times do I have to say it's over?

Except Annabeth cuts me off before I can say anything. "I completely agree. I've been telling her the same thing this whole time, but she keeps saying they're just friends. But all you have to do is watch one clip from this last week and you can tell she's well on her way to being a goner."

"Annabeth." I frown. "I'm sitting right next to you. And I'm not a goner." I glance at Eliza who's watching me with rapt attention. "Sometimes we have good conversations. But that's it, so no. I don't think we're going to be anything other than *just friends*. Besides, have we all forgotten I haven't heard from him in two days?"

Every time I say it, my stomach tightens as though someone's cinching my belt in another notch.

"She has a crush." Eliza's eyes go wide, and she reaches across the table to lay her hand on Annabeth's forearm.

Annabeth shrugs. "That's what I've been saying all along."

"We're friends." I toss my hands in the air. "End of story."

Eliza pushes her glasses up the bridge of her nose. "You can't give up. Don't give up. Do you need me to call him?"

I lean away from her exuberance. "You have his number?"

"No, but if you give it to me—"

I cut her off by shaking my head. "No. That's not going to happen."

"Okay, fine. But please, please, please promise me you'll make this right. I have to see the end of the Experiment. I have this gut feeling that you two are going to end up together."

"She won't give up," Annabeth says with authority she doesn't have. I stare straight ahead and count the bubbles in the goldfish tank next to the cash register.

"Good. I'm depending on you." I look back at Eliza in time to see her shaking a finger at me. "My friends and I will be super disappointed if you back out of this thing."

"I'm not the one who's—"

"Wait." Annabeth butts in again. "You and your friends? How many of you watch this thing?"

"Well, there's me. And Juliet. And Madeline. And Isabel." She ticks her fingers with each name. Finally, she stops naming people and shrugs. "I don't know. Maybe twenty or thirty of us."

I turn to Annabeth so quickly I'm almost certain I've given myself whiplash.

"Twenty or thirty?" she mouths into the empty air between us. I raise my eyebrows.

It doesn't sound like much. But if Eliza's twenty or thirty friends have even half of her enthusiasm, Egan's got to be closing in on the thousand views mark. And he's given up?

I glance down at my phone again, hoping to see that I've missed a text from him during this conversation. But it still sits blank.

"Don't worry, Eliza." Annabeth turns up the wattage of her grin so high I'm a little afraid she's going to over-volt. "They'll finish out the Experiment. Even if I have to go to Egan's house myself and chase him to Callie's with a Super Soaker."

I pick up the paint brush and pretend to inspect the bristles. "I'm not sure he'd run."

"Hush." Annabeth shushes me. She flutters her paint-covered fingers in the air as though she's my fairy godmother who's about to make my dreams come true. "Don't you worry, my little pessimist. All of this is going to work out just fine."

Eliza nods like she has the inside scoop. Her blond ponytail bobs. More than anything I wish I could believe them because I already miss him. But, unfortunately, Egan's silence is a lot louder than their abundance of words.

Chapter 15

I WATCH THROUGH THE BLINDS AS EGAN STARTS up the sidewalk for the third time in five minutes. Each time he's turned around before he got to the patio, but this time I don't back away from the window quickly enough and he catches my eye.

There's a clunk against the door. Then another one. And another.

I debate the merits of leaving him there and going back to the peanut butter fudge brownies I'm getting ready to put into the oven but finally decide I'd rather have answers and yank the door open.

Egan falls into me, his forehead poised to hit the door again. He unfolds his arms and wraps them over my shoulders. His cheek nestles into my hair. He smells like grass clippings and sunshine and sweat.

My hands hang at my sides, and I'm unsure of what comes next. He's been missing, at least from my world, for almost three eternal days. And now he wants a hug? What's next? A request for an apple spice cake or a rum raisin loaf to take to a fundraiser or something?

I push him away. "What the heck is wrong with you?"

"I know. I was an idiot. Like, who runs from security unless you've done something remarkably stupid?" He straightens and hits himself in the forehead, as though he can't quite believe it either.

"Not that." I shake my head. "No, I mean, yes. That was stupid. But where have you been for the last two days? Did Annabeth find you? We still have thirteen dates left in the Experiment but you just vanished." My voice cracks on the last word, and I glance away as I thrust my hands into the pockets of my dark gray joggers.

"What? No. I haven't seen Annabeth at all." Egan steps into the house and shuts the door behind him, though he keeps his entire body angled for quick escape. "I figured you were super ticked at me, so I laid low. And Mom and Dad grounded me after the food truck fair security team gave them a call. The only reason I'm allowed to be here right now is because Mr. Torrence asked if I could mow his lawn." He hitches his thumb across the street toward our middle school principal's house. "Coming over here was sort of a last-minute decision. Are you okay?" His hand hovers for just a second before his fingers brush against the tender, healing skin of the bruise on my cheekbone, a remnant from my run-in with the microphone he grabbed.

"I'm healing."

"Did you have a concussion?" He lets his hand fall away.

"The paramedics at the fair didn't think so."

"Good. How'd you get home?"

"Called Grandma. She picked me up after they took you into the security office. What'd they do to you in there anyway?" I squint at him and take a step back.

"They just asked me a bunch of questions. I guess they wanted to make sure I wasn't planning something nefarious."

"You should have told them you don't plan *anything*, nefarious or otherwise."

Egan nods once. "True."

I count the silence until I know what I want to say. "Friends don't disappear on each other, you know."

"I completely agree."

"I thought maybe you'd been sent to a juvenile detention center. Or maybe even military school."

His lips quirk with the slightest of smiles, and he scrubs his hand over his hair as he looks down at his feet. "Not this time."

I cross my arms over my chest and try to stare past him, though it's difficult to feign indifference when he's standing so close, wreathed in light from the sunset streaming in through the window behind him.

He watches me without blinking. I clear my throat and look away. "So, are you here to take me on an I'm-sorry date, then?"

"Of course I'm sorry, but I can't take you on a date tonight on account of the grounding. I'm actually here to see if you have my cell phone."

"What?"

"The kid I gave it to said he put it in your bag while you were getting checked out since I was otherwise disposed."

"You've been without your phone for the last three days?" That explains a lot.

"Yep."

"I haven't heard it ring or anything."

"It probably died. It only had like twenty-two percent battery or something by the end of the cheeseburger thing."

"Oh. That bag is in my room. I can go look for it real quick, I guess, if you want."

"Yes, please. I think I'd rather eat Mr. Torrence's grass clippings than go another few days without it."

"Hang on a second. I'll go look." I turn around and run upstairs to my bedroom.

"I'm gonna grab some ice water if you don't mind," I hear Egan call up to me.

"You know where the glasses are." I step into my room and glance around.

Everything is exactly where it's supposed to be, from the aqua throw pillows lined up against my bed's headboard to Hedwig, curled up in her favorite place of evening repose—on the window seat. And the canvas bag I took to the food truck fair still leans against the side of my desk where I dropped it when I came in two days ago.

I pick up the bag and start rifling through it. I pull out a hairbrush, a paperback, and a baggie of chocolate chip cookies I brought but forgot about as soon as I saw the curly fry truck. Just as it begins to seem like that kid dropped Egan's phone into someone else's bag, my fingers close around something rectangular and a little bit grimy.

I press the power button on Egan's phone. The screen remains dark. "Guess he was telling the truth, huh, Kit-cat?" I say to Hedwig as I reach to scratch between her ears on my way out. But then I freeze.

A sudden sense of something-isn't-right smacks me full in the face. I lean closer. Hedwig isn't moving. Her belly doesn't rise and fall. Her tail doesn't flick like it sometimes does when she's dreaming. I lay my palm flat on her shoulder. She doesn't stir awake or stretch her paws into the evening sunshine.

Nothing.

My face burns. My chest seizes. I drop the phone, and it thumps when it hits the carpet. Still, she doesn't startle.

"Egan?" I say into the stillness in my room. It was supposed to be a yell, but I sound like I'm choking. "Egan," I try again, a little bit louder.

Thankfully, he hears me this time.

"Yeah?" His voice is muffled.

"Can you come here?" My whole body feels simultaneously frozen and on fire.

"Sure thing." Within seconds, I hear him bounding up the stairs. It's clear from his footfalls that he's taking the steps two at a time. Suddenly, he's at my doorway. He presses both hands into the doorframe and leans his shoulders inside, but keeps his feet firmly planted in the hallway. "What's up?"

And that's all it takes to break me. I cover my eyes with my balled-up fists. My whole face crumples underneath the weight of my fresh loss. Tears fall fast.

Egan abandons propriety and covers the ground between us in three steps. "What's wrong? What happened? Did you hurt yourself? Are you okay?" He tugs my hands from my face with gentle, unyielding strength. His fingertips tiptoe across my cheeks, around my bruise, around my eyes. He smooths my hair out of my face.

I open my mouth to answer him, but a strangled gurgle is the only thing that escapes.

"Callie, what happened?" Egan grasps my shoulders. The lines of his jaw are so severe in this moment it looks like he was carved from a block of marble. He rubs his hands along the tops of my arms as though I'm chilly and he's going to keep me warm. "I need you to use words. Please."

Finally, my body responds. I point. "Hedwig," I wail, losing the breath I'd been holding all at once. "She's…" It takes me another twenty seconds to force myself to say it. "She's gone."

Egan's eyes go wide. "Oh, no." He crushes me to his chest, both arms crossed behind me, locked behind my shoulders. "I'm so sorry. I know she's really special to you."

When I nod, my cheek rubs against the fabric of his black T-shirt. I curl my hands up underneath my chin and leave them there. Tears keep falling for what feels like forever. And instead of filling the heavy silence with a stupid joke or a bunch of in-consequential babble, Egan stays silent. He covers the back of my head with his palm. His fingers trail the length of my hair.

As my sobs grow quieter, he breathes deeply. His chest swells. "Was she sick?" he asks softly.

"Just old, I think."

"Your grandma got her before you even started living here, right?"

"Even before we were born. But Hedwig's been mine in my heart since the day I moved in, I think." I force my clenched hands down so they hang uselessly at my hips. And then be-cause it feels awkward to stand there like that, I wrap my arms around Egan. I twist my fingers together behind him and listen to the steady thump of his heartbeat. All's fair in love and grief, apparently.

Egan rests his chin on top of my head. "I'm sorry, Callie. She's a great cat. And you know I don't say that lightly because I hate most cats."

A tiny laugh bubbles up my throat, but it gets stuck there, so I nod instead. "I know."

We stand there for a few more minutes. Egan breathes. I cry. When it seems like I can't cry anymore, I draw a shud-dering breath, steel myself for the chill of my room, and step away from Egan. Or try to. It takes a couple of tugs before he relinquishes his hold on me. And then when he does, he stands close, inches away instead of feet.

"Do you want me to move her?" he asks. "It might be better to say goodbye to her somewhere other than in your bedroom."

I swallow hard. "That's a good idea. Thank you."

Egan nods, one quick dip of his chin. "Did she have a favor-ite blanket or something?"

My heart squeezes. "Not really. Just a sweater of mine."

He reaches for me again, then seems to think better of it and lets his hand drop. "Want to get that? We could wrap her up in it."

I stare at the floor. I don't want to have to make this choice. Even though I haven't worn the purple sweater with the gray polka dots in a couple of years, I still kept it for Hedwig, balled up in the back corner of my closet for her to paw at when she got bored. Even last week I caught her pushing her head under one of the sleeves. She loved it.

Instead of answering with words, I walk to the closet, crawl into the corner, and grab the sweater. I hold it close to my heart then crush it to my face. More tears. By the time I crawl back out of the corner, Egan's there at my closet door, waiting. I hand the sweater to him, then push myself onto my feet.

He untangles the sweater and approaches Hedwig and drapes it over her. He tucks the folds of fabric around her body, then gathers her into his arms. When he looks back at me, his eyes glitter and he blinks fast. "Where do you want me to take her?"

I've started chewing on my bottom lip. "Downstairs, I guess. I don't know what we're supposed to do now."

Egan clears his throat. "We buried Luther in the backyard along the tree line."

"Luther died?" I don't know why it surprises me. Luther the black and brown mutt was old even when Egan and I were kids. Why did I think he was immortal?

"It's been a couple years. He'd lived a great life."

"Did you get another dog?"

"Yeah. *Pansy*." He wrinkles his nose. "She's a Bichon Frise, Mom's choice. That dog is dumber than a bag of marshmallows."

"I'll have to come over and meet her, I guess."

Egan touches my shoulder with his free hand. "You should. You know you're welcome any time, right?"

I didn't know.

I stumble downstairs after Egan in a haze. My mind ping-pongs between *this isn't real, she'll be there waiting for me when I go to bed* and *how am I ever going to go upstairs again knowing she won't be there.* Finally, I land on counting my breaths and trying not to think at all.

"Why don't you sit out here?" Egan interrupts my counting by opening the door to the back porch. "It's nice out tonight. Not too muggy."

It feels muggy to me. But that could also be the realization of loss, ratcheting tighter and tighter against my ribs with each passing second. I sit down in a patio chair anyway and let Egan settle Hedwig in my lap.

Though it doesn't really matter what she looks like, I still smooth her fur around her face and untangle a loose knot of puffy white fur at the end of her tail. It's very nearly automatic after so many years of constant companionship. And I can't believe our time together is over already.

"Do you mind if I say a few words?" Egan crouches in front of me. His fingers hover over Hedwig's ears, but then he seems to think better of it and steeples his hands in front of his chest instead.

"Please," I say.

Egan clears his throat. "Hedwig. You are—were—a magnificent cat. And you know I'm not just saying that because I hate cats. But you were one of the good ones. We're going to miss you for the rest of our lives."

A tear seeps from the corner of my eye, trails down the line of my cheek, and drips off my chin onto Hedwig's shoulder.

Egan closes his eyes. Seventeen seconds later, he lifts his gaze and stands up with a sigh. "Take as long as you want to say goodbye, okay? I'll finish up in the kitchen. You can come get me when you're ready."

"I forgot about the brownies." I look away from Hedwig and into his face.

"Don't worry about it. I've got it covered."

"But don't you need to get home? You're grounded, remember?"

"It's fine. I'll explain what happened. They'll understand." Egan squeezes my shoulder then goes inside, leaving me to say goodbye to the first friend I ever had.

After a solid half hour of tears, I decide I'm ready. Or at least as ready as I can be. Mostly because my head hurts so much I'm starting to wonder if someone hit me in the face with a bag of rocks when I wasn't looking. I cradle Hedwig one last time, then lay her down on the chair and cover her entire body with the sweater.

"E?" I let myself back into the house. "I think I'm ready now."

He's sitting in the living room with his feet propped up on the ottoman, watching something on ESPN. As soon as he sees me, he hits the power button on the remote. The TV screen goes black, and Egan stands up. "Did you decide what you want to do?"

I glance over in the direction of the kitchen. It's clean. Totally spotless. Even the plastic cups scattered around the kitchen, Grandpa's bad habit, have been picked up. I shake my head. "I don't know. I think we're supposed to take her to the vet to get cremated or something, but then we'd have to wait for Grandma and Grandpa to come back from dinner. I feel like I'd rather bury her in the backyard like you did with Luther, anyway."

"Okay." Egan presses one hand to my back, between my shoulder blades, and nudges me toward the kitchen. It smells like brownies and not charcoal briquettes, so apparently his baking skills have improved over the past couple of years. "Why don't you have a brownie?" he says. "I pulled them out of the oven five minutes ago, so they're nice and warm. They might help settle your stomach." He starts to leave.

"Where are you going?" I'm not ready to be alone.

"To get a shovel. I'll be back in a second."

I nod, even though it bothers me how the room feels empty when he's not in it. But he's right about how I need to eat a brownie. I grab a butter knife from the silverware drawer and slice one of the corner pieces for myself.

A few seconds later, I watch through the kitchen window as Egan traipses through the backyard with one of Grandpa's shovels. He walks to the edge of our wooded area and leans the shovel against a tree, then jogs back toward the house. He lets himself inside and smiles when he sees me nibbling on the brownie. "As good as you'd hoped it would be?" he asks.

I shrug. "I guess."

"Well, as soon as you're done we'll go ahead and take care of Hedwig."

A lump of brownie suddenly lodges itself in my throat. "Can you do it? I think I'd rather stay in here. Just make sure you mark it well enough, so I'll be able to find it later."

"Sure, I can do that for you. Would you like to watch a movie or something? I'll come back in and join you when I'm done."

I reach for a napkin and fold my brownie into it. My head still pounds. "Sounds good."

Egan holds his hand out to me, and I take it without hesitation. He leads me to the couch and pats the cushion. When I sit, he grabs a blanket from the hall closet and wraps it around my legs. He tucks the folds of fabric under my knees then kneels in front of me. "I'll be back in a few. And if you need me, just yell out the door, and I'll come back. Okay?"

"Thanks, E."

"Not even a thing, Cal. I'm just happy to be here for my girl." His girl. Like no time has passed. Like I used to be all those years ago.

I wait until Egan lets himself out, and then I turn on the TV, flipping through the channels in search of something lighthearted. I settle on an infomercial about a set of remarkable storage containers because it seems safe. I won't fall in love with the characters in this commercial. They won't die. And I won't feel sympathetic toward the polymer plastic.

Sometime later, the back door opens again. Water runs in the kitchen. I hear the flip of the trash can lid. Egan shuffles into the living room and stands in front of me, blocking my view of the TV. He's holding something behind his back. "You doing okay?"

I nod even though my stomach still feels like it's stuck underneath the business end of a KitchenAid mixer and my heart still aches. "I will be. Eventually."

"I did find something that might cheer you up while I was out there, though."

I can't help my immediate groan. "Please tell me you didn't dig up Grandma's tea roses. I like flowers and all, but—"

"Your lack of faith in me is hurtful." Egan pulls a round tin about the size of a personal pizza out from behind his back and sits down next to me. He smells like Grandma's clementine hand soap. "But I think you're going to love this."

Chapter 16

EGAN SETS THE TIN ON MY LAP. IT ORIGINALLY held Christmas cookies, apparently, because the design on the lid is Santa Claus decorating his North Pole igloo with a string of Christmas lights. But it's rusted and muddy, so it looks like Santa's relocated to the bayou.

I squint at the tin. "Am I supposed to know what thi—" I gasp. "Wait. Is this our time capsule?"

Egan grins and nods. "It's been, what, ten years now?"

"At least."

"Didn't we say we were going to dig it up after five?"

I run my fingers around the edge. "That sounds about right. Did you open it yet?"

Egan shakes his head. "Are you kidding me? We put everything in there together, and we're definitely going to open it together. If you feel up to it." He taps the top of the tin with his index finger. A clod of dirt brushes off the side and tumbles off my leg onto the floor.

I curl my fingers around the edge of the lid. "I don't even remember what we put in there."

"Me neither." Egan crosses his legs at the ankles and props his feet up on the ottoman. "Go ahead. Open it."

"Wait. We need to film this. Date number nine, right?"

He laughs. "Cal, it's fine. You've had a rough day. We already skipped two days, so we can let it go. It was a dumb idea to begin with."

My eyeballs burn from all my tears, and I'm pretty sure I look like someone hit me in the face with one of those electrified fly swatters. But he said twenty-one dates, and all of a sudden, I really want to go on every single one of those dates with him.

Because the guy just buried my cat. And, you know, it's the least I can do.

"I'm fine." I wave away his concern and the last shred of my vanity. "We can use my phone. Since yours is dead."

He shrugs. "You found it though?"

"Yeah. But I dropped it and I think it bounced under my bed. I'll get it for you before you leave." I twist the hem of my T-shirt between my fingers. "Sorry."

"It's fine. Don't let me forget it, though." Egan reaches for my phone where I left it on one of the side tables next to the couch. He holds it out to me. Our fingertips brush when I take it, and he smiles.

"You should hold it." I push the phone back to him after unlocking it. "Your arms are longer than mine. They make a better tripod."

Egan laughs. "True. Are you sure you don't want to, uhh." He circles his face with his finger and lifts his eyebrows.

"Oh." Awesome. I must look worse than I thought if Egan's saying something. "Right. Give me a few minutes." I run upstairs and avoid eye contact with Hedwig's empty space on my way to the bathroom where I give myself my best, albeit futile, five-minute makeover. I grab his phone on my way out.

When I come back downstairs, I flop down on the couch next to Egan and drop his phone nearby. "Do I look passable?"

"You look flawless." He smiles and tugs a strand of hair away from my mouth where it got mired in my peppermint lip gloss.

Egan tucks the hair behind my ear, and I may be imagining it, but it feels like his fingertips linger on the curve of my ear.

I lean away. "Hit record, cameraman. Let's do this thing." Before I lose my nerve, before I regret sitting this close, before I forget how badly he broke my heart two years ago.

"Remember, I gave you a choice." Egan winks at me then hits record. "Hi, everyone." He waves. "It's Egan."

"And Callie." I force myself to smile so I don't look like the Grim Reaper's cousin on camera. But I don't wave. Because I am who I am.

"Sorry for our absence. My phone hasn't been in working order lately, and we've had a little bit of a rough day today." Egan draws his face downward in an exaggerated frown, likely an effort to mask his actual sadness. "When I came to Callie's to pick up my phone, we discovered her cat Hedwig had passed away of old age."

I didn't know he was going to say that and just hearing the words brings a lump to my throat. My eyes fill with tears I thought I'd already cried. I stare down at my hands and chew on my bottom lip.

Egan squeezes my shoulders and rests his cheek against the top of my head. "Cal decided to pick a nice spot in the back-yard for the final resting place, so I went out to take care of it. But while I was digging, my shovel hit something a little un-usual. And we thought we'd share what I found with you all."

Apparently that was my cue, because he nudges me with his elbow after I count four seconds of silence. I blink several times in a futile attempt to clear my tears, then pick up the tin so it fits in the frame. "It's a time capsule," I say, sounding much cheerier than I feel.

Egan drums his fingers on the lid, causing more dirt to slough off onto the floor. I'll sweep it up later, I promise myself.

Egan holds the phone closer to the tin for a better shot. "Callie and I put this together about ten years ago. As you can see, it definitely looks like it's been out there that long. We'd planned on pulling it up after five years, but," he moves the phone back out and looks at me, "I guess we forgot?"

I smile and nod. "We definitely forgot."

"But it turned out for the better because now you get to experience this with us. Are you ready, Callie?"

"Ready."

"Okay. Open the lid."

I jam my fingers underneath the rim of the lid and lift. Dirt grinds underneath my fingernails. The lid raises just slightly, so I give it another tug. It flips off onto the floor, clattering on the hardwoods and leaving a dusty circle.

"Oops." I look up. Egan's face is no more than half an inch from mine as he peers into the open tin.

"Whoa," he breathes. I jerk away so fast my neck cracks, but Egan doesn't seem to notice. "This. Is. Awesome." He grabs my hand and forces my fingers open before dropping my phone into my palm. Then he digs through the tin.

"What's in there?" I ask when he keeps digging but makes no effort to show the spoils.

"Oh, sorry." Egan sits up, gripping a red, white, and blue action figure wearing a cape. "I've been looking for this thing for years. Guess that solves the mystery."

I scoot back a couple of inches and aim the phone at his face. "Why don't you go through the whole thing? Show us everything that's in there."

"Good idea." Egan grabs the tin and rifles through it again. "So, besides this guy," he holds up the action figure, "it looks like we've got quite a selection of things in here. We were seven when we did this, so it's going to be interesting to see what we thought was important back in the day."

Egan plucks a sheet of paper from inside the tin, yellowed around the edges. He unfolds it and squints at it. Then he laughs.

"What?" I lean forward. "You're not very good at this. You have to tell us what you're looking at. We need commentary."

Egan turns the full wattage of a trademark grin on me, dimple and all. "Some things never change, I guess." He holds the paper closer to me and the phone. "I don't know if you can see this or not, but this is a table of contents. Seven-year-old Callie thought we'd need one for this project." He draws the paper back and studies the page. "Though her spelling could have used some work, it looks like she did a good job."

I reach for the paper with one hand and try to keep the phone steady with the other. Egan relinquishes the list easily as he continues sorting through the contents of the tin.

"We've got a recipe for something called 'preacher cookies.' That must have been your doing, Noo—Callie." Egan hands me the recipe card. It's one of Grandma's old ones, so it says "From the Kitchen of Gail Christianson" across the top and there are tiny onions and bell peppers illustrated in the corners. I wrote the recipe in pink ballpoint pen and listed the cocoa and peanut butter and oats tight against the left edge underneath "ingredients," written in all caps of course.

"Yep. Definitely mine," I say.

"And a drawing of some sort of space creature?" Egan picks up a three-by-five notecard with neon highlighter markings on it. He grins. "Oh, look, he's eating a squirrel. That's mine. Must have been around the time my dad was having the problems with the squirrels getting into the roof."

I laugh. "What else?"

"Some banana Laffy Taffy." He drops a piece into my waiting palm. It's as hard as a chunk of concrete. "You can have it. Because I'm generous like that."

"Always a giver."

"There's a—oops." Egan wrinkles his nose. "A behavior warning my mom was supposed to sign and send back to Ms. Warshaw. I wonder if I got in trouble for that?"

"Probably."

"We've also got a couple of marbles, which is weird because I don't remember us ever playing marbles. Do you?" Egan glances at me.

I shake my head. "Probably just something we had lying around the house."

Suddenly, Egan's fingers still. "Cal."

"What?"

"I totally forgot about these." He reaches into the tin and pulls out two wads of thread.

"What is it?"

"Do you remember making these at Vacation Bible School that one summer? We were really little." He holds the thread closer to me, and I realize they aren't wads of thread at all. They're friendship bracelets, pieces of cross-stitch floss knotted up around each other with beads tied on the ends. "I made this one for you." He holds up the purple and teal bracelet with the neon green pony beads tied to the end.

"I remember that. And I made the other one for you." I nod to the navy and orange bracelet with the sparkly gold beads. "I thought you were a Denver Broncos fan."

Egan winces. "You didn't know any better. Help me tie it on?"

I hand the phone to Egan. He takes it and aims the lens at his wrist.

I pick up the bracelet I made over a decade ago. "You think it's going to fit?"

"I have skinny wrists. It'll be fine."

The knots in my childhood design are precise and detailed. I remember tying and retying some of them so it would be perfect, so he would be proud to wear it. Except he never wore it. Not back then. My fingertips brush the inside of his wrist as I tie the ends together right next to his medical alert bracelet.

I look up as soon as I loop the last thread of the knot. Our noses are so close they nearly brush.

Egan swallows. Inhales. Lowers the phone. Without meaning to exactly, my gaze skims the sharp angle of his nose and comes to rest on the watermelon pink of his lips. He presses them together. Then he leans away.

Chapter 17

IT'S UNNATURALLY STILL IN MY ROOM WITHOUT Hedwig. I keep thinking I hear the jingle of her tags on her collar or feel her nuzzling against my feet, and then I'm overcome with a fresh wave of grief every time reality smacks me full in the face. When I was sad, she used to lie in my lap and nudge my hands. She always knew what to do to make me feel better.

And it's kind of silly, I guess, but every time I notice the friendship bracelet on my wrist, it sort of feels like one last gift from her, to help me in my sadness. I hold my hand up in the darkness of my empty room. The lime green pony beads on my bracelet almost glow in the dark. And, strangely, my heart also feels a little glowy.

Egan and I moved outside and sat in the backyard for another hour after we opened the time capsule. We talked about everything from tree frogs to family vacations. He held my hand the whole time. Sure, he took a picture of our interlocked fingers and bracelet-ed wrists so he could post it to the official Great Date Experiment social media accounts. And he made sure he left before Grandma and Grandpa got back from dinner since I haven't quite figured out how to tell them we're hanging out again and tonight didn't feel like a great night to share it. But all that makes sense.

What doesn't make any sense is how I keep replaying the way my skin tingled when he brushed tears from my face with his thumb every time my fresh loss overwhelmed me. I can't shake the echo of his voice, or the gritty softness of his words when he confessed that, even though he gets caught up in all the likes and comments sometimes, he mostly just wants to make a difference in the world, however that ends up happening. Now I'm wondering if that's what I want, too. If I want to make more of a difference with my life. Next to him.

It's why I'm sitting here at thirteen minutes after ten watching every single one of our videos again. And it's how I know the exact second Egan publishes the video from tonight. I watch it as soon as it loads, even though I know it's probably going to make me cry again.

It does. A lot. This time I swipe away my tears myself.

At the very end of the video, the screen goes black and "In Memory of our Beloved Hedwig" appears. Beneath the simple white text there's a picture of me holding Hedwig close to my face. Her snowy white fur obscures my chin, making me look a little bit like Santa Claus. And the red floppy hat I was wearing didn't help matters any. I have no idea where he found that picture.

The first comment shows up almost as soon as the video ends. One by one, more comments follow in real time. It's crazy. Were people stalking our site or something?

I scroll all the comments, skipping the spammy ones and nibbling on my pinky nail as I read the rest. Right on cue, there's a super rude comment in the middle of the pack.

   This is a train wreck. Eegan—

I wince at the misspelling—

   acts like he love's her, but thats all it is. An act. He
   knows the right things to say and do and shes buying
   into the whole thing. Callie, your so freaking dumb.
   Wake up and walk away.

My head pounds in time with my heartbeat. Of course he's acting like he loves me. That's the whole point of the Experiment. I'm not buying into anything. This is what I signed up for. Kind of.

The twelve nice comments that follow don't hold as much weight anymore. Now all the rude comments, the ones I'd only skimmed earlier, feel louder. Bigger. Heavier.

"Rileyyy_Rayyyne," for instance, thinks my hair is mousy, my front teeth are too close together, and my hands look like creepy little paws. Basically, she says, I bear a striking resemblance to that French rat who cooks from the movie just without the talent.

Joke's on her. I think that rat is adorable. And so does my grandmother.

I'm about to shut everything off and just go to bed when another comment pops up at the end of the list. I glance at it, and it sucks me in. The first sentence alone makes me feel like I've been beaned with a bowling ball.

> That girl looks like her face got run over by a lawn-mower. She's so hideous. I'm surprised she hasn't broken the camera yet. Has anyone noticed her parents aren't ever around? They must have taken one look at her face and drop-kicked her to her grandparents. How can she act like she's so much better than the rest of us when she looks like that?

I haven't cried over my parents in years. Years. Because it's just a part of my life the same way some kids were adopted into families they aren't biologically related to, or like some kids' parents are divorced. It's a thing. But it's not a *thing* to me. Usually.

Except right now it apparently is because I can't help even more stupid, hot tears spilling over onto my cheeks. I tell myself it's because I'm exhausted, because I've had a really rough day, because everything feels confusing right now. These fresh tears are not because I care what some stranger on the internet has to say about my life. It's not like they know anything about why I live with my grandparents or who I actually am outside of the Experiment.

But then, it's like that last comment was kindling or something. Comments line up, shooting sparks from all directions. And most are aimed at me.

Me and my offensive desire to pray before Egan and I eat a meal together, even if we're in public. Me and the scandalous shirts I wear that don't have sleeves. Me and my love of food, which "spookygoldfishxo" has decided is indicative of some sort of eating disorder, which he or she finds disturbing.

When I read a comment about Hedwig and how she probably ate rat poison so she wouldn't have to spend another second living with me, I stuff my tablet underneath my pillow until the screen goes dark. It takes every ounce of willpower in my body not to fling it across the room too.

I grab my phone and rip it from the charger. My fingers shake as I message Annabeth.

> **Callie:** SOS. Need you at my house now. I'll un-lock the front door.

If she doesn't answer in five minutes, I'll call her. Because this really is that important.

But she does answer. Almost immediately.

> **Annabeth:** Can't. Parents at a movie. They'd kill me if I left without asking. Going to bed soon too. What's wrong?

It figures. I toss my phone back onto my bed without answering and stalk toward Grandma and Grandpa's room. They were so tired by the time they got back from dinner they didn't ask many questions. Questions like, "Hey, did you dig that hole for Hedwig in the backyard yourself?" or "Who tracked in all this dirt?"

Grandma just teared up when I said Hedwig was gone, and Grandpa hugged me so tightly I wasn't sure I'd ever be able to breathe again. Grandma would for sure come sit with me if I asked her to, but she's been handling a heavy caseload at work lately, and I know she's feeling the exhaustion. If I avoid the squeaky spots in the floor, she'll get the rest she needs and never know I snuck by. Besides, talking won't make me feel better. I have to do something.

I push their bedroom door open and pause to make sure the click didn't wake them. But Grandma's snoring, and one of Grandpa's feet sticks out from underneath the quilt. Neither of them stir, so I follow the glow of the moon into the bathroom, then push the door shut and fling open the cabinet doors underneath Grandma's sink.

Somewhere. It's got to be under here somewhere.

I move an old, broken hair dryer out of the way and rifle through a plastic crate full of lotions and hotel sample shampoos and discarded shower caps but can't find what I'm looking for. I bite my lower lip to keep my feelings from leaking out of my face again.

Why are people so mean, anyway? What satisfaction do they get from ripping me apart? I didn't do anything to them.

Just as I'm about to give up, my fingers brush glossy cardboard. I yank it out into the open and stare at the picture of the smiling woman on the front of the box of hair dye. Her teeth are straight, her face is unblemished, and nobody would even think of calling her hair mousy. It's gorgeous and auburn, like the pulp of the purest blood orange.

She probably grew up with both her parents. And her cats live forever, I'm sure.

As soon as I get back to my bathroom, I start running hot water from the bathtub faucet to get my hair wet. I rip the top off the box of dye, yank on the disposable gloves, and mix up the chemicals fast as though I'm Dr. Jekyll awaiting Mr. Hyde. When I look in the mirror, my expression is flat. Mousy. Mousy hair. Mousy personality. Mousy life.

Not. Anymore.

With a deep breath, I squirt the bottle over the top of my head. Dye splurts all over my scalp and along my hairline. It oozes onto my forehead, and I swipe it off with a nearby towel. Once I've finally drained the squeeze bottle of goo, I swirl my hair into a flattened looking cinnamon roll shape and use an old clip to secure it on top of my head. It smells like oven cleaner in here.

My phone rings from my bed. Annabeth.

I dismiss the call. Within seconds she calls back. I dismiss it again. And she calls back again. When it's clear she's not giving up, I answer, holding the phone a whole foot away from the side of my head. "Hi."

"Um, hi, yourself. What's wrong with you?" I imagine Annabeth staring at her phone as though she can see me even though this isn't, and won't become, a video call.

"Nothing. What do you need?"

"You sent me an SOS, then you walk away? It's not like you. I sense a disturbance in the Force."

I roll my eyes and dab away another errant drip of dye. "You said you were going to bed, so I figured I'd let you. I'm fine. Just trying something new. Letting loose. Turning up the volume if you will."

"On what?"

"Everything. If people think I'm mousy, I'll prove how wrong they are. It's time for me to—"

Annabeth groans. "You're kidding me, right? I told Egan he should moderate those stupid comments or something. It's too much for you to handle, reading all that junk. Consuming that stuff every night is hazardous to your health."

"It is not too much for me to handle, Annabeth Mathis. I'm strong. Stronger than you think I am, apparently." But my voice quivers.

"Of course you're strong. Why do you think I hang out with you so much? Someone needs to be the rock to my paper."

"Paper beats rock."

"Whatever." She yawns. "What are you doing? For real."

I glare at myself in the mirror. "I'm being spontaneous."

Annabeth says nothing, but I can hear her breathing into her phone. Five seconds later when she still hasn't said anything I start to get nervous and break the silence. "There's nothing wrong with being spontaneous." I clear my throat. My scalp is starting to tingle. "You do it all the time."

"But I'm me. And you're you. Only one of us gets to do irresponsible things."

"Maybe it's my turn now."

She sighs. "Fine. Will you at least tell me what this irresponsible thing is that you're doing? I don't want to wake up in the morning to see your mugshot on the news. I know they opened that new doughnut shop down the street from you, but you don't want to do anything that will get you a police record. Your grandpa would never let you back in the house."

It's like she doesn't even know me. "I'm dyeing my hair, okay? That's it. It's not too irresponsible. Just something new."

Annabeth squeaks. "What color?"

"Darker than my natural color. Like a reddish brown sugar or something. Kind of like yours."

"What color does it say on the box?"

"I don't know. It's not important—"

"It is important," Annabeth screeches. "I need you to tell me the exact brand and the exact color. This is life or death."

"Now who's being dramatic?" I walk over to my trash can where I discarded the empty box. The grinning lady on the front of the package has a streak of putrid black sludge dribbled down her nose and across the product information. I swipe it away with my fingertips and scrub them across my sweatpants. The tingle on my scalp has started to burn. "Okay, it says... well, I can't really tell. Ash something. But the lady on the box looks happy and beautiful."

"The lady on the box lies. What brand is it?"

"Glorienne?"

"No." Annabeth gasps.

"What?"

"Glorienne? Like, the company that got sued last January because their product burned holes in that one lady's scalp?"

"I thought that was because she had an allergy. Not their fault."

"Everyone thought that until thousands more people came out to say the same thing happened to them. Wash it out."

"But I can't. I still have three more minutes."

"Rinse. It. Now."

The phone beeps. She's hung up on me. I sprint to the bathtub, plunge my head under the faucet, and hold my breath.

Chapter 18

THE RECEPTIONIST AT FOREST HEIGHTS ASSISTED Living Facility peers over the top of the counter at me. Again. The nameplate on the counter reads, "Candace."

"Are you sure I can't help you?" she asks for the third time in as many minutes.

I nod and tuck a stray grayish-green tendril back underneath my knit cap. It's eighty-four degrees out right now, but there's no way I'm taking this hat off until after my hair has returned to normal.

Egan, thankfully, just tugged on the edge of the cap and asked if I was trying out a new look when he picked me up for this date. I nodded then asked how many followers we'd gained in the last twenty-four hours. He seemed to forget all about my "new look" after that. It probably helps that the cap is slouchy enough for me to pass as "headed to a music festival" instead of "adventuring in the Arctic."

When Grandma saw my hair and asked if there was anything I needed to talk about, I told her I'd just wanted to try something new and it went horribly wrong. She promised to take me to her hair girl, who can apparently work miracles, but the earliest appointment she could get was tomorrow morning.

Candace keeps me in her field of vision while she types. "So, are you here to see someone special?"

"I'm not sure."

"With a church group?"

"No. I'm—" I cut myself off. How lame does it sound to say I'm on a date? "I'm here with a friend. He's parking the car."

She nods. "I see. And what's your friend's name?" The typing stops. Candace stares at me. Her sunflower earrings sway from her lobes.

"Ah, his name is, uh…" Her scrutiny is making me sweat. My throat feels dry. I cross my arms over my chest and look around. "He's Egan," I whisper.

"Ian? I've not met any Ians lately."

"No, not Ian. E—"

The front doors open with a whoosh and Egan steps inside, still wearing his sunglasses. Candace's face transforms into a warm smile, her cheeks rising like two proofing balls of yeasty bread dough. "Egan, it's so good to see you again. How are you?"

Egan slips on his regular glasses and hands me his sunglasses. I silently drop them into my bag alongside my phone and a chocolate chip granola bar.

"I'm doing great, Candace. Hey, I'd love for you to meet my…" He pauses and tilts his head toward me. Finally, after five seconds of solid silence, he pats me on the shoulder. "Meet my Callie."

"Oh!" Candace's smile splits her face. "Callie." She presses her hand to her heart as she laughs. "I thought you were just loitering. We get kids who do that sometimes, especially if the coffee is fresh. I don't know why I didn't recognize you right away. Maybe it's your hat." She stands up and extends her hand to me. "My daughter watches your videos all the time. She thinks you two are so funny together."

"That's fantastic. Tell Kenzie thank you for watching," Egan says as I shake Candace's hand. "It means a lot to us."

Actually, it would mean more to me if I knew Kenzie wasn't

"spookygoldfishxo" or another member of my horde of detractors.

Candace sits back in her chair. "I sure will. She's going to love hearing that you two visited here together today. You plan on seeing anyone in particular?"

Egan holds his hand out toward me, fingers splayed open. I hesitate just a half-second before slipping my hand in his. It's almost natural this time, even if it doesn't mean anything.

"Lori called yesterday and asked if I could help with dinner tonight. Do you think she still needs me?"

Candace nods and taps her fingers on her keyboard again as she looks back at her computer screen. "Absolutely. I thought Luke was supposed to be here this afternoon, but he must have had something come up." She stops tapping. "No matter. I'm sure everyone will be glad to see you both. Here's your volunteer tag." Candace slips a badge with Egan's picture and name big as life on the front onto the counter. Egan loops it over his neck without dropping my hand.

"And, Callie, I hope you don't mind if I give you a visitor's badge. Unless you plan on sticking around a few months."

"A visitor's badge is fine." I force myself to sound as peppy as possible to counteract my supposed shadiness, though Egan's approval seems to be better than a background check around here.

"Did I hear something about a bingo game after dinner? Any good prizes?" Egan drops my hand and leans over the counter, resting on both his elbows.

I step up too and press my shoulder into his arm as I watch Candace type my name into a name tag template. Except she spells it "Cally."

"We've got a couple of Corner House Coffee gift cards. And the art store down the street donated some nice picture frames.

The bookstore gave us some new books too, so I thought we'd include those since the library's at capacity right now."

Egan glances down at me and winks. I can't help but smile back, even though I'm not sure why he's winking at me.

"Excellent. Sounds like those prizes might draw a crowd." Egan lays his palm flat on the counter. "Oops. It's Callie with an 'ie' not with a 'y.'" He points to the screen.

"Oh, my mistake. Sorry about that." Candace hits backspace a few times, retypes, then clicks. My visitor's badge spits out of a nearby label maker, and she pulls it off with a flourish. "Here you go. Enjoy, you two. Be sure to come back and say goodbye before you leave. If we have time, I'd love to take a picture for Kenzie."

"Of course we will. Thanks, Candace." Egan holds his hand out to me in invitation. As we walk away I lean close, partly because I'm afraid I'll get carted off if I wander too far from his side and partly because I don't want to shout in the foyer, which started to fill up with residents a couple minutes ago. "So, is this the date that's supposed to show me how much of a nice guy you are?"

"Is it working?" His voice is equally as muted.

I smile. "Maybe. You obviously come here a lot." I tap his personalized badge.

"About once a week, though I've missed a couple weeks now with the Experiment and all."

"Is this where your grandpa was?"

"Yep." Egan raises a hand in a friendly wave toward a gentleman wearing a plaid shirt and clouded glasses. "Hey, Robert. Good to see you. You coming to dinner?"

Robert grins, a slow smile that stretches across his rice paper skin. "You'd better believe it, son. You serving tonight?"

"Absolutely." Egan dips his chin and keeps walking toward a

room full of tables and padded chairs on casters. It's decorated in mauve and forest tones, but it looks reminiscent of a fancy restaurant with cloth napkins fanned out across the place settings. Glasses of iced tea and water flank each plate.

"Why do you still come here? I mean, if he's been gone so long," I ask. Another resident waves at him.

Egan shrugs and waves to his friend. "Some of these people seemed pretty lonely. So was I. I figured it would be a good match."

"You were lonely?" I raise an eyebrow. "How did that happen? You're obviously Mr. Popular."

He drapes one arm around my shoulders, propelling me forward. "After Grandad passed I didn't have many great friends left. Quality relationships are one of those things that make life worth living, and I'd run out of those."

"I guess I get that." I felt the same way for a long time before I met Annabeth.

"These people are quality. I've learned a lot from them."

"What are we doing here tonight, though? Just hanging out?"

"Oh. Sorry. That wasn't obvious? I'm going to be a server for the evening."

"And I'm going to help serve?"

"Nope." Egan squeezes my shoulders. "You're going to be the guest chef."

Chapter 19

"E." I STOP SUDDENLY.

"Yeah?" Egan peers around the dining room with one hand on his hip like a captain surveying the bow of his ship.

I wait for a resident with fluffy white hair and a floral housecoat to shuffle in front of us with her walker before answering. "You don't remember what happened last time I was in a kitchen with you?"

Egan glances at my face. "It was a fluke."

I shake my head. "No way. I'll do dishes or something instead. I learned my lesson the first time. No more cooking on camera. Too many of our dates have ended with a trip to urgent care already. Besides—I bake stuff. I'm not a chef."

He frowns and scratches the top of his head as he looks over me and across the room. "Fair enough. It's just that I told Flora she could go to her granddaughter's quinceañera tonight because I figured you could handle it."

"You. Told Flora? She doesn't have a boss?"

Egan shrugs. "Sure. Brandon is Flora's boss, but he's on a Caribbean cruise right now with his wife."

"Then what about Brandon's boss? What does he have to say about all this?"

Egan shrugs again. "*She's* taking care of her dad after he fell last weekend."

"How far up the line do we need to go? Who's making all the decisions around here?"

Egan pinches his bottom lip between his thumb and index finger. "Maybe me. I've been volunteering here for a little over a year now, and I think sometimes they forget I'm not actually on the payroll."

My eyeballs nearly pop out of my skull and roll across the floor. "You're kidding me."

"Flora was so excited, Cal. Talking about the dancing. And the taffeta. And the non-parallels."

"Nonpareils," I mumble. Doesn't he know cooking a meal for the number of people who live here requires thinking ahead? Several trips to the grocery store? A whole lot of *mise en place*? All things that should have been done yesterday but weren't.

I want to find the nearest wall and smash my forehead against it. Repeatedly.

"Well, at any rate. Think you can help out?" During the course of our conversation, he's pulled his phone from his pocket, and now he wags the camera in front of my face, recording I'm sure. A not-so-small part of me wants to rip it from his hands and stuff it into the ficus in the corner.

He continues when I don't answer. "Come on. I'll take you to Williams-Sonoma for a new teaspoon afterward. Look, our followers want you to do it."

"You're live-streaming this?" I hiss.

"Yeah."

"Why?" I duck out of the shot.

"Why not?"

Because he promised not to reveal the location of our dates in real time. Because I didn't properly prepare my tone of voice for the camera. Because I haven't looked in a mirror to make sure my hair isn't showing in the last five minutes. Because I'm not enough when I'm just me, and there are plenty of commenters out there foaming at the mouth waiting to tell me so.

Egan nudges me with his elbow. "You can choose the next date. No questions asked. Whatever you want."

"E, this is a problem. I bake stuff. I can't throw stuff together and call it a recipe like a chef. My mind doesn't work that—"

Before I finish my sentence, Egan grabs my hand and starts marching across the dining room toward a swinging door in the corner, dragging me behind him by my fingertips. "At least check out the present I got you before you hightail it out of here." He pushes the door open with his forearm and barrels through.

I blink at the sight of all the stainless-steel appliances. Notecards speckle the table in the middle of the gray-and-white-tiled kitchen, and what seems like an entire farmer's market of produce rests in a huge silver mixing bowl nearby. I spy a charcoal-gray chef coat hanging next to the industrial-sized refrigerator.

Egan follows my gaze and nods. His phone is poised to document my gradual acclimation to the kitchen. "That's it. For you. I picked it up this morning."

I step closer, touching the hemmed edge of one of the sleeves. My initials are embroidered in white across the pocket on the front. I trace the letters with my pinky. "You know what a monogram is?"

"I know what *your* monogram is." Egan peeks around his phone and grins at me, that wide-open, life-is-confetti smile.

My fingers twitch, and I inadvertently pull the coat off the hook. It falls into my hands.

Egan sets the phone on the counter, aimed toward us. He tugs the coat from my hand, and his grin settles into a lazy smile as he shakes it out and holds it in front of me. I fold into it as though it's a winter coat. It fits snug across my shoulders.

After a few seconds, Egan clears his throat. "When we were

at Henny Cakes, you said you didn't feel legit sometimes. Maybe this will help?"

My fingers can't work the buttons fast enough.

"What do ya think?" he asks when I don't say anything.

I try to measure my smile and the tone of my voice. Because it's not like he bought me a pony or something. "It'll do."

"I thought it might." He presses his palm to my cheek, then turns away and runs his thumb across a gouge in the countertop. "So. You up for adding to your resumé tonight? Maybe?"

I sigh. The collar of my coat is crisp against the back of my neck. I feel almost professional wearing this. Like maybe my dreams aren't light-years away. Like maybe I can touch them too if I just stretch a little bit. "I guess I can give it a try."

Egan punches the air. "That's my girl."

"But no promises. Put poison control on speed dial or something."

"You're gonna rock it, Callie."

"We'll see. How'd you know I'd do it, anyway?"

"I didn't." Egan shrugs.

"Then why is this here?" I point to my new coat.

"I just really, really hoped you'd do it."

I survey the pile of produce on one of the counters. Green bell peppers. Leafy handfuls of spinach in a colander. Tomatoes that look like they grew in the garden of Eden. An onion with purple skin, a deeper shade of violet than the evening sky the second before it turns into night. It's all beautiful. But it's no pecan pie or cheesecake.

"Hey. Don't stress." Egan drapes a hand over my shoulder. "It's all gonna work out just fine."

"How can you say that?" I start counting each flash of the numbers on the oven clock.

"Because." Egan's fingers move from my shoulder to my

hand, snuffing out my concentration with his palm. "What's the worst that could happen?"

I yank my hand away and tick off ideas with my fingers. "I could give someone's grandma food poisoning. I could forget to turn the oven off before we leave and take out the entire community. I could trip over my own feet and impale myself on a bread knife. I could—"

"Okay. Stop. Forget I said anything." Egan waves his hands in the air as though he's trying to clear it. "Is that what it's like living in your head?"

"All that and more."

"Amazing." He shakes his head. "But try not to worry too much. Marco should be coming in soon, and I'm sure he'll remember to turn off the oven. He's been Flora's right-hand dude for a while. You'll love him. He's pretty much the nicest guy I've ever met."

Someone else will be here. Thank God. I grasp the side of the counter in relief. "You didn't think to mention him earlier?"

Egan arches an eyebrow. "Why? I'd never expect you to run someone else's kitchen without prepping for it."

"Because you're so into prepping for things." I squeeze my eyes shut and exhale so forcefully my cheeks puff. "Is he bringing recipes? Maybe he already knows what's planned for dinner?"

"I'm not sure." Egan scratches the back of his head. "I guess I could ask Candace or someone if they know."

The kitchen door swings open suddenly. A bald man as big as a bear marches through wearing jeans and a leather jacket. He's got an eagle tattoo with wings spread across his entire neck. He stops short when he sees us. I'm afraid he's going to throw us both out into the back alley for being here when we're not allowed, but his face almost immediately melts into a massive, squinty-eyed grin instead.

"Pasko." He holds his hand out in front of Egan. It's as large as Grandma's last Easter ham.

"Marco." Egan shakes Marco's hand then claps his back twice as though Marco is his long-lost uncle. He gestures toward me. "This is Callie. She's going to be your sous chef this evening."

Marco's grin expands to enormous proportions. "Ah, Callie." He engulfs my hand in his and pumps it up and down. "I've heard a lot about you. It's an honor to work with you this evening."

I can't help the nervous twitter that escapes the back of my throat. "Maybe you should wait to say that until after dinner."

Egan laughs and folds me into his side, wrapping his arm around my shoulders. He squeezes twice. "Don't sell yourself short."

"How are your knife skills?" Marco asks me as he walks around the stainless island in the middle of the kitchen.

I stare at the floor, unwilling to meet Egan's gaze, waiting for him to spout off the story about how the last time I wielded a kitchen knife I almost needed stitches and he almost went to the hospital.

But Egan stays silent, so I clear my throat and manage a quiet, "They're okay, I guess."

"Good. That's all I need." Marco nods.

"Is that Pasko kid in here?" The kitchen door swings open again, and a woman with cotton-ball hair peeks inside.

"I'm here, Miss Judy. Be out in a second." Egan lifts his hand in a half-wave to Marco and leans close to my ear. His breath tickles my cheek. "That's my cue." As he backs out, he tosses one final admonition to his friend. "Marco, man, take good care of my girl while I work the room, yeah?"

Marco chuckles as he washes his hands in the giant double sink. "You bet, buddy." As he reaches for a towel hanging on a hook on the side of the refrigerator, he looks at me. "Have you ever made vegetarian lasagna?"

I watch Egan disappear through the swinging door, sucking all my barely-there, newfound confidence out with him. I turn back to Marco. "No. I mean, not really. My Italian food skills mostly revolve around how quickly I can use the Domino's app to order."

"Oh?" Marco hangs the hand towel back up and reaches for his chef coat, a white one that must be the size of a parachute. He shrugs into it and gestures toward me. "That's surprising. You look like a seriously professional chef to me."

I shoot him a closed-lipped smile and press my thumb into the countertop. "Right. Well. That was Egan. He's convinced that because I like to bake cookies and pies and stuff that I'm a chef."

"You aren't?" Marco smiles and winks at me.

I laugh a little and shake my head. "No."

"Well, that's too bad. We're going to be short staffed this evening with Flora at the quinceañera."

"Egan mentioned that." When I look up, Marco the Tattooed Bear is still smiling at me.

"You interested in dabbling with some veggies tonight? I sure could use the help."

I shrug. "Yeah, I can help. But don't get your hopes up too high. Like I said, I'm just a girl who likes to bake a lot."

Marco crosses his arms, which may as well be adolescent oak trees, over his barrel chest and nods thoughtfully in my direction. "I see. So, you're more of a precise kind of lady? No need to throw stuff together, you'd rather have the directions laid out in front of you and know where you're going."

"Definitely." I suddenly realize I'm sounding super enthusiastic, so I stuff my hands into my jeans pockets and look away to tone it down a notch. "I mean, exactly. You get it."

"Excellent. I need someone like you in my kitchen. Tonight, especially." His shaved head gleams underneath the fluorescents in the kitchen. "Vegetarian lasagna from scratch isn't for beginners, you know."

"That's true." The power of the chef coat is starting to wear off already. Does it cease to be a vegetarian lasagna if I accidentally chop off the end of my finger into it? "Maybe I should whip up a pound cake or something instead."

"But you just said you're good at being precise. And I really need precise." Marco sets a knife on the counter in front of me then whirls around without waiting to see if I'll get started. He hits the power button on a radio sitting in the windowsill. Suddenly it sounds like we've got an entire mariachi band in the kitchen with us. "Thanks, girl," Marco calls over his shoulder. "You're a lifesaver."

"But I'm not—"

"Can't hear you," Marco cuts me off. "Wash your hands, then start slicing up some mushrooms. Two-centimeter thickness should be about right, don't you think?" He lumbers to the beat of the music and stuffs his head in the refrigerator, his back facing me.

Sighing, I turn on the water as hot as I can stand it and hold my hands under the stream for as long as possible before it starts to look like I'm avoiding the situation. My friendship bracelet is soaked. After drying off with a black-and-white checked hand towel, I grasp a handful of mushrooms and lay them out on the cutting board.

How did I find myself in this situation anyway?

Egan.

It's always Egan.

Chapter 20

AT PRECISELY 4:30 P.M., MARCO GLANCES UP AT the clock hanging on the wall in front of us. "You ready for the dinner rush?"

I pause with my knife over what must be my fiftieth mushroom of the evening, a big one the size of my palm. "Dinner rush? It's only 4:30."

"Exactly." He leans over and eyes the bowl full of my sliced-up fungus, uniform in thickness. Marco raises his eyebrows and whistles. "Wow, you weren't kidding. That's Michelin-Star quality right there."

I look down at the stainless-steel countertop. "Well, that's what you asked for."

Marco picks up a mushroom slice and holds it in front of his face for inspection. "It's exactly what I asked for." He drops the slice back into the bowl. "Excellent work, Callie. I'm very impressed."

I let out a breath and feel a tiny smile creep over my face. "Really?"

"Absolutely." Marco claps me on the shoulder then turns to the ball of fresh mozzarella he's just pulled from the refrigerator. "Think you can add anything else to the mix?" When I frown, he holds his hands up in surrender and grins. "Nothing crazy. Just more chopping and slicing. It's clear you're an expert there." He turns around and hits a knob on the oven.

"Yeah, okay, I can do that." It is soothing and familiar. And

I haven't accidentally sliced my fingers yet, but that may be because I'm moving at the speed of a slug and paying close attention.

"Great. There's a bag of purple onions over there next to the refrigerator." He motions with his blocky chin. "Grab two or three of those."

I move mechanically toward the onions I admired earlier and pluck three of them from the netted bag. Onion skin flakes off and floats to the floor in pieces.

"While you're chopping up that onion, why don't you tell me a little about yourself?"

I set a whole onion on my cutting board and poke it with the tip of my knife. "Like what?"

"What's it like to be Callie?"

"Hard," I say without thinking. And then I want to clap my hand over my mouth because that was a dumb thing to say.

She has her own car and a cute boyfriend and this perfect little life but she still stomps around and whines like everything is so hard. The refrain from the comment I read days ago parades through my mind. *Give me a break.*

I wait for Marco to snicker at me and disagree. But he doesn't. Instead, he reaches up and turns off the radio in the windowsill. "Oh? How so?"

I tear away several layers of onion skin then drop it in the trash can at the end of the table. "I didn't really mean that." I press my knife to the onion. It slides through and hits the cutting board with a startling clunk. "I have a really good life. Actually, some of our commenters think it's too good."

I hear Marco open the oven door behind me. A warm rush of air swirls out around my legs and slips up my shoulders. "Commenters?"

"Egan's doing this experiment thing." I shake my head and

roll my eyes as though it doesn't mean anything to me. "We're going on dates and posting the footage online. He's trying to beat his brother to a thousand views."

"And the people who comment on these things aren't so nice?" Marco reaches for a large pot, dumps some chopped tomatoes into it, and slides it onto the stove with a clatter.

"Some of them are really nice," I acknowledge. "But some of them say I'm too OCD, that I need help because I don't like being spontaneous. And I live with my grandparents, so people think that's weird." I only give him the highlights. The lowlights still seem so low.

"How did you come to live with them?"

I twist the onion and start cutting again, careful to chop it into small cubes. "My parents were really young when I was born. Like seventeen or something. We all lived with my dad's parents for a year, and then my mom and dad decided they wanted to live in Seattle instead. So, we moved to Seattle, but…" My eyes sting. Must be the onions. I blink hard. "But I wasn't what they wanted to focus on, and their relationship was pretty crazy. They split up and signed some papers and next thing I knew Grandma and I were on a plane back to North Carolina together. I don't remember anything about it since I was only like two years old. But I've lived with Grandma and Grandpa, my dad's parents, ever since."

"Do you keep in touch with your mom and dad?" Marco walks over to the refrigerator and opens one of the double doors. He peers inside.

"No." I rub my suddenly very leaky nose with the sleeve of my coat. "My mom died a while ago. I think my dad lives in California now. Last I heard he was in medical school or something, but that but that was maybe ten years ago."

"I'm sorry."

"I'm not."

"Really?"

"I'm better off with my grandparents. They're responsible, and I know they love me."

"Hmm."

I keep chopping the onion, though my eyes are so cloudy now I can barely see. Marco doesn't ask anything else, but I feel like I need to keep talking. Normal people don't talk about their dead mothers then move on for an afternoon chat about the best ricotta cheese they've ever had or something. "I'm not mad about it or anything. Everything worked out for the best. Even if I am weird because of it."

"What do you mean?"

I grab another onion and hack it in half. I have to rein it in, or these onions are going to be a lot chunkier than Marco wanted. "My legal guardians are also members of AARP. What do you think that does to a girl's reputation?"

Marco laughs. "The differences won't matter so much once you find your place. And I think there are quite a few kids growing up with their grandparents same as you, so you might not be as alone as you feel."

I swipe a tear away from the corner of my eye. An onion tear.

Marco continues, graciously looking away. "The world is weird for a bald, 350-pound Latino man who cooks for old people too. I don't have commenters, but that doesn't mean a few people haven't been nasty along the way."

"But you have a place."

"Sure. Now. When I was your age, I was pretty lonely."

"Hmm." I squeeze my eyes shut.

"You've got Egan, though. He's a pretty standup sort of fellow."

I don't bother mentioning that Egan and I only rediscovered us a couple weeks ago. "Yeah, I guess."

"He thinks very highly of you."

I open one eye and peer in Marco's direction. "He's an optimist. He thinks highly of everyone." I slide the onions to the side, finished with all three.

Marco laughs. "Not everyone. But you seem very special to him. How long did you say you two have been doing this experiment? Two weeks?"

"Almost. This is our tenth date."

"Well, he's been smiling a lot more lately."

"Smiling *more*?" I drop the knife on the counter. It clatters then bounces and hits the floor. My cheeks warm. I knew it was only a matter of time before I did something stupid.

But Marco doesn't seem to notice. He plucks the knife off the floor then drops it in the sink. He grabs a different, smaller knife from the knife block and hands it to me. "You haven't noticed how much he smiles?"

I watch as Marco retrieves a bunch of herbs from the refrigerator. "I guess I've never really seen Egan without a smile."

"He'd been hurting for a while, after his granddad passed. But he seemed to cheer up every time we talked about you." Marco sets the herbs next to my cutting board. He nods toward a sprig of fresh rosemary, then picks up my onions and dumps them into a frying pan coated in olive oil.

"Oh. Yeah. Well, we're really good friends." I start tugging the rosemary from the stem, unleashing the woody, earthy scent into the kitchen where it mingles with the sweetness of the roasting tomatoes.

"Then I hope you always will be. We all worried about him after Bill Pasko passed. Weren't sure if E was going to slip back into his old habits, but a few weeks later he started talking about you and everything changed."

I drop the rosemary. "Wait. A couple weeks? He started talking about me a few weeks after his grandpa died?"

Marco stares at the ceiling like he's got to think back to remember. "Well, maybe it was…" He counts on his fingers.

I watch, silently, then resume my rosemary plucking. Egan said his grandpa died about a year ago. He showed up on my doorstep almost two weeks ago. Clearly Marco's timing is off.

"It was about three weeks after his grandpa passed." Marco nods. "Maybe even a little less. I'm sure of it."

"But that was over a year ago, right?"

Marco fishes a wooden spoon from a drawer and stirs the contents of the pot on the stove. "He's been talking about you for a while now."

Chapter 21

"I'VE GOT TO TELL YOU, CALLIE, THAT LASAGNA? IT looks like a piece of art." Egan pokes his head into the kitchen, and my body seizes at his sudden appearance. He's holding his phone, recording, of course.

I want to charge across the room and yell, "Why did you show up on my porch thirteen days ago if you've been talking about me for a year?"

But instead, I stare at the zucchini on my cutting board. I can feel beads of sweat gathering at the back of my neck, and I wish I could rip off my hat and fan myself with it.

"Isn't it gorgeous?" Marco answers before I have to. "Her precision is uncanny."

"Even Mrs. Lancaster tried a few bites, and she's never interested in anything if it involves something that grew in the ground."

I clear my throat and force myself to smile at Egan. He's going to think something's off if I can't look him in the eye anymore. "Smart lady. I had a good teacher, though." I tip my chin toward Marco.

Egan aims his phone at another pan of lasagna waiting for oven space to open up. "I think you may have found a new talent."

"It's just one dish, E." I reach for a damp washcloth nearby and start wiping down the counters even though I'm not sure that's what they do around here.

"What do you think about dessert?" Marco asks. "I was going to make lemon bars, but you're welcome to give something else a try if you two plan on staying around a bit longer."

"Of course we are," Egan confirms without consulting me. But I'm not even mad. Because lemon bars. And also? I'm not quite ready for the one-on-one time the car ride home is going to involve.

Marco hustles into the pantry and returns with an armful of lemons. He drops them on the counter. One of them rolls toward me, and I keep it from falling to the floor with my palm.

"You have everything to make these lemon bars?" I lean around Marco to peer into the pantry.

"All that and more. You can take a look in there if you want. You're welcome to make anything you'd like if you can find all the ingredients." But I'm barely listening.

A year. An entire year, Egan's been talking about me. I reach for a stack of measuring cups on the counter.

"How long until dessert's ready?" Egan holds his phone near my face.

I flinch and move away, acting like I need something else from the pantry. "About forty-five minutes. Think that's okay?"

"It's great. Dessert doesn't usually go out until six."

"Then I have to move fast." I grab a whole canister of sugar and practically toss it onto the counter where Marco's third lasagna rests. "You should probably get back to serving. We don't need more distractions in here, you know."

Egan laughs. "I see how it is. I'll get out of your hair, I guess."

"She's got a point." Marco moves his hand like a flapping mouth. "You are pretty chatty."

Egan shakes his head, even though he's grinning, and backs out of the kitchen. And this time I'm relieved.

It doesn't take me long to portion out the right ratio of sugar and flour and lemon for the lemon bars, especially with Egan gone. When I grab a hand mixer from the pantry, I also pick up a whole bowl of oranges. They're begging to be used for an orange cake with cream cheese icing.

The cake and the bars go into the oven at the same time, and while they bake Marco and I keep chatting.

He tells me about how he grew up in Mexico, and how he and his cousins used to get in trouble for playing soccer when they were supposed to be working. We talk about all the farmers markets, bake sales, and lemonade stands we've ever participated in. And by the time the desserts come out of the oven I feel like I've made a new friend. A friend who speaks Spanish, feeds the elderly, and coaches his son's soccer team on the weekends.

As Egan grabs the last tray full of lemon bars and orange cake, Marco grins at me. "You are seriously talented."

"Nah," I say, but I can't help but smile anyway as the scent of citrus lingers in the kitchen. "I'm just really good at following directions."

We both grab damp, clean washcloths from the counters and start wiping away the remnants of the last three hours. As I brush some lemon bar crumbs into my palm, I exhale. Maybe I really will come back here more often, even if it's only to talk to Marco about how weird we both are.

Egan ducks back into the kitchen with the empty tray. His face is covered in shades of hard work and humidity. When he runs his hands over his head, his hair sticks to the back of his neck with the barest beginnings of summer evening sweat.

"Hey, Callie, I know you and Marco are really busy, but do you have a minute to come out and say hi to a few of the residents?"

I glance over at Marco, begging him with every vibe I can muster to tell me I need to stay in the kitchen with him. To ask me to do the dishes or scrub the floors or clean the oven interior with a spatula and a toothbrush. Anything not to shove me out with Egan just yet.

But Marco is too busy scouring a spot near the sink to read my face. "You've already been a huge help tonight. No need to stick around any longer. As long as you promise to come back and visit every once in a while."

"Great. Come on." Egan doesn't wait for me to answer Marco. He just holds his hand out to me, palm to the ceiling. I brush by him, pretending like I don't see his hand, and push through the door to the dining room. "See you later, Marco."

"Later, chica." Marco waves at me.

As soon as I reach the dining room, it erupts in cheers and applause. I shrink backward, but Egan presses his hand to the small of my back. He bends low to whisper in my ear, and his breath sends a shiver from my earlobe to my collarbone. "They think you're amazing, you know."

I duck behind Egan, half-hiding from the crowd. But when I peek around the curve of his arm and look at the wrinkled faces and blue hair of all those seated in the cafeteria, they're grinning and nodding and looking at me as though I've just won a Nobel Peace Prize.

Egan lets me hide, but I can tell from a single glance he's proud of me. His smile curls around his entire jaw, and he doesn't even bother to pretend like he's not watching me. After an eternity wrapped up in no more than fifteen seconds, the applause dies down and the residents go back to their desserts.

One gentleman wearing a fedora with a feather tucked into it smiles at me from his seat nearby. "You sure are talented,

Miss Callie. I hope you'll come back and make a few more things for us."

Egan nudges me forward with gentle hands on my shoulders.

"I'll definitely think about it." I smile in spite of my discomfort.

The gentleman clasps his hands and rests them on the tabletop where his plate used to be. "Are you sticking around this evening? I have a grandson I think would like to get to know you and he's—"

"Whoa, whoa, whoa. Mr. Ferris." Egan slices the air with his hand. "This is my girl."

I stop breathing.

"Oh, she is?" Mr. Ferris's squirrely eyebrows raise above the rims of his glasses. "You're going steady, then?"

"We're doing an experiment. Remember? I told you all about it last week when you asked what I've been up to this summer."

I've repeated those same words hundreds of times in the last two-ish weeks, but now that Egan's saying them, the excuse seems flimsy. Like he's trying to deflect. Or is that my imagination?

Mr. Ferris winks at me but keeps talking to Egan. "Right, son. You keep saying that. But this old man is smarter than that." He tips the brim of his hat and stands up then shuffles away without another word.

Egan shakes his head. "Funny guy, Mr. Ferris." He gives me a quick side hug and doesn't even notice when I duck away after a few seconds. "Funny, funny guy."

I'm not sure I feel like laughing.

Chapter 22

"WHAT'S THAT ON THE FRONT PORCH?" GRANDMA squints and peers through the windshield as she pulls into the driveway.

I follow her gaze. "Looks like some balloons. Maybe Grandpa sent them to you for your anniversary?"

She shakes her head. "That's not for a couple more weeks, and your grandpa would just as soon send me a cooler full of fresh fish than a bouquet of pretty balloons."

"Maybe someone at church is just being nice? Or one of the neighbors felt like being sweet?" I unbuckle my seat belt as she pulls into the garage.

"It's a possibility, I guess. I did do a lot of work for the Vacation Bible School prep last week. And Monica down the street and I had a nice conversation while I was on my walk last night. It's so hot out, though, they aren't going to last long on the front stoop." She pops the trunk and hitches a thumb toward the back of the car. "Grab a couple bags of groceries on your way in, and don't sneak any of those Oreos. They're for the dessert we're taking to the neighbor who just had a baby."

I thought those Oreos were going to be my treat for going grocery shopping with her before noon. Or maybe she considered the grocery shopping my payment for the enormous bill she footed at the hair salon this morning. I tug my fingers through my recently-righted hair, now the color of an Arnold Palmer, heavy on the lemonade. Just in time, too. The commenters couldn't seem to talk about anything other than the cap I wore yesterday. Even though Egan said he liked it, the online consensus was that I should set it on fire.

As soon as I get into the kitchen and set the bag with the milk, cheese, and a package of chicken nuggets on the counter, Grandma calls for me. "Hey, Cal?"

"Hold on." I rifle through one of the other bags I brought in. If I only eat two Oreos, I'm sure the neighbor won't miss them. It's not like Grandma's just going to hand her the package.

"Sweetheart?" Grandma calls again.

I give up. The Oreos must still be in the trunk. I grab an almost-empty bag of stale Cheetos from the pantry and start walking toward the front door. "Coming."

When I open the door, the balloons tied around a shiny, decorative weight drift forward. The biggest balloon, a Mylar butterfly with orange, magenta, and yellow wings floats toward my face, and I bat it away. "Whoa. These are intense."

"And they're not for me." Grandma holds the balloon bouquet to the side and points to the sidewalk.

"Is there a…" My voice dies out on the last word. "Note?"

The entire sidewalk looks like a deconstructed MOMA exhibit. Lopsided stars in every color imaginable swirl across the concrete, drawn there in sidewalk chalk. It suddenly feels much warmer than the upper-eighties outside. I fan my face and look away.

"Why does it say, '500 views! Callie is awesome!' and 'Halfway there!'?" Grandma squints and turns her head sideways like she's having trouble reading Egan's chicken-scratch handwriting even though it's literally big as life in front of our house. "Who's viewing what five hundred times?" Grandma looks at me as though I'm involved in something illicit.

I shake my head. "Nothing. It's just a project."

Or at least I thought it was. I also thought it was going to take much longer to jump from three hundred-something to over five hundred views. Did Egan buy ads somewhere or something?

I glance up to see Grandma staring directly into my soul. My stomach squirms.

"A project with Annabeth?" she asks.

I crush the bag of Cheetos between my suddenly very sweaty palms. "Sort of. She's involved."

"So, it's not a school project then."

"Uh, no. Just a project-project."

Grandma raises an eyebrow at me. "Are we playing twenty questions today, or do you want to come out and tell me what you're tiptoeing around?"

I squeeze my eyes shut as my squirming stomach escalates to a mutiny. "It's Egan. Egan and I are working on a project together."

"Egan Pasko?" She leans forward a little. "I didn't know you two were spending time together."

"He's recording us on a bunch of dates—"

"Dates?" Her mouth drops open and her eyes go wide. "This is a big deal."

"No, it's not," I squeak, even though since last night I'm sort of afraid it might be. "It's not like we're picking out a china pattern or anything." I grind the toe of my shoe into the concrete and look for evidence of Egan's car or bike or footprints. "It's really nothing."

"How long have you been doing this nothing, then?" Grandma bats one of the turquoise balloons out of the way.

I shrug. "Just a few days. A couple weeks. Not very long."

Grandma puts her hands on her hips and frowns. "Well, a

couple of weeks seems like long enough to think about letting your grandparents in on the deal, don't you think? Especially since you've been mad at him for so long."

"I mean, I was going to tell you earlier. But the timing didn't seem right, and you know. I didn't want you to be upset if the whole thing fizzled."

"You didn't want *me* to be upset. I see." Grandma nods. "Do you have a date today?"

I shrug. "We were planning on something easy. Probably Dollar Cone or something."

"And what have you already done? On these dates."

"When you picked me up from the food truck fair? We were on a 'date.'" I use air-quotes. "He came over a couple days later, and that's when I found Hedwig, so he took care of her. We've been to the bookstore. Tubing. That sort of thing. Last night we went to the assisted living place where his grandfather was before he passed away." I scour the front yard for any sign of Egan and one of his ever-present recording devices. I don't need this little impromptu family meeting going anywhere near the internet.

Grandma's eyebrows knit together. "Bill passed? That's too bad. He was a very nice gentleman. Stern sometimes with you kids, but very nice too."

"He and Egan got to be close."

"So, all this artwork is Egan's doing." Grandma gestures toward the technicolor sidewalk. "What does he mean by 500 views?"

I explain Egan and Owen's competition, but leave out my part, how I needed to use Egan and his charisma to get me to Nichelle. Grandma nods the whole time even though the currency of likes and views is probably lost on her. She just got a smartphone a few years ago, and she mostly uses it to make actual phone calls.

Grandma finally smiles. "You all were such great friends when you were younger. I remember their momma coming to Bible study and getting on her face before the Lord, begging Him to get those boys safely to adulthood. Guess we're almost there by now. They certainly were a trip and a half."

I peer around the corner into the holly bushes. Still no hint of Egan. If he pops out of the landscaping with his phone, I can't be held accountable for my actions.

I clear my throat. "Anyway, you don't need to worry about it. We're almost halfway done, and then we'll be back to business as usual. Mostly. We might still be friends, but that's it."

"Oh?" Grandma unwinds a rogue balloon from one of the porch lights. "That's too bad."

"It is?" My voice sounds like Mickey Mouse's. I clear my throat. "I mean, no, it's not. He and I will always just be friends. I think."

Grandma leans down and picks up the weight at the bottom of the balloons. She sets it in my free hand and takes the nearly empty bag of Cheetos. "You're not interested in him, then?"

"It wouldn't matter if I were." The balloons bob over my head.

"Why not?" Grandma points inside, and I walk through the open front door. "I always thought you two would make an excellent match."

"Because we aren't like that. I had a crush a long time ago, but only because I was a little kid. You know what he did to me and how hard that was."

"Has he brought it up?"

"Yeah."

"And?"

"He apologized. A few times, actually."

"And you forgave him?"

"I think. Mostly." I chew on my bottom lip.

"Then what makes you think we're holding it over his head?"

I drop the balloon weight in the middle of the kitchen floor and watch the balloons settle before I answer. "Nothing, I guess. I just thought you and Grandpa still hated him or something. That's why I didn't want to tell you about it."

"Oh, honey." Grandma rests her hand on top of mine. "He certainly has made several bad choices in his lifetime, just like the rest of us, and we were definitely upset with his actions two years ago. It breaks our hearts when people hurt yours. But we never hated him, and if you feel ready to let him earn back your trust, that's your decision to make."

The kitchen goes fuzzy in the wake of an unexpected rush of tears. Grandma's words are the assurance I didn't know I wanted. It may not be outright approval, but my grandparents trust me. And that means more to me than almost anything else in the world because right now I'm not even sure I trust myself. Especially when it comes to anything involving Egan.

Chapter 23

"YOU DIDN'T TELL ME I NEEDED TO WEAR A RHINE-stone bikini today." I nod across the room at the other ball-room lesson participants gathered and giggling in the corner of the mirrored room. Their outfits are much shinier and made of much less material than my plain pink V-neck T-shirt and gray yoga pants.

Egan leans in. Close. "Do you have a rhinestone bikini?"

"Negatory."

"Bummer."

"What's that supposed to mean?" I nearly get whiplash yanking my chin into the air and raising myself to my full height to meet his gaze. I frown even as my stomach does a funny sort of pirouette.

Egan's eyes go wide. "Nothing. That was—" He clears his throat. "Sorry. That was inappropriate. Completely inappro-priate."

"Well, yeah."

His cheeks are turning pink. "It's not—I said it before I thought about how it sounded. You're cute, but you're more than that. I know."

Wait, I'm cute? Like he thinks I'm attractive as a woman? Or he thinks I'm cute like a puppy? Except a puppy in a bikini doesn't make any sense.

I look away. "Besides we aren't *those* kind of friends." I fight the urge to add an *are we?*

Between the wrench in the Experiment Marco lobbed at me a couple nights ago and Grandma's less-than-subtle approval of Egan's reappearance, I'm having trouble figuring out what *this* actually is. And where it's going. And where I want it to go.

"Of course we're not *those* kinds of friends. We're just us."

"Right. Just us."

"Me and you. You and me. Egan and Callie." He plants his hands on my shoulders then tilts his head like he's just noticed something's different. "Hey, are you doing something new with your hair? It looks lighter or something."

I swat him away. "I, uh, dyed it. Sort of. Just a little lighter than usual. Nothing too crazy."

"Hmm." Egan blinks a few times like he's trying to remember what it used to look like. "It looks good."

My heartbeat pounds in my head. He's never noticed anything new about my hair before—not when I cut off thirteen inches to donate to kids with alopecia in middle school and not when I gave myself the ugliest set of bangs three days before freshman homecoming. Why is he noticing now?

I start chewing on my bottom lip, wracking my brain for a way to change the subject. "Annabeth threw up last night."

Egan wrinkles his nose. "She okay?"

Ugh. Someone please revoke my small talk license. "She thinks it was a bad crab cake from when her family went to dinner or something."

"That's too bad."

"Yeah."

"Excuse me." One of the girls from the Sparkle Squad interrupts my failed attempt at conversation. Her teal halter top shimmers with bling, and it's got more fringe than a Muppet. She steps close and rests her fingertips on Egan's forearm. "My friend thinks you look really familiar, but she's too shy to come over here and say anything."

He greets her with an easy, charismatic smile. "Oh? Do you guys go to Creekside Ridge?"

He probably thinks she's hot, not cute.

She shakes her head. "No. Hopkins."

I cross my arms over my stomach, half wishing she'd do the same and half wondering how many crunches I'd have to do to get abs like hers.

"So, we don't go to school together. Maybe church?" Egan guesses again.

This time she shakes her head vehemently. "We definitely don't go to church."

Egan laughs and holds his hands up. His friendship bracelet and medical alert bracelet slip down his forearm an inch or two. "Okay, then that's not it either."

"The gym?" She smiles at him. "You look like you probably work out."

Egan pats his pockets, likely trying to figure out where he put his phone. "Nah, I don't spend a whole lot of time at the gym," he says. "I mostly run a lot. But maybe you've seen our videos online?"

"Oh?" Her perfectly-fluffed, coffee-colored eyebrows raise with interest. "Do you have any followers?"

Egan shrugs as though he doesn't actually check the exact number every hour on the hour. "We've got a few. Maybe close to a thousand or so." He finds his phone in the front pocket of his navy athletic shorts and pokes at it to pull up the Experiment website. "My friend and I are doing this Experiment thing."

Okay, see? Friend. I'm the cute friend.

The girl screeches as soon as she looks at his phone. She waves over her shoulder at her friends, Sparkly Pink Top and

Sparkly Purple Top. "Oh, my gosh. Campbell! India! You've got to come see this. It's seriously adorable."

The other two abandon their conversation in the corner and amble over as though they weren't paying any attention to us until they received the summons.

Sparkly Teal Top pushes Egan's phone toward them. "He's, like, almost famous."

I smush my arm against Egan's rib cage and try to smile with as much enthusiasm as he is. He pats the top of my shoulder distractedly.

"So, this is your thing?" Sparkly Purple Top tilts her head to the right as her gaze skims both of us, me first, then much slower down the angles and muscles of Egan's arms.

"It's our thing, actually," I say, but nobody seems to hear me.

"I'm Talia." Teal Top thrusts her hand in Egan's direction.

The willowy brunette in pink stares at me and Egan as her lips form a tiny O. "That's it. That's where I know you from." She snaps her fingers like she's just had a revelation. "T, he's not almost famous. He's definitely famous. I watch his stuff all the time."

His stuff? I frown. Do they not realize I'm the other half of the Experiment? The girl he's been cuddling up to and talking sweet with for the last couple of weeks? Two days ago, he called me *his Callie*.

"Really?" Egan draws himself up even taller, as if it were possible. "It's so cool to meet you guys. Have you been watching since the beginning?"

"I think I started watching on like your second date. I'm Campbell." Pink Top reaches to shake his hand too. She twists her hair around her left index finger.

"E?" I grasp the hem of his T-shirt. "We might want to stretch or something."

Campbell waves me away. "This class isn't intense enough for stretching. You'll be fine. So, is this your date for today?" Again, she's looking only at Egan.

He nods and his grin grows. "Yeah." He hitches a thumb in my direction. "She's always wanted to take dance lessons, so extra points to me for remembering, right?"

I frown. Maybe I wanted to take dance lessons when I was like seven, but I don't think I ever mentioned it to Egan.

"Definitely." Campbell nods, wide-eyed. "That's so sweet. I wish I could find a guy to take me dancing."

"Do you think you can take a picture of us?" Talia holds her phone out, and I realize she's talking to me.

"Oh. Uh. Sure. I guess."

Egan moves away from my side and wraps his arms around all three girls. He aims a full-wattage smile in my direction as I glare at Talia's phone and tap the screen. It snaps the photo, and I shove it back into her space.

Talia's upper lip curls. She doesn't leave the cover of Egan's arms. In fact, it seems like she's snuggling a little closer to his side. "I didn't know you took it. I think I blinked."

"Yeah." Campbell waves her fingers in my direction. "Can you count down this time?"

I grit my teeth. "You got it."

I count down as instructed, but then India reaches for her long blond hair at the last second to get it out of her face and we have to try again. It takes four tries before I finally get a photo of which all three girls approve.

I'm totally over dance lessons, and they haven't even started yet. Seven-year-old me wanted lots of twirling and spinning and billowing skirts. But seventeen-year-old me is standing here playing photographer for Egan groupies.

As soon as I hand the phone back to Talia, a middle-aged woman wearing a white T-shirt and black leggings steps into the room, blessedly and mercifully cutting off any other opportunity for conversation. She claps her hands several times before speaking. "Good morning, everyone. Welcome to Friday afternoon beginner's ballroom dancing. I'm Naomi. I see we've already got some couples here." She smiles at Talia and Egan, still standing next to each other after the picture. "You two are striking together. This is going to be fun."

Talia beams, but Egan shakes his head and finally extricates himself from the rhinestone colony. He wraps his arm around my neck, nearly putting me in a headlock. "Callie's my dance partner, actually."

Naomi frowns. "I see. Well, the height difference will make things interesting for you two, but it should be fine."

As Naomi turns around and the Rhinestone Girls go back to their corner, Egan shakes my shoulder. "How cool is this, Callie? Those girls actually recognize us." He pulls away from me and holds his hand above my head, waiting for a high five.

A high five.

Egan reaches into his pocket for his phone again. He waves it in the air. "Would anyone like to shoot for us today? It's easy. I'll put your name in the credits at the end."

"I will." Campbell leaps forward. She takes his phone, and her fingers linger around his. "Can you show me how to record?"

I have to fight not to roll my eyes. She's not my grandparents' age. She knows what to do with a cell phone. But Egan shows her how to hit record anyway, and she pretends not to get it three times before eventually "figuring it out" with a solid fifteen seconds of giggles.

Naomi finally begins our lesson, instructing us on foot placement and posture, but I'm having a hard time paying attention what with all the muffled laughter from the Sparkle Squad going on behind us. She tapes tiny boxes on the floor and coaches us into the perfect hold.

Egan extends his arm to me, and I step closer and exhale, focusing on the dip in his throat just between his collarbones. He smells like a pile of laundry straight from the dryer, and the warmth of his hands is just as familiar.

"What now?" I wasn't paying attention earlier.

Egan's eyebrows quirk upward, and he rests his hand against my shoulder blade. His hold is strong and sure even though I'm positive this is the first time he's ever done anything like this. "Put your left hand on my arm, where my skin meets my sleeve."

"I won't rip out your pod?"

"Nah." He shrugs, and my hand rises with the motion. "It's on my hip today. Go ahead. Hand on the arm."

I do. "Next?"

"Pull your shoulders back. Stand up straight." Egan lifts his chin in demonstration.

His arms are so much longer than mine that when he stretches to his full height, my arms go nearly straight. I grimace, but he doesn't seem to notice.

"Is that it?" I ask.

Egan shakes his head as Naomi begins clapping out a rhythm behind us. "Nope. Now you smile."

I curl my lips upward and bare my teeth. Egan laughs as he starts to shuffle around our square, dragging me behind him. "A real one, Callie."

I try to smile, but it takes nearly all my concentration not to crush his toes with my stomping around. He seems to have no trouble keeping up with the rhythm, though. "You want to stand on my feet?" His voice is low, even, but loud enough that I can hear him over the music.

"I'm pretty sure that's not allowed," I tell him.

"It's how you used to dance with your grandpa, though, right?"

"When I was four and we were dancing in the living room. We're more grown up than that now."

"Speak for yourself."

"Posture," Naomi calls out, and Egan yanks himself upright.

It feels like an eternity before Naomi's steady one-two-threes sink into my body and my feet begin to listen. And when it finally happens, Egan and I shuffle in tandem.

Now I smile. The knots in the back of my neck loosen, and I move a little closer into the safe space his arms have built around me. Maybe this date is salvageable still.

"Oops." Naomi interrupts and taps me on the shoulder. "This is ballroom dancing, not the prom and I don't think you're going to a hotel afterward, so take a step back from your handsome young man."

Campbell, India, and Talia snicker, and I bite my lower lip and stare at the floor. "We aren't that kind of…" I start to mumble before remembering nobody here listens.

The others dance too when they aren't volunteering to play cameraman for Egan. They're better than us, but by the end of the lesson Naomi isn't yelling at us about posture, and I only step on Egan's feet once every ten steps instead of every other. Even after the waltz music stops, the tempo keeps thundering through my mind.

Egan pulls me into a hug, drawing me near with the hand

that's rested on my shoulder blade the whole lesson. "That was pretty okay, huh?"

I nod. "I think we hit our groove."

"We should come back sometime." He rests his chin on my hair. His heartbeat thrums a little quicker than the waltz.

"Uh, yeah. Sure. I'd like that. And some water. I'd like some water." I drop away from his hug. "Be right back."

"So, is there going to be a season two of the Experiment?" Campbell rushes to Egan's side before I even hit three steps. I crouch and pretend to tie my shoelaces, even though they aren't loose, and listen for his answer.

Egan shrugs. "I don't know. I told Callie we'd go on twenty-one dates, and she made me promise not a minute more."

"Oh, I don't mean with her." Campbell laughs and hands his phone back to him. "I mean with someone else. Like, you could start all over with a different person, maybe with a stranger this time? That could be fun."

I stand up.

"That would be so fun." Talia nods enthusiastically as she joins them and sips from her bottle of water.

Egan pauses. He touches his chin with his fingers and looks up at the ceiling. "I haven't really thought about it before."

"It's just that you're so magnetic," Campbell rushes ahead. "I could watch you forever."

I can see his chest puff up from here, and I launch myself back across the room. "E," I claw at his hand, but he makes no move to take mine, "I need to get home. Annabeth needs me." I hold my phone up in the air as though I just got some sort of dire request for crackers and Sprite from my best friend.

He frowns but nods. "Oh. Okay. Well, hey, it was great to meet you all. Campbell, Talia, India. I'll definitely think about doing a second season." Egan takes the time to shake each girl's hand as he moves down the line like a politician. If he puckers up to kiss their cheeks, I'm going to take him out at the knees.

"Wait, can we get your autograph?" Campbell grabs his hand. "You can sign my shirt."

"I'd love to," he says. "Do you have a pen?"

"We can find one."

"Sweetheart?" I tug on the hem of Egan's T-shirt, but he doesn't seem to hear me. So, I try again. "Love Bug?"

I am not proud of myself.

He turns around, an amused smile on his lips. "Yes, Sugar Booger?"

"Annabeth seriously needs me now. No time for autographs."

Egan shrugs. "Sorry, ladies. Maybe shoot me a message through the Experiment contact form. I'll send you a signed headshot or something."

I don't wait to see if they pout or wave or anything before I hook my arm around his and start walking. He follows me, waving as we go.

As soon as we're out of earshot, he pulls his arm away and wraps it around my shoulders. "That was so awesome."

"You have headshots?"

He lets go of me and twists to retrieve his car keys from his pocket. "Not yet. But how hard can it be to get some? You can take some pictures for me this afternoon or something, right?"

"With what?"

"I don't know." He waves at Naomi on our way out the double doors at the front of the building. "With my phone I guess."

"I think you're supposed to hire a professional to take headshots."

"But you're good enough for now, right?"

Good enough for now.

I yank the car door open and drop into the passenger's side. "If that's what you really want."

Egan stuffs his key into the ignition then drums his hands on the steering wheel, still reeling from the apparent high of his newfound fame. "Callie." He stops, turns to me, and grabs both my shoulders. His eyes are wide and glittery. "Do you think we're aiming too low?"

I wrinkle my nose. "Because three girls at some random dance studio recognized us?" I never told him about Eliza in the paint shop and how she recognized me last week. And I don't think I ever will now.

"Because three girls at some random dance studio *loved* us."

I don't bother to point out that they really only loved him. Me, they practically shoved out of the picture like I was a pesky little sister.

"Maybe 1,000 views isn't what we should be aiming for." Egan slides his glasses off and replaces them with his sunglasses before slipping the car into reverse. He wraps his arm behind my headrest as he backs out of the parking space.

"What do you think we should be aiming for?" I ask.

He looks at me as he puts the car into drive. His grin is bigger than I've seen it this entire Experiment, maybe even in our entire lives.

"I think we should be aiming for global recognition."

Chapter 24

"WHY ARE WE HERE AGAIN?" I LEAN AROUND A shelf of business books in the nonfiction section of the library.

Annabeth tugs a book from the shelf with one finger on the top of its spine then slides it back in line. "Because I'm going to start a Limited Liability Corporation, and I needed to do some research."

"You realize we have this little thing called the internet, right?"

She wrinkles her nose in my direction. "The internet doesn't have a super-hot guy working the reference desk tonight."

I follow her gaze, leaning slightly to the right so I can see around her. Lucas Hearst sits behind the reference desk slouching in front of a computer monitor, looking like he's two minutes away from falling asleep and drooling on the mouse. "Hmm. Yeah. He's not single."

"How do you know?"

"He was my chemistry lab partner last semester. He spent the entirety of our classes trying to figure out how to alchemize his pencil eraser into a diamond for his girlfriend to wear."

"Maybe they broke up."

The front door slides open, and a leggy brunette wearing a huge white cheerleading bow rides in on a wave of humidity. Lucas sits up, and she walks around the desk to plant a kiss on his lips.

"You wanna bet?" I turn back to Annabeth, who suddenly

ASHLEY MAYS

looks slightly defeated. "But hey, at least you know more about LLCs, right?"

"And my stomach was just starting to feel settled again after the crab cakes." She hefts her whole stack of books back onto the shelf. "You're right. The internet is easier. Let's go."

I can't help rolling my eyes. "What are you LLC-ing, anyway?"

"My nannying business. I think it's time to make this thing legitimate."

"Because working thirty hours a week watching other peoples' kids didn't do that for you?"

"I'm going to hire other nannies too. Then when families start to look at childcare options, they only have to contact me, and they'll already have several quality nanny options."

I follow her out the automatic sliding glass doors. "So, basically the Baby-sitters Club?"

She stops so quickly I almost run into her back. "Cradle Rockers is so much more than the Baby-sitters Club ever hoped to be."

I decide to follow up on the terrible name later. "I guess the real question is which one are you? I was going to say Kristy, but you're nowhere near enough of a tomboy for that. Maybe Claudia? You're pretty artsy."

Annabeth smiles and shakes her head as she walks across the parking lot toward the sidewalk that eventually winds its way to my neighborhood. "You're feisty tonight."

"I'm allowed to be feisty sometimes."

"It's just that you're usually only that way when you're ticked about something." She waits a few seconds before forging into the weeds of conversation. "*Are* you ticked about something?"

"No."

"Really?"

"No."

She laughs. "Your dance lesson date yesterday was cute."

"That seems to be the word of the week." Before she begs me to explain, I rush ahead. "Did you notice the Sparkle Squad?"

"The other girls? They seemed nice, I guess. They weren't on camera very much."

"Egan forgot to have them sign a release so we couldn't show their faces."

"That's professional of him."

"Right? Sometimes he cares about weird details and forgets to pay attention to the big picture. Like, those girls were so rude. They barely even acknowledged my presence. It was like the Experiment was all about Egan. How he's so funny and so sweet and so perfect and 'Wow, Egan, *your* show is so amazing.'" I kick a hunk of mulch away from the sidewalk. "And even when we were at the coffee shop this afternoon these two girls came over and talked to him for at least half an hour. In the middle of our date."

Annabeth tilts her head toward me. "Well, can you blame them?"

"Yes. And so can you. You're supposed to be on my side."

"I am on your side. But maybe they're just symptoms of a bigger issue."

I stop in the middle of the sidewalk. "What's that supposed to mean?"

Annabeth grasps my wrist and pulls to keep me walking. "Just that maybe they didn't feel a connection with you. You read the comments." She tugs on a strand of my color-corrected hair. "It seems like a bunch of the Experiment fans have trouble connecting with you."

"Why doesn't Egan have this problem? They all love him,

but they think I'm walking through life with some sort of superiority complex. We grew up together. His story is my story."

"You've never really talked about anything more in-depth than what you like to read on camera. The snippets we see of you on camera are polished."

"Did you even watch the one when Hedwig died? My eyes looked like puffy, pink ping-pong balls."

"Being real means more than looking like crap." When I scowl at her, she shakes her head fast. "Which you didn't anyway. But what I mean is, you usually let Egan do most of the talking. And when you do talk it seems kind of like you're reading from cue-cards off camera. You seem pretty perfect even if your eyes were puffy that one time or whatever."

"What's the problem with seeming perfect? Maybe I just don't think it's appropriate to tell all to everyone."

"It's awfully hard to relate to pretty perfect, Cal. You're kind of the flawless queen of the Experiment, you know? Maybe if your viewers could see a couple of chinks in your armor every once in a while they'd be a little nicer."

"Egan doesn't show any chinks in his armor. He doesn't get nearly as many negative comments as I do."

Annabeth rolls her eyes. "If you're the queen, Egan's pretty much the court jester. Everyone knows he doesn't have it all together because they watch him screw up all the time. Maybe that's why people don't think you're right for each other. Because he's so real and you're so..." Her voice trails off.

"What? You can say it."

"Plastic."

I walk faster, intentionally putting some distance between us. "I can't be like Egan just so people will like me more."

"I'm not asking you to be like Egan, Cal." Annabeth catches up to me and touches my elbow, stopping me in the middle of the sidewalk. Lightning flashes in the distance. "I'm asking you to be more like you. The real you. The one I get to see all the time when you trip over cracks in the sidewalk and laugh at yourself or when you talk in your goofy, fake Julia Child accent when we're baking. Maybe if your viewers see you as more relatable, they'll quit thinking you and Egan are so wrong for each other."

"We are wrong for each other."

Annabeth smirks. "Yeah. Sure."

I shake my head and start walking again, faster this time. We still have another five minutes to go, and I don't want to get stuck in this storm rolling in.

Annabeth's flip-flops slap the concrete behind me as she rushes to keep up. "You remember that video you did for church's series on overcoming?"

"Two years ago?"

"The one where you talked about being adopted by your grandparents."

"Oh, come on." I shake my head so fast my hair sticks to my sweaty upper lip. I swipe it away. "I'm not putting that story online for the rest of the world to see."

"It showed all the best sides of you—your vulnerability and your strength. They played it right after we got my mom's diagnosis. It was the first time I remember thinking, 'Wow. Guess her life isn't as together as I thought it was. Maybe we really can be friends.'"

"It's all about my parents and what miserable failures they were. It's more their story than mine, and I shouldn't have recorded it to begin with. I felt bad about it for months afterward." I twist the ties of my friendship bracelet until it stretches tight against my wrist. "No. Not interested."

Annabeth pauses underneath a streetlamp. "Oh, right. They

only left you with your grandparents when you were barely two years old. Because that didn't drastically change *your* life and make it *your* story."

I stop too. "I'm real enough without having to air out my issues online. It's not an option, AB." My voice sounds like gravel, and I hate myself for it.

Annabeth shakes her head and shrugs. "Fine. Like I said, it's your story. But it's something you might want to think about, even if you don't end up going in that direction. It doesn't hurt to consider all your options, right?"

I can't answer her around the growing lump in my throat. We stay silent for most of the rest of our walk back to my house where Annabeth parked her car in the driveway, sharing only occasional musings about the weather or Annabeth's babysitting.

Still, when she hits the unlock button on her key fob, she leans over and gives me a hug. "Sorry if I'm being too pushy," she whispers.

"Sorry if I'm being too negative." I return her hug. "Want to meet at Corner House tomorrow morning? I'll buy you an iced tea."

She nods. "Yep. Eleven?"

I love that she knows morning means almost lunch. "Perfect." I give her an extra squeeze even though I was so irritated a few minutes ago I would have rather pushed her into a hedge. "See you then."

As Annabeth backs out of the driveway and I let myself into the house through the side door next to the garage, my phone buzzes from my pocket. I pull it out and swipe the screen, then freeze. My heart pounds. Time stops. I can't feel my face.

It's an email. From Nichelle Melendez. The subject line reads, "Thank you, Callie Christianso!"

This is it. The email I've been waiting on. The reason I even agreed to the Experiment in the first place. The good news announcement, because if it were bad news, wouldn't the subject line say, "We're sorry, Callie Christianso!"

All the awkward dates. All the horrible comments. All the disasters. It was all worth it for this.

How am I going to tell Egan? He's going to want to throw a party for me. A big one. Maybe I can convince him to record that, too, for a little extra publicity.

I tap the email with my thumb. My hands are shaking.

> *Dear Callie Christianso,*
>   *Thank you for your contest entry. Nichelle has many stellar fans such as yourself, and she is grateful for each and every one.*
>   *We've had thousands of excellent applicants, and while we appreciate your passion and dedication, we regret to inform you that you have not been selected to continue.*

It says more, but my vision is suddenly blurry, and I can't recognize the words. All I know is that I wasn't chosen. I haven't been picked. I'm not wanted. And now there's a stupid voice in my head whispering that if I'd been less plastic in my application, then maybe this would have turned out differently.

Chapter 25

THE GREEN LIGHTS OF MY ALARM CLOCK GLOW A bright, bold 11:32 p.m., and I've been alternating between staring at the back of my eyelids, literally, and staring at the ceiling for the last hour. Usually, I power through the insomnia. But tonight my brain won't turn off.

I keep thinking about Nichelle Melendez and how my dreams aren't going to come true. Probably ever. And those thoughts morph into questions about the Experiment: what's going to happen after it's over, if I want to keep doing it at all considering my mental state, whether Annabeth is completely wrong or just mostly wrong, and therefore slightly right, about how standoffish I might appear on camera.

I punch my pillow down and lie flat on my back, crossing my hands over my stomach and squeezing my eyes shut so tightly they water. I will fall asleep. And I won't dream about baking shows or parents or Egan.

But twenty minutes later all I have to show for staying in bed are my chilly elbows poking out from beneath my summer quilt.

This is never going to work. Not with all the junk rolling around in my mind. I fling my quilt away, and it tumbles onto the floor. I need a seven-layer bar.

Good thing I made some this morning because I'm never baking again after that email.

I pad downstairs toward the kitchen, hunt down a clean

butter knife, and start sawing the corner piece out of the glass baking dish.

"You're up late."

"Grandma." I accidentally fling my hunk of seven-layer bar over the edge of the dish and onto the floor, but gather it quickly like I meant to do it. "What are you doing up?"

She shrugs and shuffles farther into the kitchen, her feet stuffed into her sheepskin-lined slippers even though it's June. "Having a hard time sleeping tonight, so I was going to grab my book from the living room. I thought I heard something going on in here, so I decided I'd check it out." Grandma points to the dish and raises an eyebrow. "Are you having a hard time sleeping, too?"

"Yep." I don't want to get into the whys of it all. It doesn't matter anyway.

Grandma leans against the counter. "Where did you go for today's date?"

I take a huge bite of my bar and immediately heave it out into a napkin. The bottom is charred. Now I *know* Nichelle Melendez was justified in rejecting me. I can't even bake a basic dessert anymore. I peel the burnt bottom off with my fingernails while I answer Grandma's question. "We just went to the coffee shop."

"Oh? That seems nice enough."

"It was fine."

"Only fine? Did something happen?"

I lift one shoulder. "Not really. It was a pretty standard date. Egan had unsweetened black tea. I had something chocolate." Maybe if I concentrate on the date, I won't start crying in the middle of the kitchen and she'll go back to trying to find her book.

"Sounds pretty normal to me."

"It was. Super normal."

"Were you hoping for something more than normal?" Grandma's voice is extra soft. "With Egan."

"No."

But my traitorous stomach tingles in spite of my turmoil and my shoulders feel suddenly warm, as though they remember yesterday even better than I do, Egan's palms resting against them, fingers tapping out the rhythm of the music against my shoulder blade.

I flatten a piece of salvaged seven-layer bar between my thumb and pointer finger then jam it into my mouth.

"So, you're not ruminating about Egan then." Grandma tilts her head toward me in question. "Annabeth?"

I half-groan, half-growl. She's going to keep asking questions. "Yeah, but no. Do we really have to talk about it? I just came downstairs for the baked goods."

Grandma reaches for the butter knife. She cuts a seven-layer bar for herself, trims off the bottom, then savors a bite. "Well, what else should we talk about while we eat?" She swallows her mouthful of chocolate, coconut, and butterscotch. "How about that contest? Have you heard back from the baking show?"

I crumple instantly. My seven-layer bar lands on the floor next to me, and I bury my face in my knees.

"Oh, sweetheart." She slides down next to me. "You heard back. I'm so sorry."

It takes me a full five minutes before I can dial back my tears and take a deep enough breath to choke out a few words. "I gave them my best, and it still wasn't good enough."

"You were pretty courageous to step out and apply at all. I'm sorry it didn't turn out like we'd hoped," she says, rubbing circles across my back.

Her kind words skim right across the surface of my hurt. "They don't want me."

"They saw your application and felt like something there wasn't a good fit." She makes a disgruntled noise in my ear. "I doubt it was personal on their part."

"Well, it's personal on mine," I mumble, using the edge of my T-shirt sleeve to wipe underneath my eyes. When my nose starts to unclog, I pick up my seven-layer bar from the floor and dust it off before taking a bite. "Am I interesting enough, you think? Maybe they felt like I'm too boring." I rush the rest of my words out when her arm tenses next to mine. "Am I too quiet? Or uninteresting? Or plastic?"

Grandma stays silent for at least a full minute before leaning forward. "I'm too old to be sitting on the floor like this," she mumbles then pushes herself to a stand, her knees and elbows creaking with the effort. She reaches down and helps me up then wraps her arm around my waist.

I nestle my head in the crook of her neck between her ear and her shoulder. "Well?" I ask.

Finally, she sighs. "You're just you, Callie Gail. Not too much or too little of anything exactly, just the way God made you."

I wrinkle my nose. I know Grandma actually is a licensed counselor, but sometimes I wish she'd give me advice that's a little more concrete and a little less therapist-y. "That doesn't answer my question."

"Did that email say something about you being boring? That would be awfully unprofessional of them." Grandma gives me an extra squeeze and moves to the kitchen cabinet for an empty glass. She gets a gallon of milk out of the refrigerator.

"What about un-relatable? Do I come across like I think I'm better than everyone else?"

"I don't believe so. Where is this coming from?"

I count the thrum of my pounding pulse as I watch her pour her glass of milk. When she turns to set the milk back in the refrigerator, more words spill from my mouth before I have a chance to moderate them, the totality of the evening's events melding together and crushing my chest like an enormous boulder. "Annabeth wants me to share my story, like what I did for church a couple years ago, but on Egan's website. She thinks it would help."

"Hmm." Grandma sniffs, but she doesn't seem as offended as I feel. "Is the Experiment in some sort of trouble?"

"I don't know. Maybe. Some of our commenters think I'm one-dimensional or something. And we haven't been able to get more than about 500 views. Egan's goal is 1,000. To beat Owen."

"So, Annabeth thinks that you might be more relatable if you share some of your story, and therefore you'd get more views." Grandma nods slowly. "That's an interesting theory."

I cram the rest of my seven-layer bar in my mouth and start chewing. "It's a terrible theory. Mom and Dad aren't anyone else's business except mine, right?" I look away. "And yours, of course."

"Your story is certainly yours to share or not. It's not something you owe to anyone else. And there are other ways to be relatable too."

Even though I have a feeling I'm not going to like any of her suggestions, I still ask. "Like what?"

"Hmm." She sips her milk then folds her napkin in half and throws it into the trash can. "Asking for help when you need it is always a good idea. And admitting when you've made a mistake then being quick to apologize is important too."

I was right. I don't like her suggestions either.

"Anything else?" I ask.

She laughs then leans over to kiss my forehead. "You know, I think we'll feel a lot more clearheaded in the morning after we've had some sleep. We should regroup then. I'm so sorry for your tough news. You try to get some rest tonight, anyway, okay?"

I blink after her in the darkness. "Seriously? Aren't you going to tell me what to do?"

"About which part?" Grandma pauses in the doorway between the kitchen and the living room.

"About Dad." My voice sounds high and reedy. "And Mom. Nichelle is already over and done with." And my baking career probably is too at this rate.

"Sweetheart, I'm not sure what all these commenters are saying on Egan's site or why they even matter. And I don't know why Annabeth thinks it'll change things or get you more views if you talk about your mom and dad." She steps back into the kitchen and squeezes my shoulder. "But I do know you're strong and loyal and smart. I'm sure if you think about the whole situation, you'll make the right decision."

"Are you sure?" I bite my lower lip. It tastes like chocolate. "Because I'm not."

Grandma pulls me into a hug. "It's okay to be unsure, Callie. Most of us are more often than we let on. Nobody gets GPS for real life. But if you feel like it would help, you could always give your dad a call and ask his opinion."

My shoulders tense up, and I press my nose into Grandma's shoulder. "I don't think that will help. It's been at least ten years since the last time I talked to him."

"It's just a thought. A thought for some other time, though." She kisses my forehead. "We can talk about it again tomorrow if you want, and if you need to cry some more, I'll buy extra tissues." She leans away and frames my face between her hands. "I don't know if it makes a difference, but I'll support you in whatever you decide about this situation. I don't think there's a wrong choice here." She kisses my nose. "Good night. Sweet dreams. I love you."

"I love you, too."

Once she's gone, I saw into the seven-layer bars again, this time taking a bigger slice and avoiding the bottom layer entirely.

I love my grandma, but I don't care about or need GPS or a map or anything like that right now. What I need is to start over.

Chapter 26

WHEN EGAN SAID HE THOUGHT IT WAS TIME FOR me to come over to "meet the parents" on Sunday afternoon after church, I laughed at him. I've known Mike and Kristine as long as I've known Egan and Owen, obviously. But he insisted it would add another layer of reality for our fans.

And because all I can think about is where not being "real" got me with Nichelle Melendez and Annabeth, here I am on the Pasko family's front porch with a loaf of warm banana bread, which I only baked because I'd bought the ingredients before I got Nichelle's email.

It doesn't seem to matter that I've been here at least a thousand times before or that Egan's mom is the one who taught me how to figure out what bra size I needed when I was thirteen, suddenly all of this feels brand new and strange and intimidating. It's not exactly the "new beginning" I was looking for in my life.

The door swings open. My breath catches in my throat.

"Callie Christianson. Whoa. It's been—what, just about forever? How's it going?"

It's Owen. And he still looks exactly like Egan, only fifteen months ahead and all solid and steady where Egan is wiry and tangled up. Owen forgoes a handshake and pulls me straight into a hug. I feel like I'm being suffocated by a Kodiak.

"Hey, Owen," I say, muffled into his chest, but he doesn't seem to hear me.

"Gosh, you're all grown up and stuff. And your hair is longer, too." He plants his hands on my shoulders and holds me at arm's length. "I never could figure out why E stopped hanging out with you all those years ago. What a complete—"

"Moron. Yes. I know. You've said." Egan interrupts his brother as he walks into the foyer, barefooted and wearing a dark red T-shirt and khaki cutoff shorts.

Owen shrugs. "As long as you know it." He glances down at the loaf of banana bread in my hands. "Is that for me? You shouldn't have."

I roll my eyes, my apprehension starting to evaporate. I know this, the back and forth with Owen. "I didn't. It's for your parents."

"Oh. Then you really shouldn't have."

Egan pushes Owen out of the way. "Don't listen to him. Thanks for coming."

"Of course. I'm excited to be here again."

"Me too. Excited you're here again, that is. Cute outfit." He does a chin-up gesture and drops my hand.

"Cute *outfit*?" Owen's eyes nearly bug out of his head.

I tug on the hem of my black eyelet lace shorts. Annabeth picked them out this morning, along with my necklace and coordinating topaz stud earrings. She says the ensemble will make my blue eyes pop on camera.

"What?" Egan raises his arms in a gesture of innocence. "It is."

"Yeah, okay." Owen smirks.

Egan ignores his brother and turns back to me. "I hope you're pretty hungry. Dad's grilling, and Mom made enough macaroni salad to feed the entire National Reserve."

"I'm always hungry."

"I know." Egan grins.

"We're all hanging out in the backyard. Want to play some bocce ball?" Owen looks from Egan to me and then back to Egan's hand, which is drifting closer and closer to my fingers, probably out of habit on account of all the time we've been spending together on camera.

I leap forward and away from Egan's touch. "Yes. Definitely. I love bocce."

Egan frowns. "Have you ever played bocce ball before? Maybe we should play cornhole instead. It's safer." He steps around me and begins to lead the way through the house.

"What's cornhole?" I follow him.

"Like a beanbag toss. You take turns throwing these bean-bags full of dried corn at boards with a hole in them, and you get points when the beanbag falls through the hole." Egan shrugs. "It's fun. And the beanbags don't break windows as easily as bocce balls do."

I set the banana bread on the kitchen counter as we pass. Owen picks it up and starts unwrapping the cellophane bag, which I tied shut with a piece of dark green raffia. I follow Egan onto the back porch into the sunshine. The lemony tones bathing the backyard wash away the rest of my anxiety entirely. I take a deep breath as the clouds of my lingering bad mood start to evaporate a little bit as well.

I probably have just as many memories here as I do at Grandma and Grandpa's. The trees are a little taller and stronger and the backyard swing set is gone now, but everything else still seems like home.

"Hey, she's here." Mike grins from beside the grill and waves a large metal spatula in the air at me in greeting. "It's good to see you again, Callie. How've you been? Egan's showed me some of your videos. How're Gail and Bruce? Gosh, you've turned into such a kind and patient young woman. They must be so proud of you."

I can't help but smile when he asks questions but doesn't wait for an answer. All the Paskos do it. I used to wonder if it was because they didn't care about the answer to their questions, but now I realize it's because they want to know everything all at once.

"It is *so* good to see you, Callie." Kristine finishes tethering a tiny white dog to one of the patio table legs with a hot pink leash. She reaches to hug me, and I can smell the essence of her floral perfume when she folds me in close.

"It's good to see you again, too."

"I hope you're hungry because we've got a ton of food here." She releases me from the hug and picks up a bowl of chips from the table. "I hear you've still got your bottomless appetite."

I glance over my shoulder at Egan who's smiling, watching me, and he shrugs unapologetically. I tear my gaze away and nod. "It's true. I think I lost my braces and maybe added some freckles since the last time I saw you, but my love of food hasn't changed."

"Good girl." Kristine squeezes my upper arm. "You still like sweet tea?"

"Yes, ma'am."

"Let me get you a glass."

Egan points to the cornhole board at the opposite end of the yard where a pile of blue beanbags rests in the grass. "You want to be blue?"

"Sure."

Owen tumbles out the back door, a large slice of banana bread in his hand.

"Hey." I cross my arms over my chest, but I can't help my

smile. "You aren't supposed to eat that. I told you it was for your parents."

"It's good," he offers by way of explanation, stuffing half the piece in his mouth all at once.

"It is?" I hate that I need the affirmation now for something I was confident about less than twenty-four hours ago.

Egan tilts his head, almost like he's not sure he heard me correctly. "Why are you even asking that? You know you're awesome at that stuff."

Before I can say anything, Owen answers. "Best banana bread I've ever had." He wipes his fingers on his jeans and claps his hands together. "I'll be blue."

"Callie's already blue," Egan calls over his shoulder, already walking away. "Besides, we didn't invite you."

"We can invite him." I shake my head in Egan's direction. "You're invited, Owen."

"Callie says I'm invited, E. You're out of luck." Owen shoots his brother a closed-lipped smile and makes his eyes all squinty.

Egan's lip twitches. He looks at me like he's trying his hardest to will me to take it back, but I only smile.

"Fine." Egan finally concedes with a sigh. "But you'll have to be red. And you can't whine and cry when Callie and I whip your tail. You'll have to lose like a man."

A cough of a laugh spews from Owen's mouth. "Nah, Callie's on my team."

"She's not on your team."

"She just told me. She said, 'I'm totally Team Owen.'" Owen speaks in falsetto and flutters his hands around his face.

I hold my arms in front of me like I'm waving in a truce and try not to laugh. It'll only encourage the rivalry. "I'm totally Team-Whoever-Plays-Better."

"Same difference." Owen winks at me.

"Fine." Egan lifts his chin toward his brother. "So, losers go first?"

"Whoa," I say. "I thought this was supposed to be a friendly game."

Egan drapes his arm around my shoulders and lets his fingers rest along my collarbone. "You're such an only child," he whispers in my ear.

I glance upward. "And you're such a little brother."

He's watching my face, his molasses-eyed gaze full and warm. Flecks of amber shimmer throughout his irises like they've been dusted in brown sugar. I blink but can't look away.

"Hey, Callie?" Mike calls to me from the grill. When I don't answer, he says my name again. "Callie?"

"Oh." I shake my head, tear my gaze away, and force myself to focus on the blades of grass beneath my sandals. "Yes, sir?"

"How do you like your burgers?"

"Medium-rare, please."

"As you wish." Mike nods and flips another burger with his spatula.

"Thank you." I turn around in time to see Egan chuck a beanbag at Owen's head. Owen catches it easily and throws it back in one swift movement. It thuds solidly against Egan's chest.

"I'm ready when you are." Owen grins at me. He slings his arm around my shoulders, almost the same way Egan did seconds earlier. "Teammate."

"I'm ready."

"Okay, well now that we've established that you're both ready. Let's go." Egan claps two beanbags together and stands behind the board farthest from me and Owen.

"You want to toss first, Sugar Pie?" Owen bumps me with his hip. His arm is still solidly secured around my shoulders.

"No. You go first." I hold the beanbags toward him. "And Sugar Pie? Really?"

Owen shrugs and takes a beanbag from me. "It's gotta be better than Noog. Does he still call you that?"

I look away. He hasn't in a while, and I feel a little wistful for it. "Not really. Not when we're on camera."

"On camera?" Owen tosses his beanbag in Egan's direction. It skids up the wooden slope and comes to rest in front of the hole without going in. He winces.

"Yeah, you know. For your competition. First person to a thousand views."

"Oh, that thing." Owen keeps tossing. Two of his beanbags go through the hole. He glances at me then turns back to watch Egan who's now gathering the stack of red beanbags. Owen rubs one hand over his mouth then plants his hands on his hips. "I quit that thing like a week ago."

"You quit?" I repeat.

If Owen quit, and I already got a no from Nichelle, then what's to keep me in the Experiment anymore?

One of Egan's beanbags smacks Owen full in the face like a sack of concrete.

Owen sputters. "What do you think you're doing, stupid?" he hollers across the yard. "Your aim's better than that."

I stare down the yard at Egan, expecting to see him grinning and laughing. But he's not. In fact, his face is stony, and his lips look pinchy. His eyebrows hover low over his eyes.

"You're standing in the way." Egan launches another bean-bag at his brother, not even pretending to lob it toward the board anymore.

Owen leaps out of the way, and it narrowly misses his shoul-der. He tosses an apologetic half-smile in my direction. "Can you believe that guy? What's gotten into him?"

I shrug like Egan's behavior isn't a big deal, but it kind of is.

Egan and Owen may be competitive, but they don't pick fights with each other often. At least not that I know of. The last one I remember was when we were like eleven and Egan whacked Owen in the face with a pool noodle and knocked out one of his teeth. The whole thing devolved until it was WWE at the country club. Pool chairs were thrown, and the boys weren't allowed back the rest of the summer.

Owen turns back to Egan and shakes his head. "That was a waste of a turn. You're not even close to the board."

"Shut up." Egan jogs to our side to pick up his discarded beanbags. "Your turn," he grumbles at me.

Owen raises an eyebrow, and I grimace. I don't know what's going on either.

"You okay?" I reach for Egan's wrist.

He nods and seems to lean into my hand, but his Adam's apple dips. "Fine. Just…never mind. Keep playing."

"Okay." I take a slow step away, half hoping he'll reach out to stop me and half wondering if he's suddenly been taken over by some brain-munching amoeba or something.

My Egan never frowns. He never grumbles. And he definitely doesn't glower.

I follow Owen to the other side of the yard where we pick up our beanbags. "He must be having a bad day or something," I say, unsure as to why I feel like I'm supposed to make apologies for Egan. "Sorry."

Owen semi-smiles, but he's not watching me anymore. Instead, he seems to be analyzing Egan's every move as though he's a hyena stalking his prey.

"Or something," he says in a tone so low I almost miss it. He steps closer and wraps his arms around me from behind. "You game to play along?"

It catches me off guard, and I stutter. "Play what?"

"Follow my lead," Owen whispers then starts talking loudly. "It's just like bowling, or slow-pitch softball." He drops a blue beanbag into my palm then lines his right arm up with mine and moves our arms together, slowly, as though he's teaching me how to throw.

My face glows as hot as the barbecue coals.

"If you score, we'll be up by three, so try to be accurate with your throw," Owen continues. He presses his cheek against mine. "Need me to help you aim?"

I pull away and look up at him. His grin, though not contagious like Egan's usual expression, is mischievous and full. I smile too but still push him away with a confused chuckle.

"No, thanks. I'm good." I toss all my beanbags without pausing to line up my shots, flinging them one after the other with abandon. Every single one misses.

I wave at Egan, though he never looked away from us during my entire turn. "It's your turn again." I glance over my shoulder at Owen. "And I think you'll want to get out of the way."

Owen clears his throat and winks at me. "Don't worry about him, Noog," he says loudly. "You're probably right. E's just having a bad day."

Egan pretends like he's not listening to his brother, but even from fifteen feet away I can see the way his jaw twitches as he hurls more beanbags in our direction.

When it's finally my turn again, I aim well, draw my arm back, and let my beanbag fly just like Owen showed me earlier. It soars through the air in a miraculous arc. I hold my breath. It falls onto the board, skids a couple inches, and drops through the hole.

A breathless laugh escapes my mouth. "I did it," I say quietly, almost to myself.

"You did it," Owen yells and laughs. "Great job. I knew you would be a natural."

He nearly hoists me into the air as he jumps up and down in celebration. Then suddenly Owen stops leaping. He leans down.

And Owen kisses me.

Chapter 27

IT TAKES ME FOUR WHOLE SECONDS TO BACK away from Owen's lips pressed to the edge of my hairline, just above the curl that runs the length of my ear.

"What are you doing?" I push him away with an incredulous laugh. My heart pounds.

But Owen's not paying attention to me. Not really.

Egan yells like a *Braveheart* extra and takes off across the yard toward us. He hurls his beanbags to the ground and leaps the final three feet between us, hands outstretched toward Owen's neck.

Owen leans down and juts his shoulder out. Their bodies collide. They fall to the ground and roll around, a cloud of elbows and knees and manly sounding grunts and thuds. One second, it looks like Owen's got the upper hand, pinning Egan's shoulders to the dirt. But the next second it looks like Egan's stronger. He straddles Owen's chest and rears back his arm, elbow pulled back and fist clenched. His chest heaves.

My feet, frozen to the ground the second this started, finally catch up with the chaos, and I rush toward them.

"Stop it," I yell, grabbing Egan's upper arm because he's the closest. His muscles feel like thick rope beneath my fingers. He doesn't budge.

But he also doesn't punch his brother.

"Boys," Mike roars behind us.

I turn to see him standing there, the barbecue tongs still in one hand.

"What do you think you're doing? Stop it." He waves the tongs.

Owen's eyes are glittery and bright with adrenaline. He's grinning, though I can't figure out why.

Egan stares at Owen's face, and each time Owen blinks Egan's muscles tighten against my hands. His breathing is ragged and gritty. His glasses are crooked, the right side higher than the left. His neck is sinewy and red.

"E." It's all I can do to whisper.

Immediately, he looks into my face. His gaze softens the slightest bit, and he licks his lips.

"Behaving like this at all, but especially with company, with *Callie*, here?" Mike shakes his head. "You two are better men than that."

Egan swallows. His shoulders slump a little bit. He plants his foot into the grass next to Owen's chest and uses his other knee as leverage to push himself up off Owen's sternum. Owen grunts and winces.

As soon as Egan's upright, he tugs the collar of his shirt which got stretched in the scuffle. I just stare. Mostly at Egan. He avoids my gaze and rubs his hand over his hair, smoothing over the cowlick in the front. Finally, he extends his hand to Owen and helps pull his brother to his feet.

"That's what I thought," Owen grumbles close to Egan's ear when they drop hands. He brushes the grass off the back of his jeans.

Mike hovers close to my shoulder. "I'm sorry about that, Callie. These guys are all testosterone and adrenaline sometimes. Everything's fine now. Isn't it, boys?" He holds the barbecue tongs toward Egan and Owen threateningly.

Owen presses his fingertips to his top lip as he nods. He's bleeding a little. "Sorry, Callie. I was just being stupid." Owen's gaze flicks from me to Egan's face and back to me.

"Really stupid," Egan grumbles, still without looking over at me.

"Egan," his dad warns.

"Sorry, Callie." Egan finally looks at me. "I'm really sorry."

My heart wrenches inside my chest. His perma-smile is gone. He's not bleeding like Owen is, but a stray piece of dried-up grass is stuck in his hair next to his ear. I want to reach over and brush it away, but instead I keep my hands clasped in front of my body.

"Sorry that took so long, Callie. As soon as I went inside I got a phone call and…" Kristine's voice dies off as she steps out into the backyard. "What in the world happened out here?"

Egan's cheeks grow even redder. Owen hangs his head.

"Just a little disagreement, Kris." Mike has already gone back to the grill. He flips a burger. "Go get cleaned up, boys. These burgers should be ready in just a few minutes. Callie, you can go ahead and wash up too if you'd like."

I force myself to nod. "Sure. I think I will. Thanks."

Owen slinks inside and Egan follows, only slightly slower. We all hit the kitchen at the same time before Owen diverts. "I'll take the upstairs bathroom," he says. His hands are stuffed in his pockets, and he gives me a quick nod which I think is another non-verbal apology.

Egan keeps walking to the downstairs half bathroom.

I trail after him, though I could probably wash my hands in the kitchen sink instead. But I have things to say.

He yanks the door open and plants himself in front of the mirror then turns his face from side to side, probably inspecting for damage.

"You're not bleeding anywhere," I say.

"Good." He sniffs and his nose twitches.

"That was…" I don't know where to start or what to say. So, I stop and look down at the floor.

"That was not how I saw things going today." Egan yanks the hot water handle. He plunges his hands into the stream then pumps two whole handfuls of basil and citrus hand soap into his palms. He scrubs his fingers and nods for me to do the same.

I take a lot less soap and swirl it around over my knuckles before I put my hands in the water next to his. Our wrists touch.

As soon as the bubbles rinse from his skin, Egan grabs a cream-colored hand towel from the rack on the wall. He holds it out to me. I take it and press it against the backs of my hands.

"Owen's not into you, Callie. You know that, right? None of that meant anything." Egan takes the towel from me as soon as I'm done and slings it back over the rack.

My cheeks grow warm, but I refuse to watch it happen in the mirror. "Of course it didn't. It's Owen. He was just be-ing…" I scroll through the dictionary in my mind looking for the right word. Funny? Obnoxious? "Owen. He was just being Owen." I shrug. "Besides, it's not like he was doing anything that strange. The girls who fawn all over you when we're on our dates are way worse."

When I glance back at Egan's face, he's staring right at me. "You think so?" he asks.

"I mean, yeah. A little. They're sort of obsessed with you, in case you haven't noticed." I mean to look away but I can't, so I chew on my bottom lip instead.

We're so close, the heat radiating from his chest sweeps

across my cheeks. This half bath isn't meant for two bodies, especially when one of them is over six feet tall.

The corner of Egan's mouth twitches. "He was trying to make me jealous, I think."

"Oh." I force myself to chuckle. "Joke's on him, I guess. It's not like we're actually together or something."

"Right." Egan nods.

"I mean, it was still stupid." I plow forward, desperately trying to fill the space between us with something other than his molasses gaze and heat.

"Totally stupid." Egan rocks back on his heels. He reaches up like he's going for the towel again but instead his fingers settle against the back of my neck. His thumb rests in the hollow under my jaw in front of my ear. My whole body stills, except for my heartbeat which begins to gallop wildly inside the confines of my rib cage.

"After all, how could he make you jealous when we're just," my words get stuck on my tonsils, "we're just friends."

Egan leans closer. His foot catches the edge of the door and it swings closed only enough to block us from the view of anyone who might walk by.

"Exactly." He pauses as though he needs to consider what he wants to say. "This is all for the Experiment. To help you win that contest, and so I can get the views to beat Owen. Then we'll both reach our goals."

"Yes. For our goals." I try to keep my voice even. Steady. Calm. So he'll believe I believe what I'm saying even though both our goals are obsolete now, if what Owen said is true.

My hand strays to Egan's wrist, and I hold onto it. The only thing grounding me in this moment.

Egan glances at my fingers and drags the pad of his thumb

across my earring down around the curve of my earlobe. "Sometimes I wonder if we're doing this all wrong."

"Doing what wrong? The Experiment?"

"I'm not sure." Egan's invading my personal space bubble to the point that if he moves any closer we might float away together.

He tiptoes his fingers across my hairline where Owen laid one on me not even five minutes ago. Our noses brush. His eyes flutter closed, and my lashes skim the lenses of his glasses.

There's a rapid knock outside the door. "Burgers are ready. Let's go."

Owen.

Egan yanks his whole body away and almost hits his head on a framed picture of some seashells. He drops his hands from my face and rubs the back of his head, no longer looking in my direction.

"Sorry. That was—I got caught up in the pretending." He chokes on a chuckle. "But I bet our fans are going to love it."

"For sure." I nod too fast.

Egan slips around me, avoiding my gaze. "We'd better go."

"I'll be there in a minute," I say. My fingers and my voice tremble. What did he mean "our fans are going to love it?" Egan didn't record any of that.

And, now that I think about it, I'm not sure he's been recording any of this date at all.

Chapter 28

A SHARP RAP ON THE FRONT DOOR DRAGS ME away from the glossy pages of the several-years-old scrapbooking magazine I found on the giveaway shelf at the library. Now that baking is dead to me, I've decided to explore other avenues.

"Grandpa?" I call out. "Someone's at the door."

But then I catch a glimpse of Grandpa through the living room window in the backyard on the riding mower. Mondays are his mowing days. Another knock echoes throughout the house.

I sigh and close the magazine then set it on the end table as I unfold my legs from underneath my body and step away from the couch.

Another knock. "I'm coming," I yell. Then, under my breath, "Patience is a virtue, Annabeth."

It has to be her. Egan said he had to work this afternoon.

I pull the door open. My topknot slips and falls into my eyes. Someone grabs my wrist, and I tumble out the front door with a screech. "Hey!"

"No time to explain." It *is* Egan. He's already got his phone out and recording. "I have *the best* date idea. And we've got to go now."

"But. Wait, what—"

"Do you trust me?" Egan whirls around and stops so quickly I bump into his chest. My hand presses against his heart.

I blink, my pulse pounding wildly. I tell myself it's from the unexpected leap out of the door even though I know that's a complete and utter lie.

Just like the lie I've somehow managed to convince myself of about how Egan and I don't need to talk about whatever it was that almost happened yesterday at his house. Or that I don't need to tell him about my Nichelle Melendez rejection.

"Do you trust me?" Egan repeats himself when I don't answer.

"I, um, it's—I mean, I guess?"

"Good enough." Egan turns around and tugs me forward.

"Shoes, E, I need to put on shoes." I glance down at my outfit: a stretched-out pair of black yoga pants and a neon purple T-shirt with blotches of white paint all over the hem from the time I helped Grandma paint their bathroom. "And maybe a new shirt."

Egan pauses just long enough to glance at me. "Yes, shoes. Your shirt is fine. Adorable, even." He twirls me around and gently shoves the small of my back, propelling me up the front steps and into the house.

I roll my eyes but hustle toward the stairs, taking them two at a time. Once I make it to my bedroom, I grab at the hem of my shirt and look around for a suitable replacement.

"Just shoes, Callie," Egan calls up the stairs. "We don't have time for you to raid your closet."

I stifle my complaint and cram my feet into a pair of dingy white flip-flops instead.

A glimpse of my reflection in the full-length mirror propped up behind my bedroom door makes me wince. I tear my hair out of the topknot and rake my fingers across my scalp as I power walk out of my room and down the stairs. "Where are we going and why is this so important?"

"Just come on." Egan grabs my hand again, pulling it away from my hair, which tangles around my friendship bracelet.

I trot after Egan and try to disengage my hair from my bracelet at the same time. "I thought you were supposed to be working. This isn't some plot to get me to come over and finish your shift for you or something, is it?"

"No." Egan wrenches open the passenger's side door for me and waves me inside as though I'm a bull and he's wearing red. He's aiming his phone at me the whole time. "But that's a brilliant plan. I'll keep it in mind. But this time I told my boss I had an emergency and a couple other guys covered for me." He slams the door shut the second I pull my legs inside and drops his phone into the pocket of his silver athletic shorts.

As soon as he sits in the driver's seat, I clutch at his arm. "What's the emergency?"

He smiles but doesn't look at me. "You'll see," he says as we speed through the neighborhood. The rest of the trip is as frenetic and harrowing as my kidnapping. Several times I think about trying to leap from the car at stoplights purely out of survival instinct. Then Egan pulls into the parking lot at the animal shelter.

"Are you adopting a new pet?" I look up at Egan when he opens my door.

"I might be. But that's why you have to hurry. Wouldn't want some other family to get him." He tugs me down the sidewalk and into the building.

"Did you look at the website? You shouldn't have. Your heart is way too big to walk away without the whole shelter and your mom would—"

"Egan, hey. You made it just in time." A woman with short, curly brown hair smiles at us from behind a reception area desk.

Egan sighs so heavily his breath makes my hair flutter around my shoulders. "Great. Can we see him?"

"Absolutely. I've got him all ready for you."

"Him?" I may as well be tin cans tied to the back of a pick-up truck as I bounce down the hall, tethered to Egan by our hands, totally out of control. "You're really serious about this aren't you?"

"Of course I'm serious about this. It's important. We're saving a life tonight."

"Saving a life? Eesh. Someone's dramatic." I force myself to chuckle to add some levity to the situation. Because right now concentrating on the way our palms fit so nicely together is making me feel lightheaded. I really need to think of him as the boy who used to pull my pigtails and not the guy I might gladly kiss given the opportunity.

I smile at a woman standing next to an aquarium with some sort of lizard in it as we jog by. An elementary-aged boy wearing a maroon polo shirt and khaki shorts pokes at the glass with his pointer finger.

We pass a room full of kittens. Kittens with blue eyes and gray and white fur. Black kittens with curled up tails. Even little ginger kittens with stripes all along their bellies.

I screech to a halt, forgetting the hurry. "Ohh," I breathe. "E. Look. Kittens."

It's been almost a week since Hedwig passed away. Grandma asked if I wanted another cat, but I told her I wanted to wait at least a couple of months. Except that was before I saw all these marble-eyed kittens tumbling over each other, batting at invisible butterflies.

But Egan pulls me away. "No, not those."

"Hey," I protest. "I wanted to look at them. Can't we wait just a couple of minutes?"

"No." Egan steers me to the end of the hall. "I need you to see something."

"Fine." I bounce along after him, leaning away for a last glance at the kittens. "But once we've checked this off your list, I want to come back and see the one with the gray spot on his forehead."

"Deal. But I have a feeling you're going to change your mind." Egan stops, and I bump into his solid back. He reaches around with the ease of a ballet dancer and puts his hands on my shoulders to propel me in front of his body.

"Check it out, Cal." His lips are so close to my ear it tickles. He points beyond the glass window.

I peer through into a cozy cubby housing the most ancient, decrepit cat I've ever seen. His fur is scraggly, matted, gray, and patchy. He barely lifts his head to regard me with a wary black eye, then he lays his chin on the edge of the litter box as though he's entirely unimpressed with me.

And it's love at first sight.

Egan clears his throat and speaks softly. "I wanted to do something great for you. To make up for yesterday. I was being immature. And stupid."

All I truly remember about yesterday is the way the air hummed between us when he leaned close enough for a kiss. "When we were downstairs?"

His eyebrows draw together and release in a flash. "No. When Owen and I had our argument."

"Oh. That." Of course. I swallow and shake my head. "It's fine."

"No, it's not. We shouldn't have fought, especially not in front of you. And we're sorry. But mostly me. I'm sorry."

I glance up and regret it when my stomach starts to swim in the sparkliest sort of way.

Egan's chin dips as he levels me with his gaze. "It took me a little bit to find the right fit for you, but I think I'm on the right track." He nods at the cat. "He's been here for three days. Apparently two college kids adopted him a month ago. But he didn't fit in with their lifestyle, so they brought him back here. Dropped him off."

The ancient cat flicks an ear at me.

"They left him?" My voice cracks.

Egan's chest rises and falls against my shoulders. "But it's okay. Because he's got you now."

"Me." I blink furiously. "But I'm not getting another cat."

"I already cleared it with your grandma. She's all for it."

I want to say more about how I'm not ready to love again. I don't think I have it in me to be a part of the kind of long-term commitment a cat brings to a person's life. Or short-term, if this cat's appearance is any indication of how long the rest of his lifespan will be. I can't possibly be the best person for this cat.

But all those thoughts flee the second the old cat raises his paw and bats at the glass between us.

Egan's leaning against the window, one shoulder pressed against it, with his legs crossed at the ankles. He holds up his phone and raises an eyebrow in question.

I nod, and he touches the screen to start recording. "His name is Errol," Egan says.

"Errol?" I could kiss his whiskers. The cat's, I mean.

Egan nods. His hand falls to the top of my arm. He squeezes. "It seems fitting. After Hedwig. That you'd have an Errol."

"Thank you." I risk another glance at Egan's face.

He's smiling, but it's soft this time. No blinding headlight grin. Or even a sixty-watt. This is the warm glow of an Edison bulb and equally as magical.

"What do you think?" he whispers, stopping a tear from sneaking across my cheekbone with his pinky finger.

I tuck my bottom lip between my teeth and hold my breath before I answer. "I think he and I might have more in store for us than I originally planned on."

Egan nods. He stops recording, drops the phone into his pocket, and loops his arms over my shoulders as he peers beyond the glass at Errol. His chin tickles the side of my face as he answers.

"I was hoping you would say that."

Chapter 29

TWO SECONDS AFTER I SEND ANNABETH AN SOS message, she calls me. "You're not looking at hair dye again, are you?" she asks. It sounds like she's in a train station or something. Lots of clanging and yelling and loud noises.

"What?" I grimace. "No. Of course not."

"Just making sure. What's up?"

My stomach flutters. "I think I want to do it."

"Do what?" There's a muffled scramble, then I hear her say to someone else, "Please put Michelangelo back into his Tupperware. Turtles aren't allowed on the dinner table."

"Are you babysitting the Lozanos?" They're a family from our church. Annabeth has been their main babysitter since last summer, and they're the only ones I know who have household turtles.

"Yeah, just until seven though. Is everything okay?"

I glance over at Errol, who's crouched underneath my bed. "It's good. I was just thinking about everything you said and wondering if maybe I should give it a try. With sharing my story. And stuff." The last little bit rushes out like if I don't force myself to say it, I might not say it at all.

"Wait. Did I hear you correctly? You're going to take my advice?" I imagine Annabeth pressing her hand to her chest in shock.

"Maybe not if you make too big a deal out of it."

Annabeth sighs. "You're so contrarian."

"You're such a drama queen."

"And you love me for it."

"Maybe not *for* it." I can't help but smile. We're so different, but I can't deny the amount of awesome she's brought into my life over the last couple of years. "So, seven? You'll come over right after you're done there?"

"Yep. As soon as possible. Can I have dinner there? All they have here is Easy Mac."

"You got it. I'll set an extra plate at the table."

And true to her word, Annabeth shows up as soon as possible, ten minutes after seven. We barely make it through our Italian chicken and green beans before she takes her plate over to the sink.

"Ready?" she asks.

"For what?" Grandma asks.

Annabeth starts to answer, but I cut her off with a raised eyebrow. "Nothing," I say. "We thought we'd record a little addendum for the Experiment. We probably won't use it." I shrug and grab my water glass. "But try not to come up and knock unless it's an emergency. You know, just in case we've got a good take or whatever. I don't want to have to rerecord."

Grandma nods. "Ah, yes. I see. Well, have fun."

Annabeth has already started bounding up the stairs toward my room, so I can't wait to figure out if Grandma's wise to me. Or if she's rethinking her life-doesn't-come-with-GPS advice from the other night.

By the time I get to my room, Annabeth has already attached a flexible tripod to one of my bedposts. It's aimed toward my desk chair, which she's dragged across the room so it's next to the window instead of in front of my desk. When she sees my frown, she grins. "I read that it's better to have natural light for video." She grabs the cord to the blinds and pulls them up with a long and loud *ziiiiiiip*.

"You know Egan doesn't put this much thought into it when we actually shoot for the Experiment, right?"

Annabeth puts her hands on her hips. "Do you want people commenting on your shadowy under eyes or not?"

I'm about to call the whole thing off on account of her nit-picking when Errol sticks his head out from underneath my bed and lets out a rusty mewl.

Annabeth pulls her chin to her chest and wrinkles her nose. "Is that—what did you call him?"

"Errol. Isn't he perfect?" I nearly melt into a crouch and run my fingers through the fur between Errol's ears. He purrs and winds between my legs.

"He's something. Yesterday when you said Egan got you a new cat, I was sort of thinking of something fluffier. And may-be less one-paw-in-the-grave."

I cover Errol's ears with my palms. "Annabeth, don't say things like that."

She holds her hands up in the air. "I'm just being honest."

"He's wonderful. Aren't you? Yes, you are." Errol flops onto his back and bats at my hand.

"Are you ready or do you want to keep making kissy faces at the cat?" Annabeth's voice is flat.

"You're just ticked because you don't have someone who will give you presents that are as awesome as Errol."

A slow grin creeps over Annabeth's mouth. "And you do? Have someone, I mean? Because wasn't it like two weeks ago or something that you said once the Experiment was over, Egan would be out of your life again?"

Warmth blooms over my cheeks quicker than I can turn away. "I mean, I'm probably not going to be able to get rid of him after this, to be honest. He'll keep coming around, kind of like seasonal allergies."

"He'll keep coming around, or you'll keep finding excuses to bring him back around?"

I squeeze my eyes shut and shrug.

"I knew it." Annabeth explodes across the room and rockets into me, wrapping her arms so tight around me I'm afraid I might pass out. "I knew you two weren't going to be able to call it quits. There's too much history there. Too much chemistry."

"You sound like you're reading my school schedule. Maybe we should just get back to what we're actually supposed to be doing?" I slide out of her hug and make a big deal about combing my fingers through my hair.

"Use a real brush." Annabeth picks my phone up from the corner of my desk where I dropped it and shoves it into the tripod. Despite her admonition, she's grinning.

"Actually, I'm good. Let's do this." I drop into my chair in front of the window before she can say anything else. I press my palms against the tops of my thighs, suddenly feeling queasy. Instead of counting, I force myself to exhale, long and loud.

"Do you want to plan something to say? Or just wing it?" Annabeth sits cross-legged on my bed.

"Wing it. I can't think about this too long or I'll never do it."

"Well, that's out of character. But fair enough. I'm hitting *record* right...now. Want me to ask questions?"

"Yes, please."

"Okay. Um, well, start from the beginning, I guess."

"That's not a question."

Annabeth shakes her head. "Fine. How did the whole adoption-by-grandparents thing happen?"

"They signed some paperwork, and here I am." I cross my arms over my chest.

"But like, for real. And uncross your arms. You look mad. Take a cleansing breath or something."

I force myself to breathe deeply again, enough to push the tension out of my shoulders and into the air around me. When I do this three times without taking it any further, Annabeth gets fed up.

"Look, do you need me to go first or something?" She hops off my bed and hip-checks me off the chair, then drops into it, fluffs her hair around her shoulders, and looks into the camera with a tame, closed-lipped smile pressed onto her face.

"I'm Annabeth Mathis," she says. "And this is my Sixty-Second Story of Strength."

From the floor, I can't help but interject. "Did you just think of that? It's catchy."

"Yes. Thank you. Are you going to get behind the camera or not?"

I flop over onto my mattress and tuck my hands underneath my chin, interested to see how this is going to go. "Yep. Continue."

Annabeth nods once, quick. "Okay. Take two. I'm Annabeth Mathis, and this is my Sixty-Second Story of Strength." Again, she smiles. "A little over four years ago, my mom started having weird things happen to her. She had trouble seeing things clearly, and she was super exhausted all the time. Every once in a while, she said it felt like she'd stuck her finger in an electrical socket or something. It took a couple of years, but she finally got a diagnosis. She has Multiple Sclerosis.

"It's a disease that means her immune system attacks her healthy body and pretty much makes life difficult for her on a daily basis. We don't know how it'll progress in the future, and to be honest, I don't like thinking about it, either.

"The day we got her diagnosis, my boyfriend sent me a text message to say he liked me but thought we should just be friends. And just like that he was gone. He didn't know about the diagnosis, but his timing was still really crappy. It was hard.

"A couple months ago, Mom had some new symptoms show up, and it's getting harder for her to move around. She has a cane she uses now. She used to do triathlons, but she had to give those up a little bit after her diagnosis."

I can see the shimmer of unshed tears in Annabeth's brown eyes from here, and I have to pinch myself so I don't lose it too.

"But you know what?" Annabeth sniffs, and a watery smile takes over. "My mom is awesome. She pushes through every single day. When she feels sad, she lets herself be sad for a little bit, but then she gets up and works through it. She's not interested in giving up, and she's taught me to be the same way.

"I have big dreams, and sometimes they're scary and it's really hard and I don't think I'll ever reach them. But I'm not interested in giving up either."

Annabeth folds her hands in her lap and looks away. I take that as my cue to stop the recording.

I slip off my bed and lean into Annabeth, wrapping my arms around her and squeezing as tightly as I can. "I'm so proud of you, AB. I hate that this is a part of your life."

"Me, too." She returns my hug. We stay there for a solid two minutes until Annabeth leans away and swipes her pinkies underneath her eyes. "Don't think I've forgotten what we came up here to do."

"Of course not." I shake my head and drop into the chair. My stomach still seizes, and I can't help but count the polka dots on my T-shirt, but now that Annabeth has given me a roadmap of sorts, I know what I want to say. "We're just recording this, right? In case I decide to use it sometime in the very-far-off future. Right?"

"We don't even have to send it to Egan at all if you don't want to. This is just for you right now." She nods so earnestly I can almost feel her confidence buzzing like an electrical current across my bedroom.

"Okay. Yeah." I take a deep breath, pull my shoulders back, look into my phone, and shoot it a half-smile, half-power-stare. "Let's do this."

Chapter 30

ERROL LICKS HIS PAW ONE LAST TIME THEN FLOPS over against my thigh. His tail flicks at my phone, which I've been staring at for a full twenty minutes now, though it's just sitting there. Dark.

"This is stupid, Errol. Egan's done so much for me. I need to suck it up and do this for him." Even if he isn't trying to beat his older brother anymore, I know he's still drawn to the idea of making it. Of being someone. Of—how did he put it—having global recognition.

I know my story probably won't bring global recognition, but every little bit helps. Or something.

Besides, I still need to sell my part. He's going to get suspicious if I quit trying, and I'm not ready to tell him exactly how much of a failure I am.

I run my fingernails underneath Errol's chin. He purrs but doesn't move otherwise. I'd thought recording my story was going to be the hard part. I was wrong.

The hardest part is picking up the phone.

I know I'm probably overreacting, but what if someone figures out where my dad is and eggs his house or something? I mean, he deserves it and all, but if anyone's going to do it, it should be me, not some anonymous internet troll.

I reach for my phone.

But then again, the trolls are truly terrible. Last night I read a comment that said I'm out of touch with the harsh realities of the world because I live in a home where we can afford wooden blinds instead of vinyl ones, which is a standard of luxury I had no idea existed.

I shrink away from my phone and sit on my hands.

I used to think that when I put stuff out there into the world, I could still control it. People would see my heart and think logically and maybe empathize a little and everything would be okay. But if there's one thing I've learned in this experiment, it's that information can be a weapon. And people brandish that weapon without doing any fact-checking or heart-checking along the way.

I think I've been a victim of that. Except I'm sure some people would be upset that I'd even use a word like "victim" in the first place. What with my wooden blinds and all.

Errol flinches, and I realize I've started digging my fingernails into his chin.

"Oops. Sorry, buddy. Didn't mean to hurt you." He lets out a rumbly meow which I decide is an offer of forgiveness. But we are still getting to know each other, so it could also be a request for another one of the chicken-flavored treats I got him on the way home from the shelter. I miss Hedwig more than I thought possible, and my room still feels empty without her. But I'm glad to have Errol to help me work through the grief.

"You still don't happen to have any suggestions, do you?" Errol doesn't answer, so I decide to go on a fact-finding mission to prep for the phone call I may or may not make.

Grandma and Grandpa don't talk about my dad often. I don't think they know much about what he's doing now, and stories about his childhood don't interest me. So, he isn't a popular topic of conversation in our home.

It's easier to pick up my phone knowing I'm not using it for a phone call. I search for my dad's name and 660,000 results populate my screen almost immediately. My eyebrows raise to my hairline at the first couple.

Paul Christianson, aspiring muralist and "professional coffee taster" in Seattle. Possible.

Dr. Paul Christianson, plastic surgeon in the Bay area. Possible, but not probable.

Paul Christianson of Christianson Extermination and Pest Prevention Services. I open that one because it seems the most plausible. A raccoon chitter rips through the nighttime silence so loudly I nearly chuck my phone across the room.

Errol barely stirs.

Once my heart rate has recovered, I pick up my phone again. "This is stupid," I whisper to Errol. "I'm just going to call him. I'm a big girl. I'm practically a legal adult. We'll chat. I'll see what he thinks. No big deal."

Errol flips over onto his back and wraps his paws around my arm. He licks my palm with his sandpaper tongue. I decide that's an affirmative and pick up my phone, open my dad's contact info, and hit send before I can talk myself out of it.

Grandma gave me his cell number a few years ago in case of an emergency. But I've never used it. Until now.

After two rings, I realize I'm holding my breath and force myself to let it go.

"Paul Christianson." The voice is clipped and tight.

I open my mouth to answer. To say hi. To say I don't know what. But nothing comes out. My mouth goes completely dry.

"Hello?" He tries again. "I can hear you breathing."

I snap my mouth shut.

"Who is it?" A feminine voice floats across the airwaves.

"Just some weirdo."

I drag in a deep gulp of oxygen. "Dad?"

"Lucy?"

"Who's Lucy?" I ask.

"Who's this?"

"Callie."

"Oh. Oh! Callie. Wow, it's great to hear your voice. How are you, sweetie?"

My upper lip curls immediately. Sweetie? We barely even know each other. "I'm good. I think. How are you?"

A kid screams in the background. It's better than a raccoon, I guess. My hands are shaking, so I grasp the edge of my quilt as though it's the last thing keeping me grounded on earth.

"Good. I'm good too." I hear muffled footsteps and a door closes. The screaming goes away. We both fall silent.

I plan everything else in my life. Why didn't I plan this moment? Did I really think I could just blurt out, "Hey, I'm going to tell the story of how you abandoned me to hundreds of strangers on the internet. Is that okay with you?"

"So, how's school?" he finally asks.

"Great. It's great." I shake my head. "I mean, no. I'm done. It's out. For the summer."

"Right. Of course. It is June, I guess." He chuckles, but it sounds strained. "You're, what, going to be a sophomore next year?"

"Senior, actually." My heart feels like it's suddenly sunk into my toes.

"Wow. Time flies. You thinking about going to college?"

I shrug, even though he can't see it. "I have a couple state schools I might apply to. Grandma and I visited them a few months ago, but I don't really have my heart set on any in particular."

"Good. Good. How is your grandma?"

Why does he call her my grandma? She's his mom. He should just say, "How is Mom doing?"

I shake my head to pull myself back on track. "Um, she's doing well. She still does counseling, just with a few clients here and there. And she volunteers at church and around town a lot, too."

"And your grandpa?"

"Still working for the police department. But mostly as a consultant these days."

"Sounds like the General." My dad's voice sounds flat, and I imagine him rolling his eyes or smirking even though I'm not sure what he looks like these days.

Again, silence.

"My cat died," I blurt out when the heaviness of the quiet settles around my shoulders. Then I grimace.

"Oh. I'm sorry to hear that. How long had you had him?" Dad sounds bewildered.

"Her. Hedwig. I got her when I moved in with Grandma and Grandpa. Really she was Grandma's cat. You remember seeing pictures of her, right? In our Christmas cards and stuff." I think Grandma still sends him Christmas cards.

"Absolutely." He clears his throat. "Of course."

"Egan got me a new cat yesterday. He's old. But I have a lot in common with him." Because he was abandoned, too. "Because he likes to drink milk. And sleep." I keep babbling because I'm not sure what else to do.

"Who's Egan?"

It's so weird that I have to explain this to my own dad, even though our only tie is biological. "He's my best friend. And we're going on dates. We went to a Little League all-star game today. It was fun."

"You're dating? Wow. I forget you've grown up."

"We're not really dating." I say it like that's going to clarify things. "I mean, not like in a relationship or anything. Just going on dates. We're doing this thing he calls the Great Date Experiment. You should look it up sometime."

Here it is. My opportunity. I just need to say, "Is it okay if I post a video of me talking about you and my mom?"

But I can't.

A dog barks in the background on Dad's end and he yells for someone to shut up that stupid animal and the moment evaporates. When he turns back to the phone, he apologizes. "Sorry about that. My wife's dog is obnoxious. But yes, I will look up your thing. I'm writing it down now."

His wife. I wonder when that happened. I wonder if he'd even thought about inviting us or if she knows I exist.

"How is she? Your wife, I mean," I ask, wrapping a stray string from my quilt tightly around my index finger.

"Ellen? She's great. She stays home with our kids, Lucy and Reid. Lucy's at summer camp right now."

It feels like all the oxygen has been sucked from the room.

Siblings. I have siblings.

Why didn't I know this? Nobody wanted to call me after their first ultrasound when they saw a flickering heartbeat on the screen? I have a brother and a sister, and nobody thought they should let me know? Do Grandma and Grandpa know?

My finger is turning purple. I yank it away from my quilt, snapping the string, and scoop Errol close to my heart, one-handed. He growls in protest but doesn't struggle to get away. I draw my knees closer to my chest. "How old are they?" I whisper, almost choking.

"Lucy's ten. Reid is almost six." Dad recites their ages like he's talking about the highs and lows in the forecast. I don't miss the fact that he couldn't remember how old I am.

"How nice for them," I finally manage. My throat feels full, and my voice sounds like I'm underwater.

"Well, is there something you need? Or were you calling to say hi?" my dad asks.

Oh, sure. We haven't talked basically ever, but I'm just calling to say hi on this random summer night. "That's exactly it." I squeeze my eyes shut and bury my face into Errol's fur. "Just saying hi."

"Okay, good." He lets out a heavy breath. "I was afraid for a minute you were calling to ask me to fix your ears."

"My ears?" I drop Errol into my lap and press one hand to the side of my head.

"Do they still stick out? Your mom and I used to call you Little Dumbo."

I'd never thought my ears stuck out. Until now. "No, they're—"

"Great. Because I don't operate on family. I could give you a referral, though." He chuckles. "Let me know if you'd like to have one of my colleagues add a couple of cup sizes for you in a few years. If genetics are to be trusted, you're going to need it."

My stomach riots. I need a trash can.

"I gotta go. Bye," I spit out and end the call, dropping my phone on my bed before he can say anything else. My entire body is shaking now, and I feel like I need to rinse my mouth out to get rid of the vile taste rolling around my tongue. As carefully as I can, I put Errol back onto the floor. He stares up at me and meows as though he's offended, and I sink down next to him and hang my head between my knees.

Deep breaths, I remind myself.

My room is so silent I have nothing to count. So I tap my fingers together in a steady rhythm and count that instead.

All these years I thought my dad was nothing. A loser. All those Christmases and birthdays and family reunions I thought he was the broken one who couldn't get it together enough to be a part of our family. But now I know all that was a lie.

My dad is a successful plastic surgeon in the Bay area. And he thinks I'm the one who's broken.

Chapter 31

THE PLUNK OF ANOTHER STRAWBERRY INTO THE plastic bucket drags me back into the present. The air around us is thick and heavy with humidity, and when I glance at the horizon, I can see blue-black clouds roiling and tumbling over each other even though it's sunny on top of our little patch.

Egan waves his fingers in front of my face. "Are you going to pick any, or am I going to do all the work today?"

I look up at him from my spot in the middle of the dirt footpath where I dropped after my lower back started burning from all the crouching. Slowly, very slowly, I stretch to pluck a single berry and drop it into the bucket.

I wait for him to roll his eyes or nudge me with the edge of his shoe or tell me to knock it off. But instead, Egan sinks to the footpath next to me. "I thought for sure I had a winner of a date today, but it doesn't seem like you agree." He slides his fingers down a nearby plant and slips a berry into his palm. "You still like strawberries, right?" He holds the berry in between his pointer finger and thumb. It glistens like a ruby in the sunlight.

"I do." I take the fruit from his hand and pop it into my mouth, then discard the stem over my shoulder.

"Then what's going on? We've been here for twenty minutes, and you've been mopey the whole time. That's only the fourth strawberry I've seen you eat, and the other three were also ones I picked for you. What happened to the girl who ate more than she picked? At this rate we're barely going to have enough for a single recipe."

Recipe. Right. Like those even matter anymore.

"Actually, I think I'm going to take up scrapbooking instead of baking."

Egan looks at me as though I've told him we should build a snowman here in the middle of the strawberry patch. "Isn't scrapbooking, I don't know, obsolete or something?"

"Yeah. You're right." I tuck my bottom lip between my teeth then let it go immediately in case that sort of thing causes extra wrinkles my dad could critique or something. "It's not the date, E. This is fun."

"Could have fooled me," he mumbles.

When I don't say anything else, he leans over and nudges me with his shoulder.

"No. Really. It's great." I force myself to smile, but I know it registers flat when his trademark grin doesn't appear in response. "I just had a hard night last night. But it's fine. I'll be okay." As I say the word *okay*, my throat starts to clog with tears, so I pop up from the ground. "Let's pick some berries." Now my voice sounds more chipper than an entire pep squad.

Egan follows, picking up the bucket and letting it swing from his fingers as he follows me. "Is it the comments? Did someone say something super stupid last night?"

I shake my head. Oddly enough, I've forgotten to read the comments over the last couple of days.

"Is Errol okay? Did he hack up something disgusting on your favorite shirt?"

"No. Errol's still great."

Egan's footfalls slow behind me. "Is it me? Did I do something dumb?"

I stop. "No, not at all."

He steps in front of me and touches my shoulder. "Are you sure?"

I stare at my feet, the bucket of strawberries dangling from my fingers. A piece of hair slips from behind my Dumbo ear. Tears roll hot and free down my face, dripping off my chin and plopping to the dirt.

"Callie." Egan grasps both my shoulders in his hands, then he must decide that's not close enough because he crushes me to his chest. "What happened? What's wrong? You have *got* to use some words here."

He smells like sunshine, and it's not fair because all I can do is cry and let my mascara run down my face and into the cotton of his T-shirt. I uncurl my fingers from the bucket handle, and it drops to the ground with an echoey thud. Bright red berries skitter across the dirt.

It's a solid two minutes before I manage to choke out, "My life. That's what's wrong. All of it."

"There are so many good things in your life. Right?" Egan's voice is soft and a little shaky, almost like he's afraid. "Please tell me what happened."

"Everything." I press my palms to his chest and force myself away. "Everything happened." I can't keep it to myself anymore, even if it means Egan will think I'm unmotivated to stay in the Experiment. "I heard back from Nichelle Melendez."

Egan merely blinks at me.

I wipe my cheek with the back of my hand. "It was stupid anyway, to think I was good enough to work with her."

"No, Callie. You *are* good enough."

"Stop. I'm not. She didn't choose me. So, it's over, and I guess I try to figure out something else to do with my life. Because clearly I'm not cut out for baking or whatever. Even when I have a platform like the Experiment."

"Come on. Quitting something you love because of one little—"

"It's not little." My voice breaks.

"I know. I'm sorry. I didn't mean it like that." Egan steps
closer again. "Did you get the email last night?"

I count the eyelets in his black tennis shoes, where the neon
green shoelaces loop in and out. It helps, but not enough.

"Seriously, Callie. She really should have chosen you, and
I'm not just saying that because I…" Egan clears his throat.
"Because I'm your friend."

"There's more." The heat of shame climbs up through my
chest, leaving a trail of searing pain in its wake. I squeeze my
eyes shut. "I called my dad."

"What?" Egan sounds as shocked as I felt last night. "Your
dad. The real one?"

I grimace and frown. "What do you mean the real one? He's
my dad."

"But you haven't talked to him. Like ever."

"I did last night."

"Wow." Egan reaches up and scrubs his jaw. "Wow."

"Yeah, wow." I cross my arms over my chest.

The air is so heavy and hot, dark and dull. Lightning flashes
over Egan's shoulder, but the leaves on the trees surrounding
the strawberry fields are still.

"Well, what did you say?"

"I said hi."

"And?"

"And he called me Lucy." I look up.

Egan's brow furrows. "Lucy?"

"Because I have a sister. Whose name is Lucy. She's away at
summer camp. He thought I was her on the phone."

His eyes are the size of Oreo cookies, and his Adam's apple dips and rises. "A sister."

"And a little brother too." The tears are coming so fast now my eyeballs may as well be faucets. I raise my hands in the air and wave my fingers. "Surprise, I'm not actually an only child."

Egan is standing so still he could be mistaken for a manne-quin with mascara stains on his shirt.

"But wait, there's more," I say.

His eyebrows raise.

"He's a plastic surgeon."

"Did he offer to help you pay for college?" Egan's mouth tilts with a tiny, wry smile. "Because that would be sorta nice, right?"

"Nope. But he did offer to have one of his colleagues pin back my Dumbo ears."

Egan growls, literally growls like he's transforming into a werewolf or something. "He said that?"

"Yep. And much worse." I wince, remembering the cup size comment.

"What a complete waste of breath. Do you have his address? I might need to take a road trip. Alone. With a baseball bat." When I sort of frown at him, he shrugs. "For his mailbox, not his face. I promise."

Thunder cracks overhead.

"I just…" My hands are shaking. "I don't even know what to think anymore. Is that—do you think they always thought there was something wrong with me? And that's why they gave me up?"

Suddenly, Egan's lips are on mine, sweeter than crème brûlée custard and just as smooth. His thumb brushes the top of my right ear, following the curve of it. I think I'm supposed to move away. But, instead, I lean closer. Into the kiss, into his space, into us.

Eternal split-seconds later, he breaks the kiss and rests his nose against my forehead. He hooks his pinky on my friendship bracelet. "Noog." His voice is ragged, and he shakes his head. "There is absolutely nothing wrong with anything about you. I mean that with every cell in me."

"Did you—" I'm blinking rapidly, like one of those dolls with the crazy eyelids. "Did you mean to do that?"

The corner of his mouth twitches. "Are you asking if I accidentally kissed you?"

"Well, I mean, you didn't record it or anything, so how are we going to put it on the Experiment page and get more views and…" I run out of steam when I glance up and notice his grin is growing.

"You don't think it'd be weird to broadcast our kisses to the rest of the world?"

My heart throws a spark at the mention of multiple kisses, like this is maybe, possibly, perhaps going to be an ongoing thing. I force myself to shrug. "If it would get you more views."

"And you don't think it's weird for me to be kissing you?"

Memories of Dr. Pepper over chewy ice at the pool and PB-and-J picnics in the woods and playing pirates in our old tree fort flood my thoughts before I settle back into the newness of our kiss. Our first kiss. My heart suddenly feels as effervescent as fresh seltzer.

All my best adventures have always been with Egan.

"No." I shake my head, forehead still pressed against his chest. "It's not weird at all."

And, in fact, kissing Egan today feels like the least weird thing that's happened in the last twenty-four hours.

Chapter 32

AFTER EGAN PELTS ME IN THE FACE WITH AN OVER-ripe strawberry for the third time, he grabs at my phone, which I'd been using to snap pictures of the roiling clouds, of the berry blossoms, of his profile.

"We need to commemorate this carnage," he says, barely stifling fits of laughter.

"You're only saying that because you've hit me three times, and I only got you once."

He doesn't deny it, but he does grin and hold my phone in front of us, camera pointed at our faces. One touch to the screen and he's captured the moment, his full-of-life smile and my raised eyebrow and tilted lips. I was trying to look chagrined, but the strawberry rouge on my cheeks sabotaged that, and instead I merely look content.

Egan leans in and touches a kiss to my brow bone, and this time I can't keep my smile hidden. He snaps another picture.

"I know you had a really crappy night leading up to this, but I have to say, this is my favorite date we've ever been on. Hands down," he says.

I crouch and pluck another strawberry then test its ripeness between my fingers. It's not ripe enough to throw at his face, but it is ripe enough to drop into the bucket, so I do. "I think I agree."

"Really? You like this more than the food trucks?"

The next berry I touch is perfect. A little mushy, but not disgusting. Just enough that it'll explode upon impact. I glance up to see if he's watching me, but he's still engrossed in my phone.

"Well, you almost got arrested at the food truck date and then we didn't talk for two days. So, yeah, I think this is better." I straighten and hold the squishy strawberry behind my back.

"But if you leave that part out, the food truck date was still awesome, right? You did win that cash."

I nod and take a step toward him. "That was pretty cool."

"What did you end up doing with that, anyway? We never did make it to that fancy kitchen store. Maybe we should do that for our date tomorrow." Egan tilts his head. "Why are you looking at me like that?"

"Like what?"

"Like that. Your face is weird."

"Your face is weird."

"You're hiding something." He swipes his thumb across my phone, pokes the power button, then drops it into the pocket of his navy athletic shorts so he can investigate. With minimal effort, he leans over the top of my head just as I smash my strawberry into his nostrils.

He sputters then, lightning-fast, grasps both my wrists in one hand, while he swipes at his nose with the other.

"That was sneaky," he chuckles close to my ear then smashes another berry directly onto my forehead and smears it across my whole face. Half my bucket and seven irreparable berry stains on my shirt later, thunder rumbles low and long. The skies split with warm, pelting raindrops as fat and heavy as chocolate chips.

There's a tiny shed, if you can call it that, at the end of one row of strawberries, where they've left extra buckets and baskets for people too shortsighted to grab one at the beginning, and Egan and I run to that, laughing.

Laughing. After last night, I didn't think I'd laugh again until Christmas break. At least.

I fall into the doorway of the shed, gasping, and Egan tumbles in behind me. He sets his bucket down inside and grimaces. "Looks like I lost a few."

I peer into it and drop my also-lacking bucket on a nearby workbench. "If by a few you mean three-quarters of the bucket." The rain intensifies, and I move to the doorway to watch as it begins coming down in heavy gray sheets.

"So, uh, I have a question for you." Egan scoots his bucket farther into the shed with his foot. He crosses his legs at his ankles then leans sideways over me, resting his forearm on the doorframe above my head.

"Yeah?"

He squints at me from behind the lenses of his rain-speckled glasses. Warmth radiates from his rib cage. I rub my bare arms, covered in goose bumps, but don't lean in because what if we're the kind of friends who kiss now, but not the kind who snuggle?

"Do you still want to finish out the Experiment?" He holds his hand toward me, fingers waiting for mine.

I lay my palm in his. Fast. "Of course. Why wouldn't I?"

"Because the only thing keeping you in this thing was that Nichelle lady. If she said no, does that mean you're done too?"

"Nichelle is old news. I haven't been in it for her in a long time." I remember why I chose not to tell him in the first place, and my fingers tighten around his inadvertently. "Do *you* want to finish out the Experiment? Even though Owen dropped out?"

"Even though—" he stops abruptly. "Wait, how'd you know about that?"

"He told me. At your house." I bite my bottom lip and lean

into his chest, deciding in this second that we are most definitely the snuggling kind of friends.

He wraps his arms around me and rests his chin on top of my head. "Noog, I'm sorry. I didn't mean to let it go so long. Why didn't you call me out on it?"

I close my eyes and count his heartbeats. "I'd found out about Nichelle the night before. I was afraid if I told you I'd been eliminated you'd back out too since both our reasons for sticking with it were totally obsolete. So, we were both being kind of dumb."

He exhales once, forcefully, like he's laughing at something that isn't the least bit funny. "I could have come up with a couple more reasons to keep it going." He pauses for a long rumble of thunder. "You know competing with Owen was just an excuse, right?"

When my brow furrows, he continues. "I was in it for you the whole time."

"I don't think I follow."

He speaks slowly as he traces a swirl on the back of my hand, still resting on his chest. "The hippo. The Moon Pies. Julia Child. The Experiment. I did all of it for the same reason, and it had nothing to do with my brother. I did it all for you. Because I missed you, and I needed you back in my life."

Marco's story about how Egan talked about me months before he showed up on my doorstep suddenly pops to mind. I'd been too confused and scared to hope it meant anything. But now? "You mean, you wanted to be friends again?" I ask.

Egan smiles and ducks, reaching backward to rub the top of his head. "I was prepared for that, but I was hoping for something more like this." This time he captures my chin between his thumb and index finger and tilts my face upward.

I press into the concrete floor with my tiptoes to cover the distance. His lips taste like strawberries and coming home. The kiss is slow and lingering, more purposeful than spontaneous. When he breaks it, I tuck my bottom lip between my teeth.

"That's what you hoped for even back then?"

Egan nods. "Even then. And before that, too, if you want me to be totally honest." He teases the fringe of my friendship bracelet with his fingertips. "I don't know what happened or what changed the first day of ninth grade, but you walked into that high school like you owned the place with your color-coded planner and your Julia Child biography, and—and I don't know." He stares down at me, his eyes a little shinier and more caramel than usual. "I couldn't deal, Callie Gail." He whispers my full name with such wistful tenderness and sweet nostalgia, I have trouble remembering what year it is.

I look away and clear my throat, fighting the urge to kiss him again, this time until neither of us can breathe. "That's funny." I try to force some levity into my voice, but it sounds hushed and reverent instead. "Because that's right about the time I started having trouble dealing, too."

He exhales then leans away and holds his hand out for me to take, which I do. Our fingers weave together as though we've actually been holding hands since ninth grade. Egan stares out the doorway, into the rain and over the horizon, but I watch him.

"Hey, E?"

"Yeah."

"I know I said it was dumb in the beginning, but I was thinking. It might be kind of cool to see that view count tick over a thousand. So, maybe we shouldn't give up on that too fast?"

He nods a few times, jaw set and gaze straight ahead. Then

he turns and shoots me a crooked half-smile. "I'm okay with that. If you're serious, that is."

"I wouldn't have said it if I weren't."

His smile grows into a grin that takes over his entire face and then his whole body. If I look into his eyes for long enough, I'm convinced I'll see little idea elves already churning away in his brain, trying to come up with that viral element that will propel us beyond seven hundred fifty views and into success.

Egan squeezes my hand. "So, we're for sure going to finish this thing out, then? With twenty-one dates."

I pause like I need to think about it, but I'm already nodding, betraying myself. "Yes. Definitely."

He angles himself toward me again. His face and the lenses of his glasses are covered in a fine mist from the rain. "Can I date you after twenty-one too, even though a certain someone said that would never happen? I'm a man of my word, you know, and I did promise to abide by that stipulation."

"I think I may have been a little hasty in making that decision."

"Good." He smiles that confetti smile of his and it feels like the sun has broken through the clouds right over us, even though the thunderstorm hasn't let up. "Because I'd like to take you on a lot more dates in the future. Like, at least a thousand more."

I can't help but grin right back at him. "I think I'd like to go on those dates."

Chapter 33

EGAN WEAVES HIS FINGERS THROUGH MY HAIR AT the nape of my neck. "It's awfully hot out tonight. How do you not sweat to death every summer with all this hair?" He drops a kiss underneath my ear.

I shiver and clasp my hands together behind his neck. "I guess I'm just used to it. And I usually have it up in a ponytail." He leans back and tilts his head in a question I interpret easily. "Tonight felt too special for a plain old ponytail, even if it was putt-putt and slushies."

"I see." He smiles. "Well, they're both good looks for you, if you ask me."

"Thanks."

The world of compliments and kisses feels so foreign-yet-familiar even twenty-four hours after we decided to make things official.

The porch light flickers. I frown.

Egan laughs and tugs his fingers from my hair and loops them together behind my lower back. "Your grandpa must be watching."

"No, if Grandpa was watching, he'd be chasing you with a shotgun and a shovel by now."

"Your grandma?"

"Maybe." I close my eyes as he presses another innocent kiss to my hairline. "But it's after nine, so I think she's probably already gone to bed."

"Electrical issues?" he asks.

The lights flicker again.

My stomach sinks. "I wish that were the case, but I have a feeling." I look toward one of the windows next to the front door without leaving the safety of his grasp.

A pair of brown eyes stares back at me through the slats in the blinds. I shriek. Egan nearly drops me off the edge of the porch, but he recovers quickly enough to yank my body back close to his.

The front door pops open, and Annabeth pokes her nose outside. "Cal, we need to talk. This is serious."

"No, this is seriously disturbing." She's been texting me all evening, but since I didn't want to be the girl who looks like she can't leave her phone alone for more than three seconds at a time, I've been ignoring her. "I don't know if you've noticed, AB, but my date *is not over*." I struggle free from Egan's hold and push the door open all the way.

"This is really important." She glances up. "Hey, Egan," she says without inflection.

I look over my shoulder at Egan who's standing with one hand on his hip. He pinches the bridge of his nose with his other hand. "Hey, Annabeth."

"Can you two say goodnight already?" Annabeth's eyes are wide, and her skin is the color of sausage gravy.

I sigh. "Fine. Whatever." I pull myself onto my tiptoes with a hand to Egan's shoulder and press a quick peck of a kiss to his cheek. "Goodnight, E."

He shoots me a soft smile. "Night, Noog. I'll call you in the morning."

"Please do." I smile too. It seems like I've been doing an awful lot of that over the last day or so.

"Cal," Annabeth interrupts.

"Seriously, Annabeth." I tear myself away from Egan's gaze and march through the front door. "This had better be good. Like earth-shattering and life-changing."

She closes the door behind me before I have a chance to wave to Egan one last time. "Earth-shattering and life-changing? Maybe. Good? Probably not."

"Quit being so dramatic. Don't tell me you went on a date with that guy from the ice cream shop. I told you he kept trying to look down your shirt." I follow her into the living room where she drops onto the couch as though she lives here.

"So, you two are kissing now?" She crosses her arms over her chest.

"Just little kisses."

Annabeth groans. "That makes things so much worse."

"Wait. I thought you just knew this was going to turn into a real thing. 'I wrote my thesis on rom-coms,' you said. Because this," I point in the direction of Egan's retreat then back at myself, "is a real thing now. Like really real. Shouldn't you be throwing us a party right now or something?"

She shoots me a pained glance. "I probably would have, but that was before I saw this."

She holds her phone out to me. I roll my eyes when I catch sight of the familiar bow tie logo. "It's the Experiment website. So what?"

"Scroll down." Annabeth looks like she's going to throw up, and I wonder if I shouldn't be taking her more seriously right now. Yes, she's dramatic. But usually only in an excited sort of way.

"Fine." I sink onto the sofa next to her and move the page upward with my index finger. Then I freeze.

My finger hovers over a still of my face. My face from two days ago, in high-contrast black and white.

"What is this?"

"It's your Sixty-Second Story of Strength. The one we filmed about your parents," Annabeth whispers.

"I know. But why is it here?"

Annabeth shrugs.

I touch the screen and the video comes to life. "My parents terminated their parental rights on June twenty-second. I'd already been living with my grandparents for a year. But both my parents were there in court. My mom left that afternoon, and it was the last time I ever saw her. We got word when I was four that she had passed away."

The shot and the camera angle change, so I'm staring directly into the lens, right at the viewers, just like Annabeth suggested. "I'm Callie Christianson. And this is my Sixty-Second Story of Strength."

I watch the entire thing. I'm not sure why, though, since it's not like I need a refresher on my own story. Especially since we filmed it two days ago, and my last conversation with my dad is all I've been able to think about when my mind hasn't been hinged on Egan.

"People say I'm strong once they find out my story." On-camera me shrugs. "And I guess that's okay because what they're really saying is that they see God's strength through me, whether they know it or not. My parents may have rejected me, but He never has. It's still not easy, but at least I know I'm not alone."

The video goes black, and my stomach aches. "Whatever happened to just filming that for me? I didn't want to share it with anyone. Not with Egan, and certainly not with the entire internet."

She peels her phone from my hands and tucks it underneath her leg. "I didn't share it."

"Really, Annabeth?" I shake my head. "Who else knows it exists?"

She raises her eyebrows, and I can see embers in her eyes. "I don't know how it got out, Callie. I never even watched it back. But that thing's been edited and worked on. You know we didn't shoot it in black and white. There's only one person we know who does video editing *and* has access to that website."

"No. No. He wouldn't." I press my hands to the side of my head and squeeze my eyes shut so tightly stars pop up and explode.

Annabeth continues. "It's his website, and he's the only one who adds stuff to it, right? I kind of doubt someone else hacked it only to add that video."

"How would he have gotten it, though?"

She sighs. "I'm just gonna keep saying the same thing I've said all night. I don't know, Cal."

It's like my brain has suddenly turned into a highlight reel from the last almost three weeks. I watch a playback of our favorite dates, and our hesitancy and awkwardness and renewed friendship. And then, from yesterday and today, our kisses.

But threaded through the sparkly, fun memories are also strings of unease. Like how excited Egan was over the fact that the Sparkle Squad sort of recognized him. And how I all but signed away my future firstborn yesterday when I told him I wanted to hit 1,000 views, even though it wasn't my goal to begin with. How excited he was when I admitted it.

"He wouldn't do *that*. Would he?" I choke out. I hate that it's even a possibility.

"Are you going to call him?" Annabeth asks. She has that sad, sympathetic look in her eyes, the same one she gets when she tells a parent she thinks their kid has lice.

"No." I shake my head, deciding in that second. "I'm not. I trust Egan. He didn't do this. It's a mistake. He'll see it, and he'll take it down, and it won't even be a big deal."

Annabeth draws a deep breath in through her nose and lets it out with one word. "Okay."

"You think he did it on purpose."

"I think he might be enjoying the spotlight a little too much."

It feels like I've swallowed an iceberg. But I shake my head anyway. "No. Maybe it's something he would have done two years ago, but he's different now."

Annabeth pats my thigh. "I really, really hope it's true. For both of your sakes."

Chapter 34

THE BABY RACCOONS ARE FIGHTING IT OUT
against the glass in the woodland habitat at the zoo. I watch as
they gnaw on each other's legs and cry when someone bites too
hard. Right now that's what my heart feels like too. Gnawed
on. Chewed up.

Last night was rough. After lots of deep breathing exercises,
I finally fell asleep around midnight. Then at two a.m., Errol
hacked up something and woke me up with his gagging. After
that, all I could do was circle around every possible explanation for my video being on the Experiment site. Over and over
again.

I kept praying that when I checked the site this morning,
my story would have vanished. But as of 7:42 this morning, it
was still there.

"Hey, they didn't have any Dr. Pepper, but they had lemonade, so I got that for you." Egan leans over my shoulder and
hands me a sweating cup of lemonade.

"Oh. That's fine. Thanks."

"You're welcome." He swoops in and kisses my forehead.

I flinch, and he frowns as he leans away. "You okay? You've
been super quiet all morning."

"I'm really tired. I didn't sleep well last night." I grasp the
lemonade with both hands so he can't reach for me.

"Did your dad say something else monumentally stupid?
My baseball bat offer still stands."

I shake my head. "No. I haven't talked to him again since the first time."

"Okay. Too much excitement after putt-putt last night, then?"

"Something like that."

"Hey, I know what will make you feel better. Hippos. I heard they had a baby hippo born here a couple months ago."

I nod, but all I can think of is the stuffed hippo that started this whole thing sitting at home on my bed, hippo-ing we could hang out sometime. And about how I went back and forth about the whole thing, scared of Egan and scared of humiliation. I think I'm going to throw up.

I shove the lemonade back into Egan's hands. "I don't feel so well."

"Do you need to find a bathroom?" He's in my space immediately, gathering my hair up and away from my sweaty neck with one hand. "Are you too hot?"

"I need to sit down," I choke out.

"Okay. Somewhere to sit." His head swivels back and forth so quickly he looks like an owl. "Let me find a bench. Or a stump. Why are there so many people here?" he mutters to himself then grabs my hand and pulls me toward a huge red and white cement toadstool in the middle of a flower bed. "Here. Sit on this."

"It's not a bench, E," I protest but sink down onto it anyway.

"I don't think they'll mind." He sets my lemonade on the ground and crouches in front of me. His hands find my knees. "Is it too sunny here? I can find a shadier place."

"It's fine. I'm fine."

"You don't look fine." He rests his palm on my forehead. His hand is cool and damp from the sweating lemonade cup. "How can I help?"

I bite my bottom lip and force myself to meet his concerned gaze. I travel the lines of his face as though they're a road map of the last three weeks and of the years before that. Like they might give me any hint of direction for moving forward.

At every exhibit, I've stayed silent. Waiting. Hoping Egan would speak up and explain it all away. But he hasn't. And I can't sit alone with all these questions for another second.

I close my eyes and lean into his touch.

"Callie?" Egan whispers my name. Somehow I manage to hear it over the shouts of a screaming pack of children nearby.

"E, have you looked at the Experiment website today?" I ask.

He frowns. "No. Why would I? Is it down?"

My heart pounds wildly, and my stomach threatens to stage a mutiny. "No. I don't think so. But there's something there. Something that shouldn't be."

He pulls his hand away. "Oh? You mean like more nasty comments?"

"No." I shake my head. "Like a video Annabeth and I made earlier this week. About my parents." I open my eyes and wrap my arms around my torso before I ask the question I wish I could forget. "Do you know how it got there?"

All night long I imagined this moment. I imagined his face screwing up in confusion. I imagined his cheeks turning red with barely tamped down anger at whoever got into my personal business and made it public. I even imagined the worst-case scenario: his sheepish admission of guilt and subsequent, immediate apology.

But Egan doesn't do any of that.

Instead, he shrugs. "Yeah. Of course I know how it got there. I uploaded it."

My face goes numb. "You did what?"

"Yesterday. Before putt-putt. I accidentally texted it to my-self when I sent myself the pictures from your phone of us in the strawberry patch."

"And you decided to post it? Without asking me?"

He blinks, and his eyebrows knit together. "Well, yeah. It's so good, Noog. I know everything about your past and your parents and stuff, but it even made me kind of emotional. I knew the second I saw it that it would be that thing, that push, to get us over a thousand. Our viewers needed to see that side of you. Don't you think?"

"No. I don't think." I grip either side of the toadstool with every ounce of strength I have left in my body. "I wasn't ready to share it with anyone else. And I definitely didn't want our viewers to know any of that. You've seen how they've ripped me to shreds in the comments throughout this entire thing." I stare at him full in the face. "And that was before they knew I was abandoned by my own parents. What do you think they're going to say about me now? What do you think they're going to say about my dad?"

Egan shrugs. "I didn't think you'd care. Since you were so mad at him and all a couple days ago."

"I am mad at him. Still. But that doesn't mean I want to drag him through today's equivalent of the public square and throw him in the gallows. Maybe you didn't realize it, but if he's there, I'm there too, Egan." I'm talking so fast I have to gasp to breathe. "You know I told him about the Experiment. He's go-ing to Google us, see this video, and then he'll sue me for libel or something. He's a successful plastic surgeon in the Bay area." My voice sounds like the screech owls in the avian exhibit.

"You're overreacting, Callie." Egan stands and looks around as though he's embarrassed by my outburst.

"I'm not overreacting, Egan. I'm angry. Really, really angry. I'm pretty sure I have every right to be."

"I thought you said you'd done something like it for your church one time. How is this any different?"

"Nobody at my church would ever tell me they'd have dumped me off a bridge instead of leaving me with Grandma and Grandpa because then nobody would have to look at my face ever again."

Egan's fists clench. "Did someone actually say that to you? On our site?"

I look away, crossing my arms over my chest as hot tears simmer behind my eyes. "They didn't have to, okay? They've said it before in a thousand different ways on all our other videos. This one won't be any different."

"Mommy, she's mad."

I glance over to see a little boy wearing shark-shaped sunglasses and dragging a stuffed elephant by the ear as he walks across the sidewalk next to us. He's pointing at me.

"Don't stare, son." His mom grabs his hand and pulls him farther away from me as though I'm one wrong word away from shooting flames from my nostrils.

I launch myself off the mushroom and start walking.

"Where are you going?" Egan shouts after me.

"Anywhere," I yell back. "As long as it's far away from you."

The sound of his footsteps behind me picks up as he breaks into a jog. "You can't walk home, Noog. We're like twenty miles away from your house." He reaches for my elbow.

I wrench it away and keep walking. My hair falls around my face like a shroud. "I'll call Annabeth."

"Didn't you say she's filling in at that day camp all day?"

"I'll call my grandma."

"It's Friday. She's at work."

I stop.

The sun beats down on my shoulders, impossibly hot and heavy. My happiness, my hope, my dignity, they've all poured from my body along with the rivulets of sweat carving pathways from my scalp to my chin. I want to sit down. On this scorching pavement. And weep.

"I can't be in the same car with you right now," I whisper when Egan inches closer.

"Then I'll buy you a bus ticket. You can sit in the front. I'll stay in the back until I know you got home safely."

"Fine." I start walking again, mostly to get away from him.

"I'm sure nobody's even seen it yet." He argues with my back. "We're not *that* popular."

"Annabeth did. Last night."

"Is that what her whole cloak and dagger routine was about?"

"She knew right away this was your fault. I kept giving you the benefit of the doubt. 'No, Annabeth,' I said. 'Egan wouldn't do something like that. He…'" My voice cracks, and I have to concentrate to finish my sentence without breaking down entirely. "'He loves me.'"

Egan moves effortlessly in front of me and puts his hands on my shoulders, acting as a roadblock. He stares into my face, and this time I meet his gaze head on. "I *do* love you, Callie. Really." His molasses eyes search mine, and I remind myself they actually look more like mud or old coffee grounds.

When I don't respond, he sighs and drops his hands from my shoulders. He clears his throat. "I'll go home and take it down, okay?" His voice is deeper now, more subdued. "Will that make you happy? It'll be like it never happened."

I stop just short of physically covering my barely beating heart with my palm. "Would that make me *happy*?" The tears I've been holding back since last night spill over and sear my skin. "You can take down that stupid video, and you can pretend like it'll take care of everything. But you've betrayed me. You've destroyed our friendship. You've humiliated me. So no. Just taking down that video? It won't make me happy."

When I stop talking, Egan seems shocked. Dazed, even. He opens and closes his mouth like a guppy.

I push past him and hope I'm heading toward an exit.

Nothing will ever make me happy again.

Chapter 35

MY PHONE CHIMES. AGAIN.

"I swear, if this thing goes off one more time, I'm going to cram it down the garbage disposal." I stomp across the kitchen toward my phone with the eight-inch chef's knife in my hand.

Annabeth raises an eyebrow and leans far out of my path of destruction. "Is it Egan?"

"Is it Egan. Of course it's him." I poke my phone with my pinky to clear the latest notification.

She reaches for my wrist and gently pries the knife from my fingers. "How many times has he messaged you, though?"

"Since I got off the bus yesterday?" I pretend to think about it, but I don't need to. It's the only thing I've counted today, surprisingly enough. "Seventy-four times."

Her eyes go wide. "That's some dedication."

"You know what would have been a better use of that dedication? Not posting that video." I cross my arms and lean against the counter while Annabeth takes over chopping the pecans for my carrot cake cupcakes.

I've started baking again. I should have known I wouldn't be able to quit it for too long. It's the best coping mechanism I've got.

My dad saw the video. I knew he would. I just didn't think it was going to be so fast. And I also didn't know he was going to call Grandma about it.

He was ticked. So was I. He yelled at Grandma about it, and

I'm pretty sure he would have yelled at me too except Grandma refused to let him talk to me. And then I was glad she wouldn't let me talk to him because somewhere along the way I decided all this was his fault too.

If he and my mom had worked a little harder, loved a little better, cared a little more this wouldn't be my story.

"How much cinnamon, Cal?" Annabeth stops chopping pecans and holds up the red-and-white spice tin.

I shrug. "I don't know. A couple teaspoons maybe."

"Where are the teaspoons again?"

"Probably in the dishwasher."

"Would you mind getting them?"

It takes mammoth effort for me not to throw my hands in the air. "Why don't you just eyeball it, Annabeth? Seriously. It's not like it matters."

Annabeth slams the cinnamon tin onto the countertop, and a tiny rust-colored plume puffs from the top. "It does matter, Callie Christianson. It *does*. You don't get to go belly up on everything you've ever cared about because Egan screwed up, okay?"

I bite my bottom lip as more ridiculous tears rush to my eyes. "He didn't forget to feed my fish for a couple days, AB. This is serious." My voice cracks.

"I know it's serious. You just told me to eyeball ingredients. So, believe me—I know this is a big deal." She grabs both my wrists and stands so close I can see the way her eyes fill with tears too. "And I'm just as upset as you are. You two are—"

"Were."

"Were ridiculously perfect for each other. I don't care what some of those trolls online said about you. When the two of you are together, you're incredible. Callie, you ground him, and he helps you fly." She shakes my hands, and a tear slips from the outside corner of her eye.

I crumple onto her shoulder. "He's an idiot."

She nods, and I can smell the plumeria of her shampoo. "He is an idiot. A spontaneous, clumsy, bumbling idiot." She draws back and wipes underneath her eyes with the pads of her pinkies. "But he's not mean." My phone chimes again. She ignores it. "I don't think he posted that video because he wanted to hurt you."

I choke on a mirthless laugh. "No, he did it because he wanted more views on that stupid site. Which is almost as bad."

"He wasn't thinking."

"Clearly."

"Cal, I'm so sorry." Her mouth twists, and she looks away.

"For what?" My voice gurgles, and I lean over to rip a piece of paper towel from the holder next to the sink.

"For telling you to do this stupid thing in the first place. Really if you think about it, it's all my fault you're in this miserable place right now."

"No. It's his fault, not yours." I blow my nose into the paper towel then crumple it up and toss it in the direction of the trash can. And then I freeze.

Something looks different. On my arm. Something's missing.

"My bracelet," I choke. "It's gone. Where is it?" I wave my arm through the air as though I'm a magician who can make it reappear on command.

Annabeth frowns. "I thought you took it off because you were mad at him. Maybe it's upstairs in your room? Did you take it off before bed last night?"

I shake my head so hard my hair starts to fall out of my greasy topknot. "I'd remember doing that."

"Go check." She grabs an oven mitt from the counter. "I'll babysit the cupcakes."

I know I look like a lunatic, and I know it makes no sense that I'm distraught over something I got from someone I loathe so much right now, but I'm not ready to let go of it.

Or of him.

At least not in my heart, even if I've cut ties with him everywhere else.

Annabeth shoos me toward the hallway leading to the stairs. She knows I need it even if I don't need him. I run upstairs. When I get to my room, I fling the door open so hard it whacks against the doorstop and almost bounces back in my face. I drop to my hands and knees and scramble across the hardwood floor, searching for any glimpse of those horrible neon green pony beads. They were so hard to miss when they dangled from my arm, but now I don't see any sign of them. When I push myself back up, I pull a muscle in my shoulder, but it doesn't matter. I have to find that bracelet.

I fling the quilt off my bed and dump my pillows onto the floor, but my sheets are empty.

It's not in the bathroom, either.

Or in the closet.

Or on my desk.

Every search leaves me empty-handed, and my stomach twists tighter and tighter until I can barely stand straight through my panic.

Twenty minutes later, Annabeth knocks on my bedroom door. "Want me to help you look?"

"Yes," I nearly yell at her. The desperation in my voice scares me. I clear my throat and start over. "Yes. Please."

I watch as she picks up my blankets, shakes them out, then

folds them with meticulous precision. We must be living in a parallel universe. Suddenly I'm chaos and Annabeth is order.

We pour over every surface in my room. And it's not until I start yanking biographies and cookbooks off my bookshelf that Annabeth reaches for me and shakes her head.

"It's not going to be back there. I don't think it's here. Do you think it fell off at the zoo?"

I wrack my brain as I try to recall how things happened yesterday, but all I can think about is the way Egan shrugged as he admitted to uploading that video. "I can't remember. I can't even remember if I had it on yesterday morning when we left."

Annabeth rights the last book on my shelf. "Do you want to go look for it?"

"Where?"

"At the zoo. That makes the most sense, don't you think? Since we can't find it here."

"It rained. It probably washed away."

"But you might feel better if you cover all the possibilities."

I know I should let it go. I told him our friendship was over, and I meant it with everything in me. We are done. Our relationship, our friendship, it's all over. But that doesn't mean I want to forget we ever existed.

So, I nod. "Yes. I'd like to go look for it."

Chapter 36

EGAN WAS RIGHT. OUR DATE TO THE FOOD TRUCK fair is my favorite.

After re-watching every single date three times and crying so much my entire body pounds with my pulse, I've decided that's the truth of it.

Errol meows and butts his head into my palm as a hollow knock sounds on my bedroom door.

I hit pause at the four-minute-twelve-second mark. Egan's face freezes on my tablet. In the warm sunlight of the early summer, his skin looks almost as golden brown as a turnover on its last thirty seconds in the oven.

Another knock.

"Come in." I push Errol until he drops off the bed and goes to sulk in the corner.

"Just checking on you." Grandma opens the door a crack and peers inside.

"I'm fine," I try to say. But it sounds more like, "I'b fide," so I'm pretty sure she knows I'm lying.

She opens the door the rest of the way then sits next to me on my bed. "Can we chat for a minute?"

I shrug as though I don't really care either way. But the second she wraps her arm around me and I feel the strength in her grasp as she holds me close, I lose it.

All my obliterated hopes, my fears-that-came-true, and my broken and muddy feelings rise up in my chest and bubble from my eyes. Tears carve hot paths down my cheeks as I beg myself for the hundredth time today to let it go. To let Egan go.

Grandma rubs my back as I cry gut-wrenching sobs that grab my entire body with greedy fingers and shake me around until I'm puny and flat. Once the sobs cease and I feel about as useful as a wet piece of newspaper, she smooths my stringy hair away from my face.

"Sorry," I apologize and swipe my arm over my eyes.

"For what, sweetheart? Feeling confused and hurt? I think I'd be more worried if you stuffed all this inside and pretend-ed it didn't exist. You and Annabeth weren't able to find your bracelet?" She runs her hand up and down my bare forearm.

We searched the raccoon exhibit. The orangutan exhibit. The aviary. Even the cheery toadstool of my demise where I pulled hunks of mulch apart with my bare hands. But the only things we found were a bunch of weird looks from people walking by and two twenty-dollar-ticket stubs for our efforts.

Annabeth broke up with a guy she dated for a couple of months at the beginning of junior year, and we went out to an empty parking lot and burned all the letters he'd written to her. She was totally fine after that. So, why can't I pretend we burned my bracelet and be done with it?

"No," I finally manage to say. "We didn't find it."

"I'm so sorry." Grandma kisses my temple. "I know it was special to you."

It's all I can do to nod when more impossible tears spring up. Grandma lets me cry for a few more minutes. Finally, when I can go a full twenty seconds between bouts of heaving breaths, she broaches conversation again. "Your dad called again this morning. This is the most I've heard from him in years."

"Jerk."

Grandma rests her cheek on the top of my head. "He's still concerned about that video. He wants you to take it down."

I half-shrug, unable to care about how my dad's feeling right now. "I can't. It's all up to Egan, so you'd have to talk to him about it."

"I see." Grandma sighs. "Well, it's no matter. I told your dad I needed to watch it before I could decide if it needed to be removed or not."

"It's not like I said anything that hasn't been shared before." I shred a tissue I've been clutching for at least half an hour. It's sweaty from the prison of my palm. "Remember when I did that video for that series at church? This is pretty much the same sort of thing."

"I know. But it's been a while. Do you mind?" She motions toward my tablet, still stuck on Egan's face.

I bite my bottom lip and hand it to her. "It's the last thing he posted, so you'll have to click over to the first page. Don't read the comments, though. They're usually pretty messed up."

Grandma shoots me a thin-lipped smile. "Noted."

She scrolls through the page with her fingertip, and I watch as flashes from the last three weeks of my life glide across the screen. Part of me wishes she'd scroll slower.

"It's this one?" Grandma's index finger hovers over the top video, and I nod.

"Yep."

Without pausing to let me prepare myself, she presses *play*.

Me-on-screen launches into the same speech she's given every time another curious person decided to take a peek into my personal life. I haven't watched it since the night after putt-putt when I was with Annabeth, but I don't really need to see it again. I still remember everything I said.

As soon as the video fades to black, Grandma sighs. "I'd forgotten how emotional it is for me to hear you talk about your mom and dad." She sniffs and pats underneath her nose with the sleeve of her navy-blue T-shirt.

She's never told me that before. "It is?"

"Of course." She clasps my tablet in both hands and rubs the corner with her thumb.

"Why?"

A flicker of a sad smile travels across the lines around her face. "Because it's hard to watch when someone you love hurts another someone you love. I think your mom and dad did the right thing in bringing you to Grandpa and me, and I'll swear to it every day of my life. But it was awfully hard to explain to that little blond-headed two-year-old who stood on my front porch with her fingers in her mouth asking when Mommy and Daddy were coming back."

"I don't remember doing that."

Grandma nods. "Every single night for about a year. Broke my heart." She turns back to my tablet. "So, you can't get on-line and take that video down?"

I shake my head. "No. It's Egan's website. I wouldn't know what to do even if I could log into his account."

"Hmm. Okay. Then I guess I know what I'm going to tell your dad, then."

"What are you going to tell him?"

"That there's nothing we can do about it. You don't give out his address or anything. There's nothing hateful there. Just the truth spoken by a very thoughtful and wise young lady. And if the truth makes him uncomfortable, I think it's high time he deals with that." She reaches over and tucks a piece of hair behind my ear. "Now, if you were putting that out there because you were hoping to get back at your parents or use strangers online to help you process hard things that would be better handled in private, well—then we might be having a different conversation."

"It's nothing like that." I look away and stare at my toenails. "But what if I want the video taken down?"

Grandma scoots back onto the bed. "Then we'd want to consider it. Why would you want to do that?"

I'd snort except my nose is too plugged up. "You haven't seen any of the terrible comments on these videos. Some people get on our site every day just so they can tell me they wish God would smite me because I'm taking oxygen from people who need it more."

Grandma only raises an eyebrow. "That seems like a very rude thing to say."

"Exactly. I don't want those personal details out in the world. Think about all the horrible things people are going to say about me now."

Actually, I don't have to think about them at all. And I don't have to read the comments either—it doesn't take much imagination to come up with the things they'll say. I've heard the same things my entire life but mostly from myself.

> She's a horrible person. Her mom should have had an abortion instead of giving birth to her.

> I'll bet her dad saw her picture a long time ago and demanded a paternity test—she looks too much like a monkey to be related to any humans.

> What a liar. Can't even be honest with us about her parents. I'll bet they live up the street in some sort of mansion. They just don't want her in the will.

Grandma makes another thinking noise, dragging me back to reality. "We've all got critics, sweetheart. Someone will always be there to disagree with you. But when you close yourself off entirely and start putting police tape around your life to keep everyone else out, the bullies win, and you end up keeping out a lot of the good people too."

"Then what am I supposed to do? It's not fair to have to listen to them all the time."

"So, don't listen. Let them scream until they get hoarse. They're probably always going to show up and do it because it makes them feel powerful. But you don't need to let them be a part of your life. You listen to the voices that matter: me, your granddaddy, and God. We'll tell the truth about you; and the truth is that you're a spectacular young woman with a strong heart and a strong mind and a strong future." When I only work my bottom lip between my teeth in response, Grandma takes my hand in hers. "Do you have to read the comments?"

I shake my head. "No. Not really. It's just hard not to when they're there all the time."

"And there's not a way to turn them off?"

"I don't know. Maybe. Probably. But Egan would have to do that." I rest my head on her shoulder.

She pats the side of my head. "I'm sorry, Callie Gail. I know this is hard, and I know it hurts. None of it feels fair at all."

"No." I try to breathe in through my nose without luck. "It's not fair at all."

Grandma presses a kiss to the side of my head. "I'll give you some space. I know you've got a lot on your mind." When she hands my tablet back to me, her finger grazes the screen, and a new page starts to load. "But you come get me if you need anything, okay? Granddaddy and I are just watching TV, so you won't be interrupting anything."

"Okay," I whisper, watching my tablet. "I will."

I've funneled an enormous amount of energy into staying away from this particular video in an effort to shield myself from the pain and suffering I know must be lurking there. But now, as the comments underneath my Story of Strength load, I can't tear myself away.

Chapter 37

I HOLD MY BREATH, STEELING MYSELF FOR THE searing vitriol. But the first comment isn't angry or even the slightest bit miffed. It does bring tears to my eyes but in a good way.

> Hi, Callie. Thank you for sharing this. I was adopted too, but I live with my aunt and uncle. Sometimes I feel like I don't fit in anywhere because most adoption stories aren't like mine. Even though it sounds weird, I'm encouraged to know yours is similar. Maybe we can talk about it sometime?

She leaves her email address, which I save. I can't help but keep reading, moving on to the next comment.

> Callie, you probably don't remember me, but I was at Corner House Coffee that night you were there with Egan. (You two are perfection, btw.)

I wince but keep reading.

> I've been watching the Experiment almost since the beginning, and I enjoyed it. But when I saw this video, it took it to a whole new level. I admire the way you talked about your parents here. It's probably not an easy topic for you, but I appreciate the way you're still working through it all even though it hurts. I'd love to hang out sometime. You seem like a really sweet person.

It's simply signed, "Audrey."

My aching heart swells. I've gone to Corner House Coffee a couple of times a week for the last two or three years, but I've never had a conversation with anyone else there. At least not one that doesn't involve how many pumps of caramel I want in my drink or whether or not I prefer my beverage iced on any given day.

I'll figure out a way to contact Audrey too, I decide.

The next comment isn't a nice one—someone thinks I'm way too "Jesus-y" and they've decided I use my faith as an excuse to hate other people. And then the literal next comment comes from a guy who thinks I don't talk about God enough. He says if I were a real Christian, I'd recite more Bible verses on camera. And he thinks Egan and I should go on a date to a Bible Study at his church.

I roll my eyes at his suggestion and keep scrolling. The comments keep coming, message after message. Some to Egan, but a lot of them are for me. Most from people who are hurting. People desperate to know they aren't alone in their pain. I wish I could raise my hand and shout, "I'm here!" loud enough for them to hear it.

As soon as I think it, my heart cinches. Maybe that's what my Story of Strength is for other people? A way for me to be there even though I can't physically be there? A way to remind them they aren't alone after all?

All of a sudden, it clicks. That's exactly what it feels like to me when people share their stories and kind messages with me. I pick up their words and tuck them into my heart then pull them back out again whenever I'm lonely or hurting. And if that's what my story is offering to other people, that sort of feels like the tiniest bit of a gift even though the rest of it is still really hard.

More tears spring to my eyes, but this time they aren't born of grief. Instead, they're tears of gratitude. Suddenly, my aching and drooping spirit feels as though someone has come alongside and wrapped it up in a splint. There's still a lot of hurt and confusion, but at least now I'm not trying to prop myself up on my own as I figure out how to heal.

I scroll back to the top of the page and hover over the video to check the number of views. As soon as I see the count, I gasp so loudly Errol stirs from his spot on the corner of my bed and blinks at me as though I've somehow inconvenienced him.

Twelve-hundred and seventy-one views. Egan was right again. My story pushed us over the one-thousand-view precipice.

I wonder if he's celebrating, or if he's decided to move on from the Experiment since I still haven't answered any of his messages or phone calls. I wonder if I'll ever be able to respond to his messages or phone calls again. Dull pain blooms from the center of my chest again. This time, instead of crumpling or holding my breath until it eases, I acknowledge it. I take a shaky breath. And then I keep reading comments.

When I finally look up again, it's nearly midnight.

My mouth tastes scummy. My shoulders ache. And I'm pretty sure my armpits are actually the source of the burnt onion odor wafting across my room. I climb off my bed, careful not to disturb Errol, and pad over to the bathroom to turn on the shower. The steam opens my lungs and irons out the kinks in my muscles. After I've drained the entire hot water tank, I put on fresh clothes and comb out my hair.

While I brush my teeth, I retrieve my tablet and lean it against the bathroom mirror so I can read more comments as I blow dry my hair.

I touch the link to the next page and wait.

And wait.

And wait.

The progress icon in the top of the window spins, but the entire page stays gray. Finally, an error message pops up.

I nearly spew my mouthful of toothpaste across the bathroom mirror and mash the refresh button. Two minutes later, I get the same error message.

Hitting the back button to get to the comments I'd finished reading before my shower does nothing either. I rinse out my mouth then grab my tablet and shake it as though that's going to make it tell me why it stopped. I type in Annabeth's brand new "Cradle Rockers" website, and it loads quickly. I try the Experiment website again.

Nothing but a flat, panic-inducing gray page.

I scramble downstairs in the dark and sit in front of Grandma's laptop in her office, but I get the same results there. Every other website I can think of loads just fine. But the Experiment site is gone. Wiped clean. Almost like it never happened to begin with.

My nose tingles, and goose bumps line my upper arms. Some of Egan's last words to me trickle through my mind like the Ghost of Christmas Past.

It'll be just like it never happened.

I have to talk to him. I don't want to. But if I'm ever going to figure out a way to help all those people, I absolutely have to.

My phone is exactly where I left it this morning when Annabeth and I were baking the carrot cake cupcakes. It was exhausting trying to ignore Egan, so I just turned it off and left it there. Someone cleaned up the cupcake mess, but they left my phone untouched. I grab it and turn it on.

After the phone flickers to life, I swipe away notification after notification from various social media accounts and texts and missed phone calls. All from Egan. But they tapered off about four hours ago. And he hasn't tried to contact me again at all in at least two hours.

Before I can talk myself out of it, I return his last phone call and hold my breath while it rings.

"Noog?" His phone clatters, probably on the floor.

I wince.

"Noog? Is that you?" His voice is muffled, but it's his and it nearly overwhelms me with longing for everything we lost.

But there's work to be done here, so I draw my shoulders back and take a deep breath. "E?"

There's more shuffling then, "Thank you. Thank you, thank you, thank you." He says it so quickly and so many times all the words run together. "I need to see you."

"We need to talk." I'm so proud of myself for speaking at all, much less saying anything intelligible. The tears are already creeping back in.

"Yes. Absolutely. When? In the morning? Wait. No. You hate mornings. Tomorrow afternoon, then. I'll come take you to lunch. Will Dairy Queen work? You can get all the ice cream you want. Extra sprinkles. Extra peanut butter. Whatever you want. I don't care."

I'd laugh if it didn't feel like I was perched at the top of a mountain's edge with my arms and legs and heart dangling over an abyss. "How about right now? Not Dairy Queen of course, but here."

"Now?" His voice cracks, and he clears his throat. "Now. Yeah, okay. Sure. We can do that. I'll be right there. Meet you on the back porch."

He hangs up before I can agree.

A wave of panic grabs hold of my entire body. I drop my phone on the kitchen table and cover my face with my hands.

He's coming here. Now.

I shouldn't have called. I should have figured it out on my own. I'm not ready to see him again. Maybe I'll just pretend it never happened. He'll show up, I won't answer the door, end of story.

No. That won't work.

He wouldn't give up. Grandpa would wake up. It wouldn't go over very well.

I rake my hands through my hair and wave the hem of my T-shirt to generate a bit of a breeze since it suddenly feels like the inside of a broiler in here.

Maybe I can leave him a note on the porch. It doesn't have to be much. Something simple. Like, "Hey, looks like the site is down. Maybe you should fix it."

I pace back and forth so many times I know exactly how many steps it is from the kitchen sink to the stove and back. On my sixth trip around I have a revelation. If I wake Grandma up, she'll talk to him. And she also won't show up with a shotgun or anything weird like that. Then I won't have to say anything or even see Egan. Problem solved.

I whirl around on my heel and stifle a scream when a shadow moves outside.

Egan's here already. Standing on the back porch. His hand is poised above the back door like he's about to knock.

The second we make eye contact, he waves. Or flails is probably a better word for it.

My heart tears around my chest. I stare at him, unblinking. He points to the door. Holds his hands up in question. Finally, I nod. Open the door an inch. And back away.

He nudges the door all the way open with his toe, watching me the whole time.

Neither of us says anything, and for a full twenty seconds

all I hear is the sound of his breath over the serenade of the tree frogs in the backyard. He stares at the ground, and I stare at everything other than him.

Finally, he speaks. "Hi."

Good. Manageable. I can do this. "Hi."

"Are you okay?"

I glance up. It's a mistake.

He looks like the stuff nightmares are made of. His eyes are sunken into his face, and his hair sticks up in every imaginable direction. The plain white T-shirt he's wearing has a hole in the armpit the size of a small crepe pan. And the plaid pajama pants he has on have got to be several years old or something because they're a good four inches too short.

He reaches for me when I don't answer and repeats his question. "Noog? You okay?"

I lean away from his touch. "I'll be okay."

His throat dips, and he scratches the back of his head. His friendship bracelet slides down his wrist. "Understandable, I guess."

I hate this. How we suddenly stumble over pauses turned pitfalls where words used to cover the gaps seamlessly. What are we even allowed to talk about now?

He speaks. "I'm sorry things—"

"There's something wrong—"

We talk over each other and stop at the same second.

Egan shoots me a closed-lipped, straight smile. "Ladies first."

I nod and look down at my bare feet. "There's something wrong with the site."

"The Experiment site?"

"Hold on. I'll show you." I leave the door open as I go back to retrieve my phone. I pull up the error page on my way back. "See? I can't get it to load anymore."

Egan tilts his head toward me. He frowns. "Right."

"And I tried it on Grandma's computer too. It's not loading anywhere else. But I get internet just fine, so it's not us."

"No." He shakes his head a little. "It's not you."

"Then there's something wrong with it. I need you to fix it." I poke at my screen so hard it bends my fingernail backward.

Egan scratches the side of his head. A crease appears between his eyebrows. He looks away. "I'm sorry, Noog. I can't do that."

"What?" I tumble out of the doorway, and he catches me by the elbows. I jerk myself away before I can get used to the feel of his fingertips again. "What do you mean you can't do that?"

Egan holds his hands up as though he's defending himself in a court of law. "It's gone."

"It can't be gone."

"I nuked it."

"Then un-nuke it." I bury my fingers in the front of his shirt and shake him. The armpit hole rips a little more. "It's important."

He takes a deep breath and stares at my hands. "I think I've gathered that much."

I drop my hold and shove my phone underneath his chin. "Here. Use this. Fix it now."

He shakes his head. "It's not that easy. I took the whole thing offline an hour ago and deleted it all."

"But you've got backups, right?"

Egan looks like he's staring down the flow of Pompeii. "Backups?"

"Yes. You know, those things you set up so when a disaster happens you can get all your electronic stuff back?"

"I guess that probably would have been a good idea."

I press my forehead to the doorframe and groan.

Egan bends low. "I'm confused." He's so close his breath tickles my ear.

"I thought I'd found my place, E. All those people." I shake my head, push him away, and look up into the night sky. "My video actually helped them. They said so. In the comments."

"Okay?" He doesn't get it.

"But I didn't answer any of them. I was too busy reading. And now they're going to think I've abandoned them."

He steps away, leaving me alone in the doorway. He holds out his hand. "Let me see your phone."

I drop it into his waiting palm, and he strides over to the double rocker and pokes at the phone's screen. His tongue sticks out as he concentrates, and he doesn't even look up when I tiptoe over and perch on the edge of the seat next to him so I can look over his shoulder.

The page he's on looks foreign. Lots of weird letter, number, and symbol combinations everywhere.

I hold my breath and draw my knees to my chest as he works.

After what feels like forever, he looks up and shakes his head. "Noog, I'm sorry. I can't get it back." He drops my phone in his lap and leans back, propping his hands behind his head in defeat.

I close my eyes and rest my forehead on my knees.

What now?

It's the whole reason I called him. The whole reason he's sitting here beside me. For the millionth time today, more tears leap to my eyes. Who am I becoming? I haven't cried in years, and now I'm pretty much an eternal, blubbering spring. I clench my fists and tilt my face toward the sky.

Egan leans forward and nudges me with his shoulder. When I say nothing and do nothing, he leans closer. And then his arm is around me, strong and sure and warm.

Ten seconds, I tell myself. Ten seconds and then I'm going to duck away from his touch and I'm going to pull it together and say goodbye again.

Ten seconds pass. Then twenty. Then thirty.

"I wish there was something I could do to fix it." Egan speaks up as my count reaches fifty-four. His fingers tighten around the top of my arm, and he reaches around with his other hand to wrap me in a hug. "And you know I'm talking about more than just nuking the site, right?"

The porch light flicks on, and the door to the back porch hurtles open. "Son, it's awfully late for you to be sitting on the back porch with my granddaughter."

I squint toward Grandpa, who's standing shirtless in the doorway with his arms crossed over his chest and his eyebrows drawn low over his eyes. At least he's wearing pants.

Egan rockets to his feet, and I tumble away from his arms, my heart pounding in my throat.

"It's fine, Grandpa. We were talking, and he was trying to help me—"

"No, sir. You're right. It is late, and I shouldn't be here. I'm very sorry." Egan dips his head like he's tipping an imaginary hat. "Goodnight, Callie."

He's leaving? Now? Without waiting for a goodbye from me, Egan turns and jogs around the corner of the house back to the driveway where his car is probably parked.

"It's almost one in the morning, Callie Gail," Grandpa says.

"I know."

"You looked awfully cozy with that boy. I thought your grandmomma said he broke your heart."

"He did."

Grandpa harrumphs. "Then what was he doing here on my porch with his arm around you?"

"I needed him." I have to stop and clear my throat to keep going. "I needed him to fix something for me."

"Was he able to take care of it?"

I shake my head. "Not this time."

Chapter 38

"HOW DO I MAKE A WEBSITE THAT LOOKS LIKE this?" I lean forward and stare at Grandma's laptop as Annabeth looks over my shoulder. The website I point to is pretty and soothing, done in pastels and white with a few metallic gold accents. The header swoops across the page in flowy, easy cursive.

She raises an eyebrow. "You hire someone."

"Not helpful."

"I'm just telling you the truth."

"Yours looks good."

"Right. Because I hired someone."

"Who? Did they charge much?" When she stays uncharacteristically silent, I know the answer. I groan. "You hired Egan?"

"I needed help, okay? And it was before you two melted down. YouTube can only get you so far when your specialty is wrangling turtles for two-year-olds. Not coding or whatever. What do you want a website for, anyway?"

"I need a distraction."

"Oh. Right. Of course." She sighs. "You want to start a cookie shop? We'll sell sparkly unicorn cookies. And campfire cookies. And seagull cookies."

I frown at her. "Your mind is a weird place."

"But it's usually a happy place."

"No. I'm not starting a cookie shop."

"Then what?"

"I don't know really. I'm thinking about putting together a

place for people to go if they want to share their stories." I lean back over the keyboard and click on another website I'm not going to understand.

"Does that mean you plan on sharing your own story again?"

"I might."

She raises an eyebrow. "Really?"

"Yes. Really. It was pretty well-received on the Experiment site, believe it or not." And I also feel really badly about all those people I'll never be able to respond to. So, maybe I'm trying to make up for it somehow.

"No mean comments?" Annabeth asks.

I shrug. "Some. But it's fine."

Annabeth whistles. "Look at you being vulnerable, taking charge, and ignoring the haters."

"It seems like the right thing to do." I pretend like I'm really interested in this FAQ page in front of me.

"Are you thinking about following the same format? The sixty-second story thing?" She runs her thumbnail along a notch in the kitchen table.

"Probably. It seems easier that way. Why?"

"What kind of stories are you interested in featuring?"

I shrug. "Just real-life stories. I'm pretty sure we've all got hard stuff we've walked through at one time or another. I'm just trying to make sure we all know we aren't alone."

"So, a story from a girl whose boyfriend broke up with her the day her mom got a devastating diagnosis—is that the sort of thing a person could talk about?"

"AB, you don't have to—"

"No, I do have to. I told you to talk about your hard stuff with your viewers, but I've kept a lid clamped down on my stuff and pretended it didn't exist for a long time now. That's not really fair of me."

"You aren't really on the other side of your pain yet," I point out.

"Neither are you." She shrugs. "But I don't want to wait too long to be real about it and miss the opportunity to help out someone else. Besides, we already filmed it. It's just sitting on your phone right now."

I want to argue with her. I know how hard she fights to stay positive, even though her mom's multiple sclerosis diagnosis rewrites what normal looks like for her family every single day. But I can't say anything because Annabeth's story is important too.

So, I only nod. "If you want to share, I think that's fine with me."

She smiles. "Good. Well, not good. I feel a little queasy about it, to be honest. But still, good. I think I'm ready to start being real about the whole situation with someone other than God."

"Then yours can be the first video we post." I click around on Grandma's laptop. "After I figure out how in the world to build a stupid website, that is."

"I noticed the Experiment site is gone." Her voice is soft again.

"It's been a couple days, I guess." I haven't told her about how I called Egan the second it went down or about the apology that made me cry or about how I haven't heard from him in the thirty-eight hours it's been since Grandpa ran him off before I was ready for him to go.

She'll have questions. And I don't have any answers.

"Did he take it down?"

"I didn't ask him to." I squint at the computer screen. "What do you think about this site? I could probably throw together something similar in Paint."

"Why are you changing the subject?"

"I'm not. We've been talking about building a website for like twenty minutes. I'm just going back to that topic of conversation." I look up to see her watching me. Intently. "What?"

"Something happened."

"Yes. Something happened. We fought. It's over."

"After that. Obviously I know about the fight, but something else happened. You know I'm half a criminal justice credit away from being a cold case detective, so don't try to hide it from me." She sighs. "What happened?"

"I called him."

"Like, yesterday?"

"Like, the day before yesterday. I wanted to see if he could get the site back. I thought it had been hacked or something."

"It wasn't."

I shake my head. "No. It wasn't."

She reaches out and lays her hand over mine on top of the keyboard. "He thought taking it down would be the right thing, and he wanted to do the right thing." When I don't say anything, she lowers her voice to an empathetic whisper. "I'm right, aren't I?"

I stare at our hands. "Yeah, I guess that was his line of thinking."

"And?"

"And what?"

"Did you make up?" Her eyes go wide. "Did you make out?"

I have never wanted to bang my forehead on the table more than I do right now. "No, we didn't make out. He came over, couldn't fix it, then Grandpa came out of the house shirtless and ran him off."

Annabeth crosses her arms over her chest. "You promise that's all there was to it?"

I nod. "Yes. That's all there was to it. He didn't even apologize, not directly to me, anyway."

It takes her barely ten seconds to process, then she's back to the interrogation. "Why didn't he apologize?"

I slap my palms on the kitchen table. "Annabeth, I don't know. Why are you asking me these things?"

"Because." She pushes herself away from the table. "It matters. I need to know what I'm working with here, even the less-than-savory details."

I cover my face with my hands and drag my fingers down my skin as I groan. "I'm not asking you to work with this."

She doesn't answer as she walks down the hallway toward the doorway to the garage.

"Annabeth? Stay out of it. I mean it."

She hums "A Spoonful of Sugar."

I jump out of my chair and run after her. "Annabeth, stop. I can't date him again. We'll be lucky if we ever get just our friendship back."

The side door slams.

Chapter 39

"WHY DID YOU GET SO MANY OF THESE FLYERS printed, AB? There are only so many telephone poles in Creekside."

She raises an eyebrow at me half a second before chunking a staple through another flyer with a staple gun. "There's no such thing as having too many eyes on a product."

"I know, but you can use the internet too. That's a thing." I should know.

"I'm about done with your negativity this week, Cal." Annabeth moves to the next telephone pole without so much as glancing over her shoulder. "You didn't have to come with me. It's not like I forced you out here." She holds out her hand for another "Cradle Rockers" flyer from my stack.

I slip one off the bottom for her. "Grandma told me if I stayed, she'd have me help Grandpa power wash the back porch to get rid of the mold outbreak."

"I'm touched that I rank slightly higher than a mold outbreak to you." The flatness in her voice gives me pause.

"It's not you. You know that, right?"

"It's Egan. I know."

I suck in a breath. Even two weeks after our severance his name still hurts like a papercut. Inflicted by cardboard. Right to my heart.

Annabeth staples another flyer to a wooden stop sign then checks her phone. "How's the website going?"

"It's…" I almost say fine but can't because it's such a blatant lie. "It's terrible. I have no idea what I'm doing, and the whole concept is confusing. You change one tiny thing, and it breaks the whole site."

"You could call him."

"He hasn't called me." Not even once. He's gone dark. Completely off the grid. Silent.

I haven't heard from him even once since the night he ran away in his pajamas. I could call him, maybe, but he's the one who broke us. And, besides, he's the kind of guy who could make conversation with a Christmas inflatable so it would be easier for him to come up with something to say. Maybe that's part of why his silence now is so scary.

My stomach feels like a swamp. I want junk food. "Hey, let's go to that movie." I hand Annabeth another flyer as she approaches a large maple tree. Warm, buttery popcorn, a box of Sour Patch Kids, and a Coke Icee sound really good right now. "We could see that one you really wanted to go to on Monday. Remember? The one with that blond girl from that weird alien space show thing in it?"

"Really?" Annabeth staples the flyer to the tree. "You were a thousand percent uninterested a couple days ago."

"I was tired. And you were being pushy."

"You were being sloth-y." She checks her phone again. "We can't go right now."

"Why not? There are only ten flyers left in the stack. You could put the rest of them up at church and we'll be good."

"Because I'm sweaty and gross."

"There's air-conditioning at the movie theater. I'll buy you some Junior Mints."

"Can't." She shakes her head. "I have a job. In like ten minutes." Annabeth takes the rest of the flyers from me and folds them in half before cramming them into her bag.

"Babysitting? You didn't say anything about it earlier."

She starts walking back toward Paterson's Pharmacy where she parked her car a couple hours ago. She's still poking at her phone. "I forgot about it. But let's do the movie thing for sure. Tonight? Will that work?"

I sigh. I see another afternoon of watching Errol shred the curtains in the living room in my future. "Yeah. Whatever. Tonight's fine. You really should start using a planner or something."

"Right. I'll look into that." Annabeth stops when she notices I've fallen behind. "Come on. Move it, Cal. I've got a lot to do."

"Who is it this time?" I kick a hunk of mulch back underneath a tree.

"The, uh, Smith...hammers. The Smithammers." When I frown, she shrugs. "They're new in town."

"Must be." The more I think about going home, the more desolate I feel. "You know what, you should just get going. I'm gonna hang out downtown for a little bit."

"By yourself?"

"Why not? Maybe I'll stop into that new boutique thing next to the bike shop on Naylor."

"Okay, sure. Let me know if you see anything cute on clearance."

"I will. Especially if it's covered in glitter."

She smiles and waves over her shoulder as she slips into her car. "You know me well. Call me if you need a ride home."

I wave back. "While you're babysitting?"

"Oh. Right. No. After I'm done. I'll come pick you up then, okay?"

"I'll just walk or call Grandma. But—" Annabeth slams her door shut and peals away without waiting for my reply. "Thanks?"

I end up staying downtown for only about twenty minutes after Annabeth's departure. The boutique is definitely more Annabeth than me, and it's not enough to keep me from feeling like I've eaten bad sushi every time I catch a glimpse of Henny Cakes out of the corner of my eye. The twenty-five-minute walk home is good for me, but I'm definitely out of shape because when I get back it's all I can do to collapse on the couch with Food Network on TV.

Three hours later, my phone buzzes next to my face, startling me from sleep that's much deeper than any I've been getting at night lately. It's a nearly unintelligible text from Annabeth. The part that is intelligible, however, is concerning. Because it looks like she's saying she's going to be here at my house in three minutes? I rub the back of my hand across my eyes and stretch until my neck cracks. Surely, she meant to say thirty minutes.

When I swallow, my mouth tastes like the back porch mold Grandpa just got rid of, so I head upstairs to brush my teeth. As soon as I plunge my toothbrush into my mouth, my phone buzzes again with another message from Annabeth. This one is just a single word:

Annabeth: here

I frown and scrub my molars. Surely not.

My bedroom door flings open, and my surprised screech blows toothpaste residue all over my bathroom mirror.

"What are you doing?" Annabeth, looking gorgeous and put-together with her hair in long, loose curls, smoky eye makeup, and dangly gold earrings, stares at me with one hand on her hip.

"Brushing my teeth?" I hold the toothbrush in the air. "What are you doing?"

"Picking you up for the movie. Why aren't you ready?"

"You literally just texted me. I fell asleep on the couch." She wrinkles her nose, and I glance down at my outfit, a pair of neon pink Nike shorts and a gray V-neck T-shirt. "What?"

"You're gonna get cold."

"I'll take a hoodie." I rinse my mouth out and drop my toothbrush back on the counter. "What time does the movie start?"

"In like thirty minutes. But I want to get there for the previews."

I grab the hoodie draped over my desk chair and pull it on then grab my wallet and stuff it into the front pocket. "You never want to see the previews. What's going on?"

"My brother said something about a rom-com he thought I'd like. I want to see the trailer."

"Ever heard of YouTube?"

"You ask too many questions. We are going to be so late." Annabeth grabs my wrist, turns around, and drags me downstairs and to the driveway.

When we get to the theater, she's equally as aggressive.

"Wait, I want some Sour Patch Kids." I reach toward the concession counter as Annabeth propels me past it, marching toward the ticket-ripper as though she's leading a coup.

"We'll get them later."

"Later? But—" My body registers recognition before my mind does, and I freeze. There's somebody loitering in front of the restrooms. Somebody familiar. I look at Annabeth, whose eyes are as wide as Reese's cups. "What's Owen Pasko doing here?" I ask. Did she know he was going to be here?

Annabeth grimaces. "I don't know." Her pinkening cheeks lead me to believe she maybe does know.

I shove her toward the ticket-ripper. "Move. Now." I don't want to have a conversation with him. To look into his eyes and see his brother or hear his voice and be transported back to the backyard barbecue and thrown punches and near kisses.

There's a thud and a crash in front of me. A six-foot-tall cardboard cutout of a fluffy squirrel grins up at me from the floor. Annabeth is on her back beside it, her purse wrapped around its enormous tail.

Owen's gaze catches mine in the aftermath of the commotion. "Hey. Callie." He's about ten feet away, too close for me to pretend I didn't hear or see him.

I make a big deal out of helping Annabeth up and righting the squirrel before I answer him. "Hey, Owen."

"How are things?" He dips his chin, and I catch that far-too-familiar flash of molasses in his eyes. My knees nearly buckle.

"Things are fine. Good. How's…everything? For you, I mean."

Annabeth clings to my elbow. "Sorry," she whispers. I dig my nubby fingernails into her arm.

"Everything could be better." Owen's face looks pinchy. "But it's fine. Or it will be."

"You here to see a movie?"

"Just leaving, actually. You guys seeing that one about the girl with the dog and the, uh, pigeon? Or something." He graciously pretends like I'm not a total moron for asking if he was at a movie theater to see a movie.

I look at Annabeth who keeps glancing down the hallway, at her feet, and anywhere other than at Owen Pasko. "I think that's the one we're gonna see," I say.

"Cool." He jams his hands in his pockets and nods. "Well, I'll let you get to it. Tell your grandparents I said hi." Owen backs away.

"I will. Thanks. Tell your, uh, your mom and dad I said hi too."

"For sure." He lifts his hand in a wave. "See you later, Annabeth."

"Bye," Annabeth squeaks then takes off toward the ticket-ripper again. She hands both our tickets to him.

He motions to his right with a quick twitch of his head without looking at our tickets. "Last door on the left."

"Thanks." Annabeth yanks me behind her.

"Wait." I wrap my fingers around her wrist. "How do you know Owen? Did you date him or something?"

"Uhh." Annabeth's face is almost the same shade as the maroon carpet squares. "We just met. Nice guy, though."

"Like when Egan helped you with your website?"

"Something like that." She shoves me into the doorway of our theater. "Here we are. Pick a seat. Which one looks good to you?"

"It's empty." I look around the theater at row after barren row.

"Huh. We must be a little early." Annabeth starts up the steps to about the middle and scoots all the way to the center. "This work?"

I follow her. "Sure. Whatever."

The second I sit down, she pops back up. "You said something about Sour Patch Kids?"

"Um. Yes. Where are you going? I thought you didn't want to miss the previews."

"I know, but you just saw your ex's brother. You need some sugar to cope, right?"

I blink at her. Finally, I shake my head and lean back in my seat. She is confusing. And I will never win whatever game she's playing, so I'm not even going to bother. "Right. Sugar will help. And so will popcorn." When she doesn't object, I keep going. "And a Coke Icee."

"Anything else?"

"That's it." I start to reach for my wallet in my pocket, but Annabeth holds up her hand. "My treat this time."

"Oh. Okay. Thanks, AB." Maybe I shouldn't have asked for so much.

She leaves, and I start scrolling through my phone. Random trivia questions flash across the movie screen, and I lean forward, looking for Annabeth and, also, anyone else. Why isn't there a single other person here? Surely this movie isn't *that* terrible. It's only been out for like a week.

The lights dim.

"Hey, Noog."

I startle and drop my phone. It clatters to the sticky floor beneath my feet.

Egan stands at the end of the row holding a box of Sour Patch Kids and a bag of popcorn in one hand and an Icee in the other. He gestures down the row with the Icee and points to the space next to me with his pinky. "Is this seat taken?"

I glance around the completely empty theater. "Yeah, actually. It's Annabeth's. But there are plenty of other seats." Like all the way in the back row next to the emergency exit.

"What about this one?" He gestures toward another seat with his chin.

I only shrug, my heart rate surging. "Whatever. That's fine."

His shoulders relax, and he starts down the row toward me. "These are for you." He sits, leaving one empty seat between us, and holds the popcorn out.

"Oh. Thanks." I take it, then accept the Sour Patch Kids and drop the Icee into my cupholder. Suddenly, none of it seems appetizing.

Egan settles into the chair, runs his hand over his hair, then leans forward and stares at the movie screen. He doesn't say anything.

After a solid two minutes of listening to nothing but the poppy soundtrack accompanying the theater trivia, I can't stand it anymore. "Why are you even here, Egan?"

He winces and rubs his palms on his jeans. "Would it be believable for me to say I'm just here to watch the movie?"

"No." I set the popcorn on top of the folded-up, empty seat between us and start to stand. "I need to go find Annabeth. I don't feel so well." The lights dim and the movie screen flickers to life.

"Wait. Callie. Not yet. Can I have one minute? Just sixty seconds. Please?" Egan touches my forearm. His whispered words taste like a tablespoon of cayenne.

I bite my lower lip, and my eyes flood with tears. Sweet, but somber, music plays across the theater. I don't want to move from him, but I need to, so I drop back into my seat and cram my fingertips underneath my thighs. "Not a second more."

Before he can say anything to respond, his face appears on the screen in front of us in black and white. He's sitting in an overstuffed armchair in a room I recognize as his dad's study. I hid behind that chair at least a hundred times playing sardines growing up.

"All my life I've been the guy who just wanted everyone to think I was worth watching, even at the expense of hurting the ones I love. But that ends now." Egan-on-screen looks directly into the camera, the lines of his jaw and shoulders thick and strong across the enormous movie screen. "I'm Egan Pasko.

And this is my Probably-Way-Longer-than-Sixty-Second Story of Strength."

I feel more than see him sigh beside me as the video continues. "The whole Experiment was basically a way for me to weasel my way back into my best friend's life because I did something dumb and lost her almost two years ago. Thankfully, she agreed to do it. And she didn't know it when I asked her to do the Experiment, but I'd already fallen for her. And then I kept falling. More and more with every date we went on.

"Unfortunately, I also fell more for the high I got every time I saw a new comment from someone who thought I was attractive or from someone who said I was hilarious. It consumed me, and that's why I couldn't see beyond myself enough to think about Callie even though our friendship is one of the most important things in the world to me." He clears his throat and glances away before looking back into the camera.

I'm not sure I'll ever be able to breathe again.

"My grandpa always warned me that my pride would take me out one day. I never believed him—I guess I thought I was better than that somehow. I thought I'd beat it. But it turns out I was completely lying to myself. In the end I sacrificed my very real relationship with one of the kindest, most beautiful, most honest souls on earth for the chance at a surface relationship with a thousand strangers. They always say pride goes before the fall, and I guess all I have to say now is that I fell. I fell hard."

The video fades out. My pulse pounds all the way from the space between my eyes down through my toenails. I'm afraid to look at him.

"Noog, I'm so sorry." Egan's voice is gritty and sweet, like turbinado sugar. He picks up my popcorn, moves it another couple seats down, and squats in front of the empty seat next to me. He holds out his hands, palms up in front of me, as though he's waiting for me to take them.

I can't.

"You were right," he says. "None of that was my call to make. I get it, why you're so mad at me. To be honest, I'm pretty mad at me right now too. It's almost like I went right back to being the same person I was two years ago, that guy who just wants everyone else to think he's awesome." His molasses eyes are warm and molten and full. "I'm working on it, really. My dad and I talked about it some, and he's going to help me figure out how to balance all that stuff somehow."

It's his final admission, that he's talked to his dad about it, that twists me from the inside out. Two years ago, he never would have asked for advice from anyone. He never would have filmed an apology and—

"Wait. Is the whole theater empty because of this?" I look up into his shadowy face.

He nods. "I rented out the whole thing. I figured you wouldn't want any of this broadcasted to a theater full of strangers staring at you and waiting for a reaction."

He's right. He's so right. And the fact that he actually thought it through enough to rent out an entire theater makes my entire body feel like the most perfectly toasted marshmallow.

"What about Owen?"

"He was here to help me take care of any last-minute issues."

"And AB?"

"She's my insider. We've been texting a lot over the last couple of weeks."

I grasp the armrest of my seat. "So, the Merry-Go-Round at the mall? And the butterfly garden? Even though she suggested those things, they weren't her ideas."

"No. We were going back and forth a lot, trying to figure out how to get you out of the house. I had plans there too." He shrugs, lifting one shoulder to his ear. "But they didn't work out."

"I was really sad."

"You were brokenhearted. Because of me. Which is fair."

"E." It's the only syllable I can get out before the tears rise enough to drown out my voice. Seconds pass as I struggle to pull myself together. It must be long enough to cause Egan to have second thoughts because he shifts and starts to stand.

I grab for him but miss. "Don't leave."

Egan meets my panicked gaze with a cautious, crooked smile. "I'm not." He eases himself to his full height, reaches inside his pocket, then cradles my hand in his before tipping it, palm up. "I have something for you."

Neon green pony beads spill into my waiting, trembling fingers. I gasp. "But how? Where?"

"On the bus. It must have caught on something." He plucks the bracelet from my hand and loops it around my wrist. As he ties, he talks. "At first I thought you were so ticked you ripped it off and left it behind."

"I didn't."

He pauses, his pinkies against my arm, and peers at me through his eyelashes. "I figured that out after Annabeth said you two went back to the zoo looking for it." When he finishes tying the knot, he looks into my face but stays silent for a full two seconds, a feat of massive self-control for him, I know.

His thumb brushes the inside of my wrist, and he whispers. "Callie, I'm so sorry. I hate that I hurt you. I didn't think it through. Any of it. And that was a huge mistake."

The tiniest of smiles unfurls over my lips even though a tear sneaks out the corner of my eye and tiptoes a path down my cheek. "Of course you didn't think it through. You're Egan Pasko. There isn't a single thing in your life that you've ever thought through before."

"I'm going to try to change that, though." He nods once, resolute, and there's no trace of humor in his face. "No more winging it in life for me. I've seen the light, and the light is day planners and making reservations ahead of time."

I choke back a giggle. Those words sound completely foreign coming from him. "Please don't do that to yourself. I need someone in my life who looks at things differently than I do."

"I know it's probably too early to know, but do you think…" He looks away, and his throat dips. "Do you think we can somehow salvage whatever's left of our friendship?"

My heart feels like I've been holding my breath for a week. And in some ways, I have been. I've missed him so much.

I shake my head. "E, we've been friends an awfully long time."

"I know." He stuffs his hands into his pockets. "It's a lot to ask. And you know what? If you want to be the kind of friends who only wave at each other from across the parking lot at the grocery store, I understand. I think I can do that too."

I raise an eyebrow. "You think?"

Egan shrugs and levels the last remaining bits of rubble around my heart with a half-grin. "What can I say? I like kissing you. It won't be easy to give that up."

I glance at my bracelet and back at his lips. "Then don't."

Chapter 40

"IS IT DONE?" I LEAN OVER EGAN'S SHOULDER AS he stares at Grandma's laptop sitting in the middle of the kitchen table.

He laughs and tips the screen downward so I can't see. "You're being a little impatient, don't you think?"

"You promised my site would be done today."

"And I'm making good on my promise. But you're making me nervous." Egan twists around, grabs my hands, and tugs me close enough to hug. "Aren't you supposed to be working on that parrot cake recipe for Marco?"

"It's a hummingbird cake. And no, I'm not going over there until Thursday, so I've got plenty of time." It's been almost a month since the Experiment met its abrupt end after nineteen dates and Egan and I found our new beginning. We've been on several dates since then and recorded exactly zero of them.

In my free time, I've been going to the assisted living center to chop whatever Marco and Flora need for dinner prep. Then they let me use their industrial kitchen to test new dessert recipes. While I've got a great track record for not poisoning the residents, there are rumors that many of them have had to invest in new wardrobes to accommodate their expanding waistlines.

And when Egan's not vacuuming cars to earn money to take me on more dates, he's been working almost non-stop on my new website. Annabeth was right. It's easier to hire an expert. But it's still been sort of stressful. I may or may not be picky.

I sigh. "Sorry. I just want it to be perfect, you know?"

Annabeth groans. "Cal, he's been tweaking this thing for almost a week now after all your suggestions. There's no way it's not going to be perfect."

I ignore her. "Are you sure people are going to want to look at it?"

"Positive. I'm leaving a little encouragement here, and... ready." Egan pushes the laptop open again and wiggles his fingers at the screen like he's using the powers of his mind to get everything to load.

I frown and lean closer as I inspect the familiar bow tie logo of the Great Date Experiment. "That's not my site."

Egan shakes his head and stands up. "No. It's not. But I think it might be important for you to look at this first." He gestures toward his newly vacated seat, offering it to me.

I frown at him, but he only winks back as I slip into the chair and touch the screen to scroll down the site.

At first glance, it looks exactly the way I'd hoped it would that night when everything went gray and I begged him to put it all back. The intro video, the one Egan made at the very beginning of all the pictures from our past, is there again. But now he's taken away the option to leave comments, so even when people have mean, rude things to say, we'll never know. It's our space, and that sort of negativity isn't welcome here.

The other new piece is a photo of us from yesterday in place of all the videos from our dates. In it, I'm tucked safely underneath Egan's arm, holding onto my sun hat with both hands to keep it from blowing away in the breeze. My grin is a wide-open, life-is-confetti smile, and Egan, all tall and tan and true, kisses my cheek.

Annabeth took it at the pool. It's already printed off and tacked to my bulletin board in my room. But on the Experiment site it's followed by a link that simply says, *The Adventure Continues*.

I tap on the tabletop with my fingernails. "What happens if I click that?"

"You email the president." Egan shrugs like he's said something completely logical, then he laughs. "What do you think? It goes to your site, Noog. Anyone who goes to the Experiment site now will click that link and end up on your sparkly new website. Take a look."

But I only sit there, my hands on the tabletop in front of me. My fingers twitch, and I count my breaths.

Egan covers my shoulders with his hands and squeezes. "Nervous?"

"A little."

Sometimes all I can think about are the mean things people said to me. The things they said about us. The terrible things they said to each other.

But then I push myself to think about the other comments too: the ones that carried light into one of the darkest corners of my life, the ones that reminded me how my isolation was an illusion. I click the link before I can talk myself out of it.

Egan wraps his arms around me and rests his chin on the top of my head as the site loads quickly in front of us, the design done in pastel pink, golden champagne, and hand-lettering. Exactly like I'd asked, he lined up the three black-and-white videos across the top of the homepage.

The first is Annabeth's.

She was, oddly enough, nervous about actually posting her Story of Strength, even though she spent a lot of the Experiment trying to weasel her way on camera. Egan edited her story too, and it turned out beautifully. Annabeth's story and her poise became the perfect combination of raw and radiant.

The second video is Egan's, all about his struggle with the spotlight and how it's a danger to him sometimes. We thought about putting his apology video online, too, but decided to save it for us instead. Because that's who he recorded it for: us. Not even Annabeth has seen it, though she said she heard snippets while she was standing outside the theater.

Egan's apologized several times over the last week or so, and I've forgiven him every time too, only partly because he sprinkles his apologies with kisses. Mostly because he means it, and his actions over the past week have more than proved his apology true.

The third video is mine. We re-recorded my story. I didn't change much about it other than my outfit and the number of times I said "um," but I'm still pretty proud of the end result. It's my story, minus a lot of the self-loathing and guilt I've battled for so many years. It might still upset my dad, but Grandma's already told me she's proud of me and I have her permission to leave it on my site as long as I'd like.

So, I think I will.

Underneath the videos, we added an invitation to meet at the Creekside Counseling Center next week. Grandma, Annabeth, Egan, and I will all be there.

We talked it over and decided on a monthly group meeting, open to anyone who's looking for a place to be themselves and find friendship. All the online stuff is fine, but I really wanted a place to connect with people in person too. Because some things in life are better shared in person with people you trust—not over the internet.

I exhale, a mighty rush of air that causes my whole body to shudder. "It's real," I whisper.

Annabeth giggles.

"It's real," Egan confirms.

He watches me navigate the other pages, reading about how the Stories of Strength came to be. I click on the contact page, where we've invited people to share their stories with me and tag their own stories so we can find them and watch those too.

"I know this hasn't been the easiest journey." Egan kisses me quickly then rests his cheek against mine. "But does a tiny part of you feel like it's worth it at least?"

I smile at Annabeth, who's apparently verklempt over our tender romance spilling out into the kitchen. She tugs a tissue from the box in the middle of the table and dabs it under her eyes.

I lean into him, pressing my cheek close to his heart without hesitation. "It's definitely worth it."

And it's true, even though nothing happened according to plan. We might not ever be happily ever after, as much as Annabeth begs and pleads for me to say it. But we're definitely happily ever right now, one second at a time.

And I have a feeling we have a whole lot of those left.

Acknowledgments

To Mom and Dad: Thank you. For everything. Full stop. I'm so incredibly grateful for you. LUAHP, and I'm so proud to be y'orchid. I love you.

To Aaron: Thank you for believing in me and my dreams every step of the way, even when they seem impossible. I love our life together. I love you.

To Granny and Grandma: I have no doubt that I am the woman of faith I am today because of your prayers and your examples. I love you and I miss you both.

To Lindsay Franklin: I'm sitting here googling "how to use words" because I just can't. Remember that time we were both so awkwardly introverted that it took us the entire conference AND someone else calling us out to realize we were besties? You're the only person on earth who's read this book as many times as I have, and it's absolutely better for your influence. Thank you. I love you. *initiate snuggle sequence*

To Dana Black: I don't know anybody else who is as supportive and encouraging as you. Thank you for sharing in my joy and celebrating this book with me. I'm so glad you're my confetti friend. You are truly a magical soul, and I love you.

To Laurel Burlew: You're sunshine in a person. It's been one of the greatest joys of my life to watch you grow up and to become your friend. Thank you for being a cheerleader for my writing. I can't wait to be the same for you and your books. I love you.

To Rachel Kent: You have been such a trustworthy, steady, and patient presence in my life over the last nine years of my writing career. Thank you for hanging in there with me. I'm grateful to call you my agent and my friend.

To Robin Jones Gunn: You were there for me through your books when I was a lonely teen whose closest friends were Christy Miller and Meredith Graham. Imagine my delight when I grew up and discovered you are just as wonderful, kind, and inspiring as the characters in your books. Thank you for praying for me, for mentoring me, and for paving the way.

To Janelle Leonard: I'm forever grateful to this book for introducing me to you. Thank you for making every effort to help it become its best. Your enthusiasm and encouragement every step of the way has made this process so fun for me.

To Roseanna White: Thank you for taking a chance on me and this book. I'm so glad it finally gets to reach readers because of you.

To the countless other supporters in my community of writers and friends: Though there isn't space here to list each of you by name, know that if you've ever sent me an I'm praying for you! message or an I can't wait to read your book! comment or an It's about time your books see the light of day! note…I'm thinking of you. Thank you.

To Jesus, my most faithful Friend: Thank you for giving me art and creativity. It's a gift I treasure now and will for all of eternity. I love you.

Author's Note

Dear Spectacular Reader,

Wow, thank you for reading all the way to the end! I know life is crazy, and you have a lot going on. It means so much that you'd spend time with me through the pages of this book.

If you're looking for other ways to connect, check out my website: AshleyNMays.com. From there, it's easy to send me a message, find my social media, or sign up for my newsletter. (It's called Inbox Confetti, and it's a party. Seriously, you're going to love it.)

I'm honored and ecstatic to be your friend. Thank you for being part of my journey.

Love always,

Ashley

Ashley Mays